GUILT

Heather Burnside

An Aries Book

First published in the UK in 2022 by Head of Zeus Ltd,
part of Bloomsbury Publishing Plc

9 7 5 3 1 2 4 6 8

A catalogue record for this book is available from the British Library.

ISBN (PB): 9781801107914
ISBN (E): 9781801107891

Cover design: Larry Rostant

Typeset by Siliconchips Services Ltd UK

Printed and bound in Great Britain by
CPI Group (UK) Ltd, Croydon CR0 4YY

Head of Zeus Ltd
First Floor East
5–8 Hardwick Street
London EC1R 4RG

www.headofzeus.com

For Pascoe and Kerry

Prologue

Laura was relaxing watching breakfast TV in her spacious lounge. Following the increasing success of her fashion boutiques, she had upgraded from her previous home in the same affluent area of Altrincham. This house was a four-bed new build, but was on a much grander scale than most modern homes, with large gardens and pillars at the entrance. Laura loved the fact that everything inside her home was shiny and fresh, from the plush pale grey sofa to the expensively papered feature wall and the glittering chandelier, which cost her a fortune but was worth every penny.

She was gazing around in contentment and reflecting on how far she had come since her days as a working girl when she received the call that would ruin her day. Laura picked up her mobile and looked at the name on the screen. It was Gina, manager of the Deansgate branch in Manchester.

'Hi, everything alright?' she asked.

'Not really, no.'

'Why, what's happened?'

'Well, I've just arrived at the shop and there's a load of graffiti all over the shutters.'

'OK. Get someone to scrub it off.'

'I will but... well... I thought you might like to take a look at it first.'

'No, it's no problem,' said Laura. 'I don't need to get involved with things like that. Just put the shutters up till you can get someone to shift it. Nobody will see it till you pull them down again. What does it say anyway?'

'It's not very nice. That's why I thought you might want to see it yourself.'

'Go on, spill. It can't be that bad.'

'Oh, I don't know if you'll want to hear it. I mean, it's about someone called Crystal so maybe they think that's you seeing as how the shop is called *Crystals*.'

Hearing the name Crystal gave Laura a jolt, reminding her of the time when she had used that name for herself. A time when she hadn't lived in luxury or been in control of her life. A time when she had done whatever it took to get the cash with which to feed her drugs habit, no matter how degrading it might be.

She hadn't gone by that name for years so why would somebody be using it now? She didn't want to go into details of her past life with Gina though, so she said, 'OK, I'll be round as soon as I can.'

An hour later Laura was rushing up Deansgate in her high-heeled Louboutins dressed in a tailored suit with perfect hair and makeup. She had made an effort to reflect her current status as a successful businesswoman and outwardly she appeared calm and sophisticated, but inside her heart was racing with anticipation. That reminder of a previous life had unsettled her.

Laura reached the shop and marched over to Gina who

looked ill at ease. 'Come on then, let's get this over with,' she said.

'What? You mean you want to do it now while we're trading?'

Laura glanced around the shop, noticing that there were only one or two customers in at this time of the morning. 'Yeah, it won't take a minute. You stay inside and press the switch while I go and have a look.'

'You sure?' asked Gina.

'Course I am,' said Laura. 'Believe me, Gina. I've seen it all in my bloody life. Nothing they've written could possibly shock me.'

'OK.'

Laura walked back outside the shop. Despite her show of indifference, she was worried about what she was going to find, and Gina's reluctance to divulge anything was not helping to put her mind at ease. She watched as the shutters began to lower. It seemed to be taking an age and as bunched-up images of the lettering appeared, she tried to make out the words.

Crystal was the first word she recognised as she'd been expecting it anyway. Then the other words appeared, and Laura put her hand across her mouth in shock. 'Fuck!' she cursed while she read the glaring crimson words daubed across the shutters of her Deansgate shop: *Crystal is a Whore!*

The words screamed out, accusatory and defiling, and a feeling of dread descended on her. But as Gina stepped outside the shop, Laura tried to mask her alarm.

'Sorry. I told you it wasn't very nice,' muttered Gina, looking sheepish.

'Put the shutters up again!' Laura responded, sharper than she had intended. She noticed the look of surprise on Gina's face when she rushed inside the shop to do what she had been told. Laura followed Gina indoors, leaving a list of instructions. 'Keep the shutters up till it goes dark then fetch someone to clear it up. I want every bit removed.'

Then she fled the shop, immediately feeling foolish for her reaction. She didn't want Gina to know how badly she had been affected. But the words had stung and as she walked back down Deansgate, memories of her sordid past came flooding back to her. She thought she had buried all that years ago when she had come off the game. But it seemed she hadn't buried it deep enough. And now that someone was onto her, she hoped to God it didn't spell trouble.

Laura was looking forward to having her daughter, Candice, over for the night. She often stayed at home even though she was in student digs in Manchester. Laura suspected it wasn't just because she wanted to visit her but also because of the proximity to her boyfriend, Thomas's, home.

It was almost the end of Candice's second year at university and she had arranged to stay at home during the summer. Most of her friends would be returning to their parents' houses up and down the country and Candice hadn't wanted to stay in the student house on her own. She and her group of friends had therefore given up the lease and arranged to rent a new property when the next academic year began. Laura had been delighted with her decision; it was always good to have her daughter back home.

By the time Candice got in from university, Laura had been in the house a while. After the nasty incident earlier that morning, she'd wandered around the shops, trying to take her mind off things with a little retail therapy. Now her new purchases were neatly stacked away in the wardrobe, she'd cooked a lovely meal for them both, and was ready to spend a chilled evening with her daughter.

Laura looked at Candice when she walked inside the house. She felt a warm glow of love as she did every time she set eyes on her wonderful daughter. At five foot five, Candice was slightly taller than her mother but like her she was slim and had the same natural strawberry blonde hair although Laura now dyed hers mid-brown.

Candice was an attractive girl, but what Laura was most proud of was the person she had become. Candice was strong-willed and not afraid to speak her mind. She was also very caring, understanding, smart and fun to be around. In fact, Laura thought that she was the most perfect daughter she could ever have wished for. It was a blessing that she had turned out so well after everything she had put her through during her years on the beat.

'Hi, Mum, what's for tea?' asked Candice, walking over to her and giving her a hug.

'Do you ever think about anything other than your stomach?' mocked Laura. 'I wouldn't mind but you don't even show for it.'

Candice grinned. 'It's called being young, Mum, and burning it off with all the stress of exams.'

'Why, it's not that bad is it?' asked Laura, growing concerned.

'No, I was only joking. It's fine. I'm on top of things.'

'Glad to hear it,' said Laura.

Even though she knew Candice had aced her first-year exams, she still couldn't help but be a little concerned. Her daughter was now sitting her second-year exams and from what Laura had been told they were more challenging than the previous ones. She wanted the best for Candice, so it was good to hear she had everything in hand.

'What would you like to do tonight?' she asked. 'Have you got lots of studying or would you like to watch something on TV? *Corrie*'s on later.'

'Aw, Mum, I've already arranged to see Thomas.'

'Bloody hell! It's getting a bit regular, isn't it? You only saw him last night.'

'I know, but I'm missing him.'

'Jesus! You have got it bad. Are you staying over at his again?'

'Yeah.'

'OK, but make sure you don't neglect your studying. Don't forget, you are in the middle of exams.'

'I know, I know, stop fussing. I've already done some work at the library and he's not picking me up till eight so I can get some more done here.'

Laura smiled. Despite her concerns over Candice's studies, she was pleased at her choice of boyfriend. Thomas was a lovely lad who had made Candice really happy in the six months she had been seeing him. Laura felt sure that he would understand all about exam demands as he was a graduate himself and he was also considerate enough to give Candice the space she needed to study.

Laura kept up her mask of happiness until Candice set off for Thomas's house, driving the black Mini Laura had bought her when she had passed her driving test two years ago.

It was only after she had gone that Laura's mind went back to the graffiti. She had received a text from Gina telling her the problem had been dealt with, but the damage had already been done.

Those few words had dragged Laura back almost ten years to when she'd worked the mean streets of Manchester. She had been a sex worker from the age of seventeen when she had left home after her mother's partner had given her a beating. For fourteen years she had put up with life as a working girl: the abuse, the drugs and the savage treatment by the clients and her pimp. But after one assault too many, Laura had finally decided to turn her life around.

As she dwelled on the past a disturbing memory came back to her, invading her senses and making her panic. She was searching for her daughter, frantically rushing around to ask if anyone had seen her. Nobody had and the recollection still made Laura's heart race and her mind fill with despair.

Laura tried to stay calm, reminding herself that things had come right in the end. She'd found Candice and she was OK now, wasn't she? But it was impossible not to think about how close she had come to losing Candice for good, or about why her daughter had gone missing. She'd been kidnapped by an ex-client who Laura had tried to blackmail as revenge for his savage attack.

The stab of guilt still felt as sharp as that day but Laura tried to shake it off. Thank God she had got to Candice in time, and that the man had been locked away for what he had done. The past was a dangerous place to return to so Laura focused on her current life instead and decided to ignore the graffiti because it was only a few words and she'd be foolish to let that get in the way of things. She and Candice were happy now. Since her days on the beat, Laura hadn't touched any drugs although she still enjoyed a drink socially.

She now had five shops in Central Manchester, Altrincham, Wilmslow, Knutsford, and The Wirral, and she enjoyed the money and freedom that her entrepreneurial lifestyle afforded her. There were occasional problems, but nothing Laura couldn't handle. After spending fourteen years on the streets, she felt equipped to tackle anything.

Despite how much she had moved on, though, the past had left its mark. You couldn't go through all that and not have it affect you. There were times like now when she thought about her many regrets: the wasted years, the harsh treatment she'd had to endure, the death of her partner and controlling pimp, Gilly, from an overdose, and the neglect of her daughter.

The latter was one of her biggest regrets but at least Candice had accepted her past. They had both been able to move on and Laura was determined that they would never go back to the way things used to be.

Candice pulled up in the spacious driveway of Thomas's home in Timperley. Like her, Thomas lived in a large, detached house. This one belonged to his father and was in an older style than the one owned by Laura. But Thomas's home was nonetheless impressive. Candice walked up to the portico entrance and rang the doorbell, delighted when Thomas appeared straightaway at the other side of the door.

In Candice's mind, Thomas had the most handsome face she had ever set eyes on. There was something about him, his warm expression, and his kind eyes that people always found endearing. Candice had met him on a night out in nearby Sale. Apart from his looks she had been drawn in by his personality. He was fun to be with, understanding and had a wicked sense of humour and, best of all, he was just as smitten as she was.

As soon as she saw him, she broke out into a smile. He leant forward and planted a kiss on her cheek then waved his hand in a flourish, inviting her inside the vast hallway. They went through to the kitchen where Thomas's father was standing at the central island.

Thomas was slightly taller than his father at five foot eleven. They were both dark-haired, although the older man's was now mostly grey, and they shared dark eyes, but Thomas's weren't as intense. And that was where the physical similarities ended as Thomas's face was rounder and softer than his father's, which had angular features.

'Ah, that's good timing,' he said to Candice and Thomas. 'I was just making a cup of coffee. Would you like one?'

'Yes please,' said Candice while Thomas nodded.

'Pam's in the lounge if you want to go and say hello,' he pointed out, referring to his girlfriend.

'Oh yeah,' said Candice who was always pleased to see Pam.

For the next half hour, the four of them made polite chit-chat. Candice didn't mind as she got along with the couple, but she was secretly eager to spend some time alone with Thomas. When he announced that they were going upstairs to watch a film, Candice happily followed him.

'Aw, your dad and Pam are really nice,' she said. 'I bet you were glad when he came home, weren't you?'

For a moment Thomas's face was shrouded in confusion. 'What d'you mean?'

'You know, after he'd been working overseas.'

'Oh yeah, course I was,' he quickly replied.

'Where was it you said he'd been working?'

'Australia. Why?'

'Oh, no reason. I was just curious.'

'Yeah, it was Australia. That was why I couldn't see him for years. Apart from the flights being expensive, it would have been difficult for him to get enough time off. It's difficult travelling all that way for just a few days because of jet lag. Anyway, Grandma and Grandad were brilliant, so I was OK, and we video-called all the time.'

'Did he do the same type of work over there?' asked Candice.

'Similar, yeah.'

Then Candice became solemn. 'I bet you missed your mum.'

As soon as she'd made the comment, she regretted it as Thomas's face clouded over. 'I still do,' he said.

'Sorry, Thomas, I shouldn't have mentioned it. Let's change the subject. Why don't you test me for tomorrow's exam and then we can watch that film you mentioned?'

She forced a smile, trying to make up for her faux pas. It had been sad to hear about Thomas's earlier life. His mother had died of a heart attack nine years ago, which had been particularly tragic as she'd been so young, and Thomas had been just a teenager.

She still couldn't understand why his father had decided to leave his children and go working abroad so soon after they had lost their mother but, according to Thomas, it was because he couldn't face life in England after the death of his wife. She supposed it was understandable in a way and Thomas didn't blame him for it so why should she?

Besides, his dad seemed a nice guy and at least he didn't have the shady past that her mother had. Candice tried not to think about that. She didn't hold it against her mother; she had always accepted it and was proud of the way her mother had turned her life around. But, for some reason, every time she decided to tell Thomas about it, she just couldn't. His dad and girlfriend were so nice, and she was worried they'd see her in a different light if they knew. And that would ruin everything.

2

As soon as Candice put her key in the door, her mother came out of the living room to meet her.

'Well, how did your last exam go?' she asked.

'Great! It went really well.'

'Oh, that's good to hear,' said Laura, flinging her arms around her daughter. 'You're well on your way to getting that business degree. Although, I must admit, I was a bit concerned that you wouldn't be doing enough studying with you spending so much time with Thomas.'

'You must be joking! Thomas is great. He's the one who makes sure I get my work done. He even tested me last night so that I was ready for the exam. Don't forget, he knows what it's like to study. That's why he got a first in his degree.'

'OK, OK, I get the point,' said Laura, holding up her hands in mock surrender. 'I tell you what, why don't we go on a shopping trip on Saturday to celebrate. I'll take you into Manchester and treat you.'

Candice smiled, aware of how different her life was now compared to her deprived childhood. 'Aw, that would be brilliant, Mum. God, you don't half spoil me, y'know.'

Laura hugged her again. 'That's because you're worth spoiling. You're a little treasure.'

Candice was looking forward to the coming weeks. Apart from the shopping trip on Saturday, she was going to take a week off to relax after the exams. Then, she planned to work in her mother's Altrincham shop for the rest of the holidays.

That Saturday Laura and Candice went into Manchester after lunch, taking the train so they could have their evening meal at a restaurant together with a few cocktails. Candice was pleased that her mum seemed to be pulling out all the stops and she was looking forward to their celebration after she'd been working so hard revising for her exams.

Having alighted from the train at Deansgate station, Laura's Manchester shop seemed the obvious place to start their shopping trip. Candice was looking forward to it. She hadn't been to any of her mother's shops for a few weeks and knew they were always well stocked with the latest fashion designs.

It would be nice to see Gina too who had known Candice since she was a kid. She was one of the first members of staff Laura had employed when she'd opened her first branch on Deansgate. Gina had been a shop assistant then, but Laura had nurtured her and as her confidence had grown, she had eventually taken over as manager when the previous manager had moved on.

Gina spotted them as soon as they were inside, and she crossed the shop to meet them. Candice could tell by the look on her face that something was wrong.

'Oh, Laura, thank God you're here,' said Gina. 'I was just about to phone you.'

'Why? What's wrong?' asked Laura.

Gina pursed her lips. 'You'd better come through to the back.'

They entered the back office where they spotted several garments hanging over a chair. 'What are they doing in here?' asked Laura, picking one up and noticing it was one of the more expensive dresses she stocked by the designer Baudelaire. 'They're the latest designs. They should be front of shop where the customers can see them.'

Gina picked up the first garment and handed it to Laura. 'Look at it. They're all the same and all Baudelaire dresses too.'

Laura took the dress and examined it, then her face dropped as she noticed two tears running down the length of it. 'Oh my God! We can't have that. Have you taken it up with the suppliers? I hope you noticed it before you put them on the rails.'

Gina didn't speak for a moment. Instead, she picked up a second dress and held it up for Laura to see. Like the first one, it had a rip running from top to bottom and Laura's jaw dropped in shock.

'Oh my God!' said Candice.

Gina finally spoke. 'They weren't like that when I put them on the rails. Somebody must have done that to them.'

'What? You're joking!' cried Laura. She examined the garments in detail. 'This isn't just a rip. Some bugger must have run a knife along them. It must have been sharp as well, probably a bloody utility knife by the looks of it. When did you spot them?'

'Not long ago. A customer brought two of them over to me. She's not long left the shop. Then I did a quick check along the rail and found those others too.'

'And did you spot anything before that? Anybody acting suspiciously?'

'No, it's been a really hectic morning. I've been run off my feet. I'm a bit worried especially after what happened to the shutters. Do you think it could be the same person?'

Candice noticed her mother's sidelong glance at her, as though she hadn't wanted her to know. 'Why, what happened to the shutters?' she asked.

'Nothing love, just a bit of graffiti, probably not connected,' Laura replied before Gina had chance to speak.

But Candice wasn't stupid. She could see how Gina had been about to speak and then adopted a look of resignation after Laura had responded. She could also tell by their body language that there was more to this. 'What did the graffiti say?'

It was her mother who responded again. 'Oh, nothing much. It was just somebody playing silly buggers, that's all.'

'I want to know, Mum.'

'Leave it, Candice! I'll speak to you later. We've got things to sort here first. Gina, please can you go through all the rails and examine the items. Get one of the staff to help you. Bring all the damaged stock through to the back straightaway. I don't want any more customers seeing them. I'll stay here to make a few calls. I want to get a bloody security guard on the door to make sure this doesn't happen again. Oh, and Gina, thanks for bringing it to my attention.'

'Do you want me to help?' asked Candice.

'Yes, you can make us all a cuppa to start with. Then you

can go and help Gina to check the garments.' She pulled out a chair and plonked herself on it, then she let out a heavy sigh before she looked up at Candice and said, 'I'm sorry, love. The shopping will have to wait till we've got this sorted out.'

Candice put her hand on Laura's shoulder. 'It's OK, Mum, I understand. This is a lot more important.'

Once they had taken care of things, Gina asked, 'Do you mind if I ask you quickly about something else while you're here?'

Laura hesitated for a moment, knowing that Candice would be eager to enjoy the day. But, as a busy businesswoman, Laura knew that sometimes things couldn't wait. 'Will it be quick?' she asked.

'Yeah, I just wanted to check with you about the plans for the coming season.'

'It's all in hand,' said Laura, smiling. 'After the end-of-season sale, I've got some great stock arriving. I've been going round the suppliers checking out all the new lines. Wait till you see the dresses. They're fantastic. And there are some lovely suits too. All the Eighties power dressing is coming back in.'

'Oh, great,' said Gina.

Laura smiled again. At least they had something positive to focus on. 'Anyway,' she said, 'It's time to celebrate the end of Candice's exams. I'll be in touch soon.'

'OK, thanks,' said Gina. 'Enjoy your day.'

They left the shop and set off on their shopping trip. Now that they were alone, Candice decided to question her mother further. 'What *did* the graffiti say, Mum?'

Laura sighed again. 'Oh, love, you don't need to know. Just leave it will yer?'

'No, Mum. Whatever it is has got you really rattled, and I want to know why. You know you can tell me anything so why are you keeping it a secret?'

'OK, OK, if you must know, it said, "Crystal is a whore".'

Candice flinched, feeling the impact of those words. Aware of her mother's painful past, she recognised the implication. It was something they rarely talked about these days; both of them had been eager to leave it behind. But now she asked, 'Do you... do you think it's someone who knew you when... y'know...'

'It looks that way, Candice. But I don't want you to go worrying about it. Like I said, it'll be somebody playing silly buggers, and they'll soon tire of it.'

'But, Mum, what if it isn't? What if it's someone dangerous. They must have been hard-faced to walk in the shop in broad daylight and do that. And they must have been carrying a knife too. You need to tell the police.'

'I will if it carries on. Now stop worrying and let's hit those shops,' said Laura as she swung open one of the doors to Selfridges.

But Candice *was* worried. She knew the sort of people her mother had dealt with in the past and now it looked as though one of them had caught up with her. Laura might have been trying to play it down, but Candice could tell her mother was just as troubled as she was.

3

Laura went through the door at the side of North nightclub and took the stairs to Ruby's Massage Parlour. As soon as she walked through the entrance, the décor spelled out the real function of the upper floors. The place had been redecorated over the years, the owner now favouring a deep red carpet and red and cream walls with light brown fabric sofas rather than the combination of cream and rose that she had chosen initially.

But there were still lots of touches that were not only fitting for a brothel but also for a more upper-class establishment. The crystal chandeliers, expensive lamps, oversized plants in large decorative pots, velour furnishings and fabric panels on the walls had all been carefully selected.

Ahead of Laura was a reception area and the slim blonde woman standing behind the desk greeted her enthusiastically. 'Hi, Laura, she won't be a minute. She's just tidying up after her last client.'

The *she* referred to Laura's close friend, Trina, known as Mistress Ruby by her clients. And the woman behind the reception desk, Tiffany, was Trina's long-standing partner.

Laura and Trina had met over twenty years ago when

they had both been teenagers working the beat. Like Laura, Trina had found a way out of that life. For fourteen years she had not only been running Ruby's Massage Parlour with Tiffany, but she also performed as a dominatrix from a room on the top floor of the building known as Ruby's Dungeon. It suited her personality as she was the one in charge and she no longer allowed the clients to touch her.

Laura chatted with Tiffany until Trina appeared in the reception area only a short while later. An attractive black woman, standing at almost six feet tall with a slim, toned body, Trina didn't take any nonsense from anybody but to those she knew and loved she was a diamond. She had helped Laura out on many occasions and was always available if she had any problems.

'Hiya, girl, how are you?' she greeted, hugging Laura.

'Not too bad,' said Laura, forcing a smile.

'Ooh, something tells me you've got trouble,' said Ruby, shaking her head in mock dismay.

'Yeah, you could say that. It might be something and nothing though.'

'Come on then, let's go and have some lunch and you can tell me all about it.' Then she turned to Tiffany. 'Is everything OK here, love, till I get back?'

'Yeah, course it is. You two go and enjoy your lunch. I'll see you later. You've got no bookings till tonight anyway so take your time.'

Ruby pecked her on the cheek. 'OK, see you after.'

Fifteen minutes later, Laura and Trina were seated inside one of Manchester's upmarket restaurants drinking wine and waiting for their food to arrive. 'So, go on, spill,' said Trina.

Laura talked her through what had happened the previous day and told her about the graffiti too.

'Fuckin' hell! What you gonna do about it?' was Trina's reaction.

'Well, I've rung a security firm and arranged to have someone on the door. They're sending a man tomorrow. Hopefully, that'll put a stop to it.'

'You need to get the police involved.' As Laura pulled a face, Trina responded, 'I know, they're not my favourite people in the world either but you can't afford to just leave this. You don't know what they'll do next.'

'But I don't want to dredge up the past again, Trina. Imagine how that will affect Candice. I put her through enough when she was a kid. And, apart from that, I don't want the staff knowing anything either. They're not gonna show me respect if they find out I used to work the beat, are they?'

'You've got no fuckin' choice, girl! It looks as though the past just caught up with you whether you like it or not.'

Laura gulped. Trina had a way with words that could really make things hit home. She must have picked up on Laura's reaction because she then said, 'Sorry, I didn't mean to worry you. Like you said, it could be something and nothing, but do you really want to take the chance just for the sake of your reputation? Candice knows about your previous life anyway and fuck what the staff think.'

'I suppose you have got a point,' said Laura.

Trina gave Laura a meaningful look and said nothing further.

*

Candice had had a lovely day. Having finished the last of her exams she wanted to celebrate so Thomas had taken her to Blackpool. After a day on the beach and funfair followed by an hour and a half of negotiating their way through traffic, they were finally back in Manchester.

As they turned into the road where Candice lived, she was disconcerted to notice a police car parked close to her home. She looked at Thomas, her expression a mix of worry and curiosity.

'They might have called at one of the neighbours', he said as he pulled up outside her mother's house.

Candice shrugged. She guessed it might be in connection with the vandalism at her mum's Deansgate shop. She was worried about Thomas finding out in case he discovered the connection to her mother's past, but she tried to mask her concern as she replied, 'Maybe. Should we go inside and find out?'

She put her key in the door and, as soon as she got inside and heard voices, she knew the police were there. She walked into the living room to find her mother sitting across from two police officers.

'What is it, Mum?' she asked.

'I'll tell you later, love.'

One of the police officers stood up. 'We were just about finished anyway so I'll leave you two to talk. We'll be in touch if we hear anything.'

As Laura saw the officers to the door, Candice and Thomas sat down on the sofa and waited. 'Well?' she asked as soon as her mother came back into the room.

'I've taken your advice, love, and reported those incidents to the police.'

'Oh, good,' said Candice, relieved that her mother had done something about the vandalism.

'Anyway, I'm late with dinner so I'll go and get on with it and leave you two in peace.' She gave Thomas a welcoming smile then left the room.

Candice felt a moment of dread as Thomas asked the question she had been expecting. 'What incidents?'

'At my mum's Deansgate shop. There was a bit of graffiti and then someone ripped a couple of the dresses.'

'Aw, that's awful. Any idea why?'

Candice shrugged.

'What did the graffiti say?' asked Thomas.

Candice had been deliberating for a while over when she should tell Thomas about her mother's past. But she'd been seeing Thomas for six months now, so she supposed it was about time she confided in him. Besides, it was either that or lie to him about what the graffiti had said.

Worried that her mother might overhear her, she lowered her voice. 'It said, "Crystal is a whore".'

'Crystal? Why? That's the name of the shop, isn't it? But your mum's called Laura.'

Candice took a deep breath. She could feel her heart thudding as she psyched herself up to reveal all to the man she loved. 'Crystal used to be her name. Well, her pretend name I suppose. She was a… a… prostitute. And, it looks as though somebody might have found out about it.'

'Shit, that's awful! I mean, not about your mum but… well… that someone could be doing that.'

Candice could tell how shocked Thomas was about her mother, but he was trying to play it down to spare her feelings. 'Well, it's all awful really, isn't it?' she said. 'But she's not a bad person, y'know.'

'No, no, I wasn't suggesting that, Candice. Your mum's sound and I'm sure she had her reasons.'

'She did. She had a bad time with her mum's boyfriend when she was younger, so she ran away from home and ended up on the streets.'

'Wow, that is bad! Was she still a, y'know, when she had you?'

Candice nodded. 'Yeah, it was bad. But at least she managed to turn things around and, to be honest, I'm proud of her for doing that. And she's gone out of her way to make it up to me ever since.'

As she spoke about her mother, Candice could hear her voice cracking.

'It's OK,' said Thomas. 'I'm glad you've told me.'

'And you won't hold it against me?'

'No, will I heck. Why would I?' He took her in his arms and Candice could feel her heartbeat gradually returning to normal. Then he pulled away and looked intently into her eyes. 'Actually, there's something I need to say to you too.'

'Really? What is it?'

Thomas hesitated for a second, gazing around the room. 'Bloody hell! I didn't realise it was that late. My dad will have dinner ready.'

'You can always stay and have it here,' said Candice.

'Thanks, but it's OK. There are a few things I need to get ready for work tomorrow. I'll give you a ring when I get home.'

'OK. But what about that thing you wanted to say to me?'

'I'll tell you another time, I promise, but I don't think now is the best time with everything that's been going on.'

He got up to go, popping his head into the kitchen to say goodbye to Laura before he left the house and got into his car. Candice stared after him as he sped off down the road. She was relieved to have got things out in the open and glad he didn't seem to have held it against her. But she was also curious. What was Thomas's big secret, and why had he backed out of telling her?

4

Laura had been acting weird ever since the incidents at her Deansgate shop. Candice could understand it really. It can't have been nice to have been confronted with what happened years ago after she'd done her best to put it all behind her.

Candice had tried to reassure her mother, but she didn't really know how she could help – other than by telling her it was probably just somebody pulling a prank. Deep down inside, though, she didn't believe that.

Since yesterday her mother seemed to have got worse. When Candice had come home from the shops her mother had still been out, so Candice had helped herself to something to eat. Then, when her mother arrived home, she had been vague about where she'd been and why she wasn't home for tea, merely saying that she'd been to see Trina.

And today she seemed tense, the slightest noise making her jump. Candice had noticed that she had been lost in thought for most of the morning too and when she jolted her out of it by speaking, her mother became snappy.

When Laura said she wanted a word with Candice, it wasn't wholly unexpected. Still, she felt her stomach quiver as she wondered what else might have happened.

'Sit down,' said Laura, taking a seat across from her in the lounge.

Candice could see that she was even more uptight than usual, and she was wringing her hands as she prepared to speak to her.

Then she came out with it, 'I don't want you to work in the Altrincham shop during your holidays.'

'Why not?' asked Candice. 'Is this because of what happened at your Deansgate branch?'

'Yes, I don't want to take any chances.'

'Then why have you waited a week to tell me when you know I'm due to start tomorrow? I've been looking forward to it, and the money would have come in handy too.'

'I'm sorry, love, but you'll just have to get a job somewhere else.'

'Where? All the summer jobs are taken by now. I was really relying on this, Mum.'

'Look, don't worry about the money. I can always help you out.'

'But, Mum, you know how much I love working in the shop and it's a brilliant chance to get some more work experience. And the Altrincham shop is miles away from Manchester so I wouldn't be taking any chances.'

Her mother hadn't mentioned any further incidents recently and Candice had mistakenly thought that it must mean there hadn't been any. But now the look on her mother's face told her otherwise.

'Something else has happened, hasn't it?'

Laura shuffled uncomfortably in her seat. 'Yes, but you don't need to know the details. As long as you keep away from the shops, you'll be OK.'

'What is it, Mum? Tell me!'

'Nothing, love – you don't need to know,' she repeated.

'But I want to know,' Candice persisted. 'Have they targeted the Altrincham shop too?'

Again, her mother's expression gave her the answer. 'What was it? Graffiti again?'

'Yes, that's all.'

'What did it say?'

'Never mind what it said,' Laura snapped. 'Just leave it, will you, and do as I say?'

Candice was annoyed that Laura was being so dismissive. Why couldn't she tell her what the words said? It wasn't as if she didn't know about her past but now it felt as though she was treating her like a child again.

Later, when she was alone, Candice thought about how her mother had been behaving lately. These attacks were freaking her out and Candice recognised her jumpiness and snappiness as fear. She could identify with that, after all she'd been scared for a lot of her childhood, and she was finding these reminders of the past deeply unsettling.

2011

Candice was home alone, and she was scared. She was ten years old, and her mother had never left her alone before, but she'd told her she wouldn't be long. She didn't have to work that night and was just going out to see a friend for a bit. That had been ages ago and, since her mum had gone out, Candice had lain in bed for ages unable to sleep.

It was winter and her mother had left the central heating on so she wouldn't be cold. But the system was old, and the water rattled around in the pipes making loud banging noises that made Candice jump. In the end she had crept downstairs, the hairs on the back of her neck standing on end.

She tiptoed through the house, her senses on full alert. All was still apart from the sounds of the central heating and the loud ticking of the clock on the mantelpiece. Candice checked the time. It was midnight and she knew her mother would be annoyed if she found her still up. She'd left strict instructions for her to stay in bed.

Suddenly Candice heard another sound and she spun round to the place where the sound was coming from. The front door. It was a key being turned in the lock. She raced upstairs and got back into bed.

She could now hear voices. Loud voices. One she knew was her mother. And the other was a man. Gilly, she thought. Candice didn't like Gilly. He talked posher than her mother, but he swore a lot too, and his tone was often aggressive when he spoke to Laura. But at least he spoke to Laura, unlike Candice whom he ignored because, she presumed, he saw her as a nuisance.

They were arguing as they often did, and Candice wanted to check her mum was alright. She crept down the stairs again, relieved when the arguing stopped. But then she could hear other noises, loud grunting noises coming from Gilly. Then her mother yelled out and, overcome by curiosity, Candice dashed to the living room door, which was ajar.

Gilly was now standing up, fastening his trousers. Her mother was lying down on the sofa but, as Candice watched, she sat up and straightened her skirt. Then Gilly sat down next to her and fished something out of his pocket. He placed a bag on the coffee table. It was full of white powder.

'Where are the fuckin' straws?' he asked.

Laura obliged by crossing the room and taking two straws out of a drawer in the wall unit. Candice remembered her mother telling her she kept the straws in case she gave her a party. That party had never happened.

Candice watched with fascination as Gilly poured some of the powder onto a saucer that had been left on the coffee table. He and Laura placed the straws over the powder and breathed in deeply. Gilly then sat up and stretched. He was facing the door now and Candice was afraid he might see her so she sped away.

Candice got back into bed as quietly as she could. For a moment she thought about the strange things she had seen. What was the white powder? And why were they sniffing it up their noses? But now that her mother was home, she wasn't afraid anymore and she suddenly felt overcome with tiredness. She fell into a deep sleep. Her last thought was the hope that her mother wouldn't leave her alone in the house again.

Laura felt bad for snapping at Candice but this whole thing was getting her down. After the incidents at Deansgate she hadn't heard anything further for a week. The police hadn't been in touch either, so she assumed they'd had no leads. Then, out of the blue, Haley, the manager of her Altrincham shop, had rung her the previous day.

Apparently, she'd found some graffiti on the shop shutters that morning when she'd arrived for work. She told Laura that she'd already arranged for somebody to clean it off so there was nothing to worry about. She merely felt that she should know. But, unlike Laura, she wasn't aware of the incidents that had already taken place at the Deansgate shop.

'No, leave it,' said Laura trying to sound casual. 'I'd like to have a look at it.'

Haley sounded surprised at Laura's interest in the graffiti, but she went along with her request. Laura didn't ask her what it said; she was too afraid of being confronted with the answer. Instead, she decided to visit the shop once everyone had finished for the day and the shutters were down. She didn't fancy having to respond to questions from her staff again. But for the rest of that day, she was on edge, wondering what the graffiti might say.

Before setting off for the shop, she called two people: Trina who had already agreed to go with her for moral support. And the police. She preferred to deal with them at the shop rather than at home where Candice might twig what was going on. She didn't want to worry her if she could help it.

When Laura and Trina arrived at the shop, the police were already there. The officers were different from those she had seen last time but there were two of them, both male and young. She couldn't see all the graffiti at first as the police were stood in front of the shutters where they seemed to be examining it themselves and having a detailed discussion.

Laura approached cautiously with Trina. The officers turned around as she drew nearer to them, their expressions inquisitive. 'Hi, I'm Laura Sharples, the shop owner,' she said. 'I rang you.'

For a few moments, her attention was on them as she told them what had been happening at the Deansgate shop too. While they spoke, she was aware of Trina in the background, staring at the shop's shutters. Laura glanced to the side and noticed that the look on Trina's face was one of shock.

Her eyes followed Trina's line of vision and she caught sight of the graffiti, spray-painted in neon green letters. *I'm onto YOU.*

Laura visibly flinched and Trina grabbed hold of her arm to steady her.

'Shit!' she muttered.

'It's OK,' said Trina. 'It's just some idiot with nowt else better to do.'

But Laura knew otherwise. Somebody was targeting her and, whoever it was, they had deliberately chosen her Altrincham shop as their next target. She had no doubt that they were aware of where she lived. The shop was only about a mile from her home and, as far as Laura was concerned, it was far too close for comfort.

5

'I'm absolutely gutted,' Candice complained to Thomas after she'd told him about the graffiti at the Altrincham shop. 'I was looking forward to working in the shop this summer.'

They were sitting on the bed inside Candice's bedroom while Laura was downstairs watching TV. Thomas had arrived only half an hour after she'd had her conversation with her mother, and Candice had told him everything.

'Yeah, but your mum's right,' Thomas said. 'If she thinks the same person has targeted both shops then you need to be careful. I'm sure you'll find something else, and you could always meet up with some of your friends in the meantime.'

'Actually, I've got a night out with my uni mates on Thursday to celebrate the end of the year.'

'OK, so that's Thursday and Friday taken care of then.'

'What do you mean?'

'Well, you'll spend most of Thursday getting ready and then most of Friday in bed with a hangover.'

'Cheeky!' said Candice, tapping him playfully on the arm.

Thomas laughed. 'You students don't know how lucky

you are with all this free time. Some of us have to work for a living, y'know.'

'Ha, you're just jealous because you're not one of us anymore,' Candice teased.

When they'd finished their banter, Thomas came up with an idea. 'Why don't I ask my dad if you could work for him at one of his businesses?'

'Doing what?'

'A bit of admin or something. He has office staff that take care of things for the car showrooms.'

'Ah, right. Yes please. That would be great!'

She paused for a moment, wondering whether to broach the next subject with him. Then, thinking *why not*, she asked, 'I've been thinking about what you said last week.'

'Oh yeah?'

'Yeah, you said you had something to say to me.'

Candice saw his face drop before he said. 'Not now, Candice.'

'Why not? Why even mention it if you're not going to tell me?'

'I slipped up, OK? I'll tell you in good time, but I just don't think the time is right at the moment.'

'Why not?'

'Well, you and your mum have got a lot going on, haven't you?'

'Why should that make any difference? Anyway, I'd rather know now.'

'Please just forget it, Candice,' he said then he pulled out his phone and started scrolling through his social media indicating that the subject was closed.

She felt a bit irritated at the way he had shut her down, especially after she'd confided in him, so she took to her phone too. She wished he hadn't said anything in the first place, because now she wouldn't settle until she knew what he was keeping from her. For a moment, the atmosphere was stifled. She kept peeping up from her mobile, but Thomas's eyes remained fixed to his screen.

She was about to break the silence when Thomas beat her to it. 'If you want, we can go to the Altrincham shop and see if we can find out what the graffiti said. But obviously, we won't let your mum know what we're doing.'

Candice knew he was only trying to distract her from whatever he was hiding from her. But she was curious about the graffiti and, apart from that, she was tiring of the awkward atmosphere that had developed between them in the past few minutes.

'Yeah, alright then, let's go. We'll tell Mum I'm going to yours.'

Thomas smiled and got up off the bed and a few minutes later they were getting inside Thomas's car on their way to the centre of Altrincham.

When Candice and Thomas walked inside the Altrincham shop, Haley, a petite brunette in her late thirties, greeted them enthusiastically. Candice was relieved because it meant Haley wasn't yet aware that her mother had forbidden her to visit the shops.

'Hi, Haley, how are you? I hope that graffiti didn't shake you up too much.'

'No, it's not as if it's the first time. It'll be kids with nothing else better to do.'

'What? You mean there's been more?'

'Oh, not recently, no. I'm talking about ages ago, someone spraying Man United.'

'Ah right. What it said this time wasn't very nice though, was it?' said Candice, pretending she already knew.

'Well, I don't think it was abusive or anything, but your mum seemed to think it was a threat.'

'Why?'

'Well, I think it was the way they put the word *you* in capitals. I don't know why that bothered her though. It could have meant any one of us.'

'Yeah, it could have. Why do you think she's taking it so personally?' asked Candice, still fishing for information.

'I don't know. It depends on what she thinks it means. "I'm onto you" could mean anything really, couldn't it?'

Candice tried not to react, keeping up the pretence that she already knew what the words had said. 'I don't know,' she said, keeping an even tone. 'It's not like she's got anything to hide. But has she told you that there's been graffiti at the Manchester shop too?'

'No. Why, what did it say?' asked Haley.

'Erm, I can't remember the exact wording, but it wasn't nice. Maybe that's what's got her freaked out as she might think it's the same person targeting her shops for some reason. Anyway, I thought it best to warn you, Haley. I don't want to alarm you or anything, but you need to be on your guard. Oh, and by the way, don't tell her I told you about the Manchester branch or that I came here today. She's stopped me visiting all of the shops.'

'Why?'

'Because of all this, I suppose. But don't let it worry

you. She's probably over-reacting. She's always been a bit overprotective of me. Anyway, it means I won't be able to work here during the summer holidays, so I thought I'd best explain.'

'Aw, that's a shame. We were looking forward to having you.'

'I know. I was looking forward to being here. Never mind, once all this blows over, maybe Mum will let me work the Christmas holidays.'

Candice was eager to get away now that she'd found out about the graffiti, so she made her excuses and she and Thomas left the shop.

'Why did you tell her your mum had stopped you going to the shop?' asked Thomas. 'She probably didn't want her to know.'

'Because I felt that she should know. There's obviously more to this than Haley knows about, so I thought it only fair to warn her. My mum should have told her really, but she probably didn't want to worry the staff. Anyway, Haley's sound. She won't tell my mum.'

But, despite her brave words, Candice was worried about going behind her mother's back. She felt she'd had no choice though. It was only by visiting the shop that she had found out what the graffiti said and, once she knew, she had felt duty-bound to warn Haley about the situation.

Candice had worked at the shop several times during her holidays from university and, apart from being the shop manager, Haley had also become a friend. And, as far as Candice was concerned, friends should always have each other's backs.

6

Candice walked into the busy city centre bar and spotted her crowd straightaway, occupying a corner table. She bought herself a drink then made her way over to them.

'Hi!' greeted Emma and Alicia in unison, and Candice squeezed into the seat that Emma had saved next to her.

Candice had met the two girls at university and the three of them had soon become good friends. Although Candice was from Manchester, she had chosen to live in the university's halls of residence when she was a fresher so she could experience student life to the full. Then, at the end of the first year, a group of eight of them had rented a house together, three girls and five boys.

Tonight, they were all there as well as other friends. The three girls spent the next half hour catching up then began mingling with the crowd. At some point during the evening Candice returned from the ladies' to find Emma and Alicia chatting to a girl called Sally. Candice sat down, deciding to check her phone for messages then grab her drink before going over to them.

Candice was just about to switch off her phone and put it away when she was joined by Ethan. Her heart sank as soon as he plonked himself down next to her. His movements were clumsy, and it was obvious he was already drunk.

Ethan had been living in the same house as Candice and her friends, but Candice usually tried her best to avoid him. The rest of the group had agreed reluctantly to let him join them in the student house as he had lived with them in the halls of residence, and they felt mean leaving him out.

He was a good-looking lad but completely full of himself and seemed to think that all the girls should fall at his feet. Ethan was a gifted maths student, and it was obvious from his attitude that he thought it made him better than everyone else. When he wasn't coming on to the girls, he was usually trying to impress everyone with his superior knowledge.

Candice nodded and smiled politely but she was already wondering how long it would be before she could make her excuses and escape from Ethan. She had already given him the brush-off a few times in the past when he'd pestered her for a date, and she didn't want his persistence to spoil her night.

'So, who is Crystal?' he slurred by way of a greeting.

Taken aback by his question, Candice asked, 'What do you mean?'

'Crystal. It's the name of your mum's shops, isn't it?'

Candice was surprised that he knew about her mum's shops as she couldn't remember telling him. She hoped it wasn't a sign he was taking an unhealthy interest in her. 'Yeah, that's right,' she replied. 'It's no one in particular. My mum just liked the name, so she chose it for all her shops,' she lied.

He smirked. 'Ah, right. And how long has your mum had the shops?'

'Erm, a few years. I'm not sure exactly when she got her first one.'

'Why, how many has she got now?'

'Five.'

'What did she do before she got the shops?' he asked.

Candice was becoming uncomfortable with this conversation, which felt more like an inquisition, and her face was burning with shame as his eyes seemed to bore through her. She dreaded him knowing something from her past that she preferred to keep hidden.

'Erm, she worked in a shop,' she replied, unable to think of anything else.

'Which shop?'

'I don't know. I can't remember. I was only a kid at the time.'

'So, who is Crystal?' he repeated.

'I've already told you; I don't know. Look, what is all this about, Ethan?'

'I was just wondering why someone wrote "Crystal is a whore" on the shop shutters.'

He deliberately raised his voice as he quoted the graffiti. The words gave Candice a shock, making her draw her shoulders and head back, and she realised how tense she had been. In her peripheral vision she could see Emma and Alicia throwing concerned glances her way. She hoped their concern was because of the volume of Ethan's voice and that they hadn't managed to pick out his words.

Spotting them walking over, she tried to recover herself and put an end to the trying conversation. 'It's just graffiti,' she said. 'We often get it at the shops.' Then she stood up and picked up her drink before adding, 'It was probably some drunk who presumed the name of the shop owner was Crystal and had nothing else better to do than to vandalise somebody else's property.'

She walked away, meeting Emma and Alicia before they had chance to join her at the table. 'What's wrong?' asked Emma. 'Why was he shouting?'

'He's pissed,' Candice replied. 'Which means he's being an even bigger arsehole than usual.'

'Why, what was he shouting about?' asked Alicia.

'Nothing that made any sense. I think it was just his way of trying to get my attention.'

'It's probably because you've knocked him back a few times,' said Alicia. 'You know what his ego's like.'

Although Candice was shaken by Ethan's aggressive interrogation, she tried to front it out. 'Yeah, probably. Anyway, let's not let that dickhead spoil our night. Come on, let's go and get some shots.'

They headed to the bar, and Candice was relieved when she saw Ethan slope off to join another group of students. As soon as they had finished their shots, Candice, who was eager to get away from Ethan, insisted they all go to another bar. Fortunately, her friends went along with her suggestion.

For the rest of the evening Candice tried to relax and enjoy herself, determined not to let the earlier discussion with Ethan ruin what would be their last get-together until after the summer break.

It was only when she was in the cab on the way home that her own words came back to her. *It was probably some drunk who presumed the name of the shop owner was Crystal.* She realised that Ethan had done exactly that; he had presumed that Crystal was her mother's name. Her words took on a new significance. Had he presumed, or had he already known about who her mother used to be?

7

On Altrincham district was a man who had recently become more acquainted with the area, especially within the environs of Crystals fashion shop. He was there for a reason and had a particular target in his sights. And tonight, that target was an easy one. It was a woman.

He stopped on the opposite side of the shopping precinct where he had a good view of the shopfront, and pretended to browse in a shop window, taking surreptitious glances to see if his target had left yet. The name *Crystals* was lit up in numerous tiny bulbs so that they resembled crystals sparkling and he couldn't help thinking what a classy touch that was.

He was already familiar with the shop's interior because he'd paid a visit a few days previously. He'd managed to persuade a girl he knew to go in with him under the pretence of shopping for clothes. A few uppers had seen her right. During his visit he had clocked the name badge on a self-assured petite brunette: *Manager – Haley*. And that was the woman he was waiting for now.

While he had been waiting, he'd seen other staff leaving the shop, but no Haley. He hoped she hadn't left early, otherwise he'd have to come back another day. But surely, as the manager, she would be the one to lock up. Most of the other shops had now shut and he watched the hordes of employees making their way out of the shopping precinct on their way home.

When a few minutes passed and the shutters came down on the furniture shop where he was standing, he decided to move along a bit. He didn't want to look suspicious, but he had to walk a few metres before he spotted a jeweller that still had its shutters up. The man wasn't quite as near to Crystals now, so he knew he'd have to keep his eye on things as he didn't want to miss Haley.

Trying to appear inconspicuous, he was admiring the watches in the jeweller's window but still glancing towards the shop occasionally. After a couple more minutes he was reassured to see Haley outside. She must have already locked up because, as he watched, she put the keys inside her handbag then took out a remote control. At the press of a button the shop's shutters came down.

Once they were down completely, Haley set off with the man in pursuit and taking care to remain a few metres behind. As she walked along, he could see which way she was heading and guessed she was on her way to the nearest car park. He was aware of it as he'd also done a recce of the surrounding areas when he'd made his bogus shopping trip.

He knew that he couldn't afford to wait till she reached the car park. As it was summer, the evening was light, and it would be too exposed. There would still be some workers and shoppers making their way home. But he knew of an alleyway just after the next junction.

The man sped up, eager to be in reach of Haley by the time they got to the alleyway. When she turned the bend at the junction he sprinted to the corner and turned into the next street. He was glad to see that he was now in close range of Haley. He was also relieved that the street was relatively quiet. Thank God she'd left work after most people had already gone home.

A quick scan told him there was only one man getting into his car much further up the road and a couple on the other side of the street who were just going out of view as they walked past a parked van.

He psyched himself up ready. He was going to enjoy carrying out his orders, and he'd also make sure it was profitable for him.

Haley was looking forward to the next couple of days as she didn't have to work. As a shop worker, it wasn't often she got the weekend off, but her husband had booked two nights at a spa hotel in the Lake District as a special treat for them. She'd sorted everything out in readiness: her packing was done, her parents were minding the children and her assistant manager, Caitlin, had agreed to step in for the next two days.

As she made the short walk to the car park, she was full of excitement. She and her husband had busy careers and it was rare for just the two of them to spend time together. The hotel had been recommended by a friend and she couldn't wait to try out the spa. She loved the Lake District and was also looking forward to leisurely walks in the countryside followed by chilled evenings eating out and sipping wine.

It wasn't until she turned into a small side street that her attention was pulled away from her forthcoming weekend.

Hearing someone behind her, she turned to see who it was. By the time she caught sight of the man, he had grabbed her and was dragging her into the alleyway. It was difficult to tell what he looked like as he was wearing a mask, which wasn't unusual given the current pandemic.

She tried to pull away, but he was so forceful that she lost her footing, her high heels scraping along the ground. Haley began to yell but he clamped his hand tight across her mouth. Before she knew it, she was in the alleyway, and he had a knife pointed at her.

'Don't say a fuckin' word!' he ordered. 'Or I'll slice you up.'

She felt her heart racing and as he took his hand away her jaw dropped in shock. When he grabbed her handbag, she didn't put up any resistance, terrified at the sight of the knife and his threatening tone.

'Please, just take what you want and leave me alone,' she begged.

He clearly found it difficult to open the bag while brandishing the knife. 'Open the fuckin' thing!' he ordered. 'And take your purse out.'

She did as he demanded, and he shoved the purse inside the waistband of his trousers.

'Right, now give me the shop keys and that remote for the shutters.'

Haley gasped realising that he must have been watching her, but she did as he demanded.

'And now you can hand me your jewellery,' he said.

Haley cried. 'You can have my rings but please don't take my necklace. It was my mother's. It's all I've got left of her.'

'You heard what I said. Hand me your fuckin' jewellery! All of it.'

Haley wept as she handed him her wedding and engagement rings then struggled to unfasten her chain as her hands were shaking so much.

'Get a fuckin' move on!' he hissed, eager to be off before anyone spotted them.

Once he had got everything he wanted, Haley prayed that he would leave her alone. But she was out of luck. He put the knife away, using his fists instead to rain blows down on her. Before he went, he grabbed her hair, yanking it upwards till she was facing him. Then he closed in till his face was only centimetres from hers and spat out his last few words, 'That's what you get when you work for a fuckin' whore!'

Haley watched him run off then she stumbled out of the alleyway and into the street. Dazed and shaken, she looked around for help then broke down sobbing when a middle-aged couple came to her rescue.

It wasn't till later that she connected the attack and what he had said with the warning she had received from Candice. She hadn't taken much notice at the time, thinking it was just a young girl over-reacting. But now she wished she had. There was obviously something serious going on.

8

When Candice arrived at Thomas's home that evening, he greeted her with a smile. He leant in for a kiss and, as he straightened back up, she smiled and said, 'You're looking pleased with yourself.'

'That's because I've got some good news for you.'

'What?'

'Dad's offered you a job at his offices.'

She kissed him again. 'That's brilliant. Doing what?'

'Not sure, probably a bit of filing, that sort of stuff. My dad will explain it better.'

'Great. I must go and thank him. When does he want me to start?'

'Monday.'

'Monday? Bloody hell, that only gives me a couple of days to prepare.'

Thomas laughed. 'How long do you need? You're going to work in an office not for a night out on the town. How did your night out go by the way?'

'Good, I'll tell you about it once I've thanked your dad.'

Candice went through to the lounge where Thomas's father was sitting alone reading a newspaper.

'Thank you so much for offering me a job,' she said.

He put his newspaper to one side and smiled. 'You're welcome. I'm sure you'll be an asset to the company.'

Candice returned his smile. 'Thanks.'

'Are you OK to start Monday?'

'Yeah, sure. What type of work will I be doing?'

'You'll be helping the other girls in the office. A bit of filing and photocopying, checking through emails, that sort of thing.'

'OK, good. Thanks again,' said Candice.

Then she turned to Thomas who said, 'Shall we go up?'

She nodded and followed him upstairs to his room where they sat down on his bed.

'Thanks so much for putting the word in for me,' she said.

Thomas grinned at her and leant in for a kiss. He began getting amorous, his hands roaming over her body until Candice pushed him away.

'What's wrong?' he asked.

'I don't like to. I mean, I know your dad doesn't mind me staying here with you but it's a bit different at night, isn't it? He's not likely to walk in on us then but he could do now. Anyway, there's something I want to tell you.'

'Oh yeah, what's that?'

'It's about last night.'

Thomas's face adopted a serious expression.

'Don't worry, it's nothing for you to be concerned about. It's just a conversation I had with one of the lads. He's called Ethan. I don't know if you've heard me mention him before.'

'No,' said Thomas, shaking his head.

'Well, he's a bit of a dick, actually. He always gets

rat-arsed on nights out and makes a fool of himself. He's got a really superior attitude too.'

Candice then told Thomas about the conversation with Ethan and how persistent he had been.

'What if it's him that did the graffiti?' she asked.

'Do you think he'd do that?'

'I don't know. He seemed to think Crystal was my mum's name and whoever did it thought the same thing, so it did make me wonder. I wouldn't have thought that was his style though. He seems smarter than that. But what if he's bitter because I've turned him down a couple of times? And it seemed strange that he knew all about the shops and the graffiti, because I've never told him.'

'Um, but if he fancies you, he might have asked people about you. And anybody could have seen the graffiti especially with it being in Manchester where all the students hang out. How long was it there?'

'I'm not sure.'

'And what about the damaged garments? You said it looked as though someone had cut them with a knife. Do you think he'd do something so extreme just because you'd knocked him back a couple of times?'

'Not really, no. I mean, he might be a pain, but I've never heard anything to suggest he has violent tendencies. If anything, he's a bit of a soft lad. Apparently, some of the crowd ran into a bit of trouble one night and he did a runner because he was so scared.'

Thomas laughed. 'Not a hardened criminal then?'

'Not really, no. What do you think I should do?'

Thomas sighed. 'Maybe you should leave it for now. Thinking about it, how would a lad of his age know about your mum's past anyway, assuming you haven't told anyone else?'

She shook her head. 'No, I haven't. I prefer them not to know.'

'Well then, from what you've said it doesn't sound as if it's him – and imagine the ill feeling it'll cause amongst your uni friends if you go making accusations. After all, no one likes a grass.'

Candice frowned. Thomas was right. It would cause problems and the last thing she wanted was to create a difficult situation amongst her friendship group when Ethan might not have done anything aside from the uncomfortable interrogation on their night out. She'd just about made the decision to leave it for now and see what happened, when Thomas spoke again.

'On the other hand, what if it is him? Can you afford to leave it?'

9

Candice came bustling in through the door of her mother's home the following morning to find her on the phone in the living room.

'Yes, we can certainly let you have a good deal, and at a good price too.' Then after a pause she added, 'No, that's not the way we do things. The discounts will stay the same as previously.'

She looked at Candice and rolled her eyes before adding, 'Then, I'm afraid we'll have to sell them elsewhere. There's a lot of demand for some of these lines, even out of season.' She nodded at the phone. 'OK, I'd be happy to talk again if you change your mind.'

When she cut the call, Candice asked, 'Who was that?'

'One of the designer outlets, trying to get our end-of-season stock at ridiculous prices, just as I was about to make some important calls too. Cheeky sods! No worries, they'll be back when they realise they can't get that kind of quality any cheaper elsewhere.'

Candice smiled. Her mother was so business-savvy and it often amused her to see her shrewd negotiating skills. 'I've got something to tell you,' she announced excitedly.

'Something good by the looks of it,' said Laura.

'Yeah, I've got a job, starting Monday.'

After much deliberation, Candice had decided not to mention the problem with Ethan. She would leave it for now and see what transpired.

'Bloody hell!' said Laura. 'Where at?'

'Working for Thomas's dad, in his offices.'

'Aw, brilliant. That's good of him.'

'I know, he's a nice bloke.'

But Candice could tell that her mother's response was lacklustre. 'Is something wrong, Mum?' she asked.

Laura's face dropped. 'Yes, Haley rang me last night. Apparently, she was mugged on her way home from work.'

'Aw, you're joking! Poor Haley. What did they take?'

'I wish I *was* bloody joking! They took her purse and jewellery including a necklace her deceased mother left her, the keys to the shop and the remote control for the shutters.'

'Oh my God! That's terrible.'

'Oh, don't worry, it gets worse. Whoever it was must have followed her from the shop as he already knew about the keys and remote.'

Candice felt a shockwave run through her. She was surprised her mother was telling her this given that she had kept the graffiti at the Manchester shop a secret from her. But the reason for her mother confiding in her soon became apparent.

'And, to top it all, she's jacked her job in. She says she's too scared to go back to work after the attack, well that and the warning you gave her when you turned up at the shop against my wishes.'

Candice could hear the anger in her mother's voice. Not used to seeing her mother like this, especially with her, she tensed, and her face became flushed. But Laura wasn't finished yet.

'That's all I bloody need! I'll have to find a new manager now not to mention changing the locks and the shutters. It's going to cost me a fortune. And Haley will probably tell the rest of the staff, so I'll be lucky if they don't walk out on me too.'

Candice suddenly became annoyed at hearing her mother carrying on about the financial implications when Haley had been attacked and obviously left shaken.

'I would have thought Haley's feelings were more important,' she snapped.

'Well of course they are. I've already offered to go and see her tonight. I was going to take something round, but she won't let me near her, thanks to you. She's fuming because she blames me for the attack, and you've made things bloody worse by warning her about what happened at Deansgate. I just hope none of this gets in the press or it could cause problems with the other shops too.'

'Don't blame me!' yelled Candice. 'It was only fair to warn the staff. You knew they were in danger, but you chose not to say anything. Instead, you were more interested in your bloody PR exercise than protecting them.'

'That's not true, Candice, and you know it! How was I to know that this person would start attacking my staff?'

'Humph,' muttered Candice and she turned her back so she could no longer see her mother's face.

Her words seemed to have hit home because her mother didn't say anything further. Instead, she went through to the kitchen, leaving Candice alone.

Once she was gone, Candice was left shaking and she

could feel the threat of tears. It wasn't often that she and her mother fell out; usually they got on well and had always depended on each other. She was disappointed at her mother's reaction to what had happened to Haley. It wasn't like her to put greed before people's emotions.

But she knew her mother. It wasn't that she didn't care about Haley, more a case of her being overwhelmed by what was happening. It was now obvious to Candice that this was more than just vandalism. The attack on Haley had shifted things up a gear. Somebody had it in for her mother, which put them both in danger. And Candice was terrified.

Laura was dashing through the shopping precinct in Altrincham on the way to her shop. Once she had calmed down after her row with Candice, Laura had rung round locksmiths to see if she could get anyone to come out on a Saturday. Thankfully, she'd been successful in relation to the door, but she hadn't found anyone to sort the shutters out. They would have to wait till the following week.

When she arrived, she was glad to see that a locksmith was already at work. She went inside in search of the assistant manager, Caitlin, and found her at the back of the shop helping one of the staff to organise some of the garments on the rails.

'Can I have a word?' Laura said then went through to the office leaving Caitlin to follow her.

At twenty-two Caitlin was relatively young for an assistant manager especially in an upmarket shop like Crystals. But she was confident and capable, having graduated from university the year previously. If Laura was honest with herself, she wasn't too keen on the girl. Caitlin's confidence bordered on arrogance at times, but Laura let it pass knowing that she was a good worker.

Laura plonked herself down in the manager's chair and

watched as Caitlin took the seat opposite. 'OK, I'll come straight to the point,' she said, intending to assert her authority straightaway. 'Haley was attacked last night on the way home, and it looks as though the attacker had followed her from the shop because he knew she had the shop keys and remote control in…'

'I know,' Caitlin cut in. 'Haley rang and told me, and the police have been round.'

Laura felt a surge of guilt. It was awful to think that Haley had got caught up in all of this. She felt bad thinking how Haley had suffered but tried to stay strong.

'OK, so what did Haley tell you?' she asked.

'Everything including what her attacker said to her before he ran off.'

Laura saw the look of contempt on Caitlin's face and for a moment it unsettled her. But then she pulled herself together and remembered she was the boss. 'What have you told the staff?' she asked.

'Nothing yet. I haven't had chance with everything that's been going on.'

'OK,' said Laura, taking control. 'Here's what we're going to do. I want you to tell the staff about the attack and advise them to be careful. They don't need to know anything else. It'll only worry them. I'll also need a manager to replace Haley now that she's left, and I wondered if you would like the job.'

'It depends,' said Caitlin.

'On what?'

'On whether you make it worth my while.'

Laura felt her temper rising. She couldn't believe this young woman was taking blatant advantage of what had happened to Haley but she knew she needed her. 'Well, I'll make sure your pay is increased to manager level,' she said tightly.

'And what about danger money?'

Laura spluttered at the audacity of the question. 'You what?'

'You heard. What happened to Haley last night was bad enough to make her jack her job in. *And* she sounded really upset when I spoke to her. I'm well at risk here, not to mention the rest of the staff who you want me to keep in the dark about some of the details.'

Laura noticed the smug smirk that played across her face when she finished speaking, and she felt like slapping her. The girl was awaiting her response, all the time eyeing her directly, her intense gaze making Laura uncomfortable. It was as though she knew all the sordid details of Laura's past and was looking down on her.

But Laura knew she was getting carried away. All Caitlin knew was that Haley's attacker had referred to her as a whore but that could be for any number of reasons, admittedly none of them good.

It took Laura all her time to keep her temper in check. She couldn't afford to lose it. With Haley gone, nobody else knew the workings of the shop like Caitlin did apart from herself. And she couldn't afford to spare the time when she had four other shops to oversee.

The little bitch had her over a barrel and she knew it. Laura decided that for the time being the best thing to do was to hand over the reins to Caitlin, but she would definitely have to keep an eye on things. Caitlin might have been good at her job but there was something sly about her that Laura didn't trust.

'Right, I'll add a five per cent pay rise and that's your lot.'

She stared at the girl, unflinching until Caitlin was the first to look away. Laura was determined that she wasn't getting a penny more out of her. Caitlin might have had the upper hand for now, but she would also be aware that she had no chance of earning more elsewhere. Laura paid good rates to make sure she recruited high quality staff. And, she had already decided that once all this was over and somebody else had learnt the ropes Caitlin would be out on her arse.

'OK, I'll take it,' said Caitlin, her lips pursed as if in distaste.

'Right, good. That means we'll need a new assistant manager to replace you. I'll leave it to you to decide who gets the job. Oh, and that'll mean we're a member of staff down so you'll need to recruit a replacement for her too.'

'Right, will do,' said Caitlin, her face lighting up in triumph.

Again, Laura felt like slapping her and at one time that was exactly what she would have done. But she was a respectable businesswoman now, so she resisted the temptation and walked out of the shop, keen to get away from the snidey little cow.

Candice didn't know where her mother had gone. She had heard her on the phone after their row but then she had left the house without saying goodbye. Half an hour later there was a knock on the door and Candice wondered who it might be. She approached the front door cautiously, making sure she had the security chain in place before opening it.

Through the gap she could see two men dressed smartly in suits. One of them had grey hair and looked about fifty. He was of average height and build whereas the other man was much younger, probably in his late twenties, and he was taller and slimmer.

The older of the two held out his ID card. 'Hi, I'm Detective Inspector Carson.' He nodded towards the younger man, 'And this is Detective Sergeant Worrall. Could we speak to Laura Sharples please?'

'She's out,' replied Candice.

'Any idea how long she'll be?'

'No, she didn't say.'

'Are you related?'

'Yes, I'm her daughter.'

'Do you mind if we wait inside till she returns?'

'But I don't know how long she'll be.'

'Well then, perhaps you could give her a call and ask. I take it she does carry a mobile with her?'

'Yeah.'

'In that case, could you tell her that we need to speak to her as soon as possible? It's an important matter.'

Candice didn't need to ask what it was about. She knew it would be about the attack on Haley, so she undid the security chain and let the officers inside. Once they were sitting down in the lounge and she'd offered them a drink, she rang her mother from the kitchen and asked her to return home as soon as possible.

'I hope you're going to tell them everything, Mum,' she said.

'Well, as much as I know, yeah, although they'll have found out more from Haley, obviously.'

'I don't mean just the attack; I mean about the graffiti and slashed dresses.' Then she psyched herself up before adding, 'Mum, you're gonna have to tell them about the past too. You know it's all connected.'

She heard her mother take a deep breath on the other end of the phone before saying, 'Tell them I'm on my way back and I'll be as quick as I can.'

Then she cut the call, leaving Candice wondering just how much information her mother would divulge to the police.

It was Saturday evening and Laura was sitting across from Trina and Tiffany in their front room, having brought them up to date about everything including her row with Candice and her visit from the police that afternoon. She was feeling stressed about the whole situation and just wanted to offload.

'And what did the police have to say?' asked Trina.

'Not much. They just asked me loads of questions and said they'd look into things, but I don't think they've got any leads.'

'Was Candice there when they came round?'

'Yes, she let them in because I was out but as soon as I got home she went upstairs and left me to it.'

'And what about Candice? How are things with her now?'

'Not good. We've hardly spoken since the row this morning. She didn't even come back downstairs to ask how things had gone with the police. I think she was still in a mood, so I left her alone.'

'Oh shit. That's not like you two, is it?'

Laura could feel herself getting emotional. 'No but I feel like she's betrayed me, Trina. How could she go to the shop like that behind my back? It makes me look bad for not warning the staff first, but the only reason I didn't was because I was so mithered about everything.'

Trina grinned. 'She's an adult with a mind of her own, Laura, and she's just as impulsive and determined as her mother at times.'

Laura was about to bite back but when she saw Tiffany chuckle at Trina's words, she couldn't resist a smile herself. Trina was the only person she knew who could tell her exactly what she thought and get away with it, and she respected her for that. When you were having problems, you needed a friend who would tell you straight rather than pussyfooting around.

'She needs to know everything,' said Trina, 'including the fact that Haley's attacker was violent towards her, and what he said to her too. If you're right and this is some sort of vendetta, then she could be in just as much danger as you and she needs to have her wits about her.'

Laura flinched at her directness. 'Fuckin' hell, Trina. Cheer me up why don't you?'

'Sorry, I don't mean to scare you, Laura, but this is some serious shit. You're gonna need to be on your guard. And you'll do that better if you and Candice are on the same side.'

Laura sighed. 'You're right. I'll have a chat with her when I get home. And I'll apologise. Maybe I should have handled it better. I was that stressed by it all, I made her think that all I cared about was the money side of things. But it's not like that. Of course I'm bothered about the staff. I mean, some of them have been with me a long time. I've watched them grow. And I'm especially bothered about Candice. I'd die if anything happened to her.'

'Well then, you need to have a chat tonight... unless you'd rather have a drink and stay here tonight then tackle it tomorrow.'

'No... no... I'm not gonna leave her on her own with all this going on.'

'Sorry, I didn't think. I just assumed she'd be with Thomas.'

'Not tonight, no.'

'Who do you think could be behind it all?' asked Trina.

'God knows! I came across that many nasty bastards when I was on the beat. It could be any one of them. You know what it was like on the streets, Trina. Some of those fuckin' weirdos would slap us around just for the fun of it.'

Trina nodded. 'Yeah, too true.'

'Anyway, thanks for listening to me ramble on,' said Laura. 'I'll finish this cuppa then I'll get going.'

It wasn't long after that Laura arrived back home. She was surprised to find Candice's car missing from the drive, and she searched around the house for her once she got inside. Candice was nowhere to be seen. Laura tried ringing her to check where she might be but there was no reply.

Candice tutted when she heard her phone ring. Curious, she stared at the screen and when she looked at the name and saw it was her mother, she ignored the call.

She was sitting inside Haley's living room drinking coffee. Haley had thanked Candice for the flowers and card she had brought. Then she had made them both a drink.

When she'd first seen Haley, Candice had been shocked.

Her left eye was still swollen and there was heavy black bruising underneath. She was wearing a short-sleeved top and Candice had also noticed the bruises that ran up one of her arms.

'Do you want to take that?' asked Haley, referring to the call.

'No, it's OK.'

Then Haley asked, 'Why didn't your mum warn me about what was going on?'

'I don't know,' said Candice. 'I think she's just a bit stressed with everything. I believe she offered to come and see you.'

'Yes, and I turned her down to be honest. I felt like it was a guilt trip. Oh, but don't worry, I've got no problem with you being here. And thank you for your warning. I wish I'd have taken more notice, but I just thought it was a bit of vandalism.'

'I think it's more than that,' said Candice.

'Well, yeah. Now he's resorted to mugging people on their way home from work I'd say it definitely is. I wonder why though.'

Candice felt a twinge of guilt. Although she had warned Haley to be careful when she'd visited her at the Altrincham shop, she hadn't told her everything. So, as far as she was aware, Haley didn't know about the incidents inside the Manchester shop or what the graffiti said. Candice had kept it to herself for a good reason though; she had wanted to protect her mother's reputation.

Despite her fallout with her mother, she remained loyal to her and had decided not to reveal everything. What would be the point anyway? It was already too late for poor Haley who'd suffered at the hands of the lowlife scum who had done this to her. So, instead, she shifted the focus.

'Did he do or say anything that might have given you a clue?' Candice could see the distress in Haley's features and guessed she was finding it hard reliving what had happened on Friday evening. 'I'm sorry,' she added. 'You've probably gone through all this already with the police. I shouldn't ask really but, it's just that, this whole situation is getting to me.'

'No, it's OK,' said Haley, recovering. 'I can't blame you for wanting to know. I would if I were in your shoes. After all, you don't want the same thing happening to you.'

Candice felt her heart racing at the thought of becoming the victim of a similar attack, but she listened while Haley went over what had happened.

After describing the attack, Haley added, 'It was what he said before he ran off that really freaked me out.'

'Why? What was it?'

Haley sat up straight and stared pointedly at Candice before speaking. Then, taking a deep breath, she said, 'That's what you get for working for a whore.'

Candice felt a cold sweat as Haley's words hit her. She'd already suspected it was somebody from her mother's past when she'd heard about the words: 'Crystal is a whore', on the shutters of the Manchester shop. But what Haley had just told her confirmed her suspicions.

No wonder her mother was getting so worked up about everything! She was worried too. If somebody could do that to Haley just because of who she worked for then what would he have done if he'd got his hands on her mum?

12

Candice woke up late on Sunday morning. She had lain awake in the early hours with everything going over in her head and had finally fallen back asleep just before nine. Eventually she tumbled out of bed and went downstairs still wearing her PJs. A feeling of dread took hold of her as she descended the stairs; she knew she needed to have a discussion with her mother today, and she wasn't looking forward to it.

When she'd returned from Haley's the previous evening her mother had suggested they have a chat. But Candice had been tired and still reeling from Haley's revelation about what her attacker had said, so she had agreed to talk the following day.

Candice still couldn't understand why her mother was keeping things from her. During her wakeful hours she had decided she would stand her ground because this thing affected her as well as her mother.

She needn't have worried because when Laura spoke to Candice, her tone was appeasing. 'Candice, I need to apologise to you about yesterday. I didn't mean to come over as though I didn't give a damn. It was just that this has all been getting to me quite a bit. I was upset about Haley's attack, and it didn't put me in the right frame of mind to deal with all the fallout from it.'

Seeing her mum so apologetic, Candice couldn't help but respond in a similar way. 'I'm sorry too. I shouldn't have snapped at you, and I shouldn't have gone behind your back. But I thought you'd go mad if you knew I was going to the shop to talk to Haley.'

'It's OK. I understand,' said Laura. 'You did the right thing. I should have told her myself about the Manchester shop, but I had no idea they'd come to Altrincham too.'

Candice smiled weakly. 'I know.' Then, still determined to get answers, she asked, 'What did you tell the police?'

'Everything.'

'What? You mean, about your past too?'

Laura nodded then lowered her head as though it pained her to admit it.

'It's alright, Mum. You've done the right thing. Did you manage to sort everything out at the shop?'

'Yeah. Well, almost. The shutters will have to wait but I've had the locks changed, and Caitlin's stepped into the manager's position.'

'OK. What do the staff know?'

'Caitlin knows everything about what happened to Haley, but I've told her not to tell the rest of the staff all the details.' Candice gave her a pointed look and she quickly added, 'It's best not to worry them, but she's going to tell them about the attack and warn them to be vigilant. And the police have been brought up to speed now so hopefully they'll catch the bugger before he does any more harm.'

'I know everything too. I went to see Haley last night and took her some flowers. She told me what the attacker said.'

Laura looked shocked. 'Oh, OK.'

'Why didn't you tell me, Mum?'

'I was going to but, well, you know…'

She didn't need to say anything more. Candice realised it couldn't be easy for her mother having to relive the past, but she needed to know what was going on. 'Who do you think it is?' she asked.

Candice could see the anguished expression on her mother's face, and she felt awful for asking.

'Well, if you want me to be honest, it could be anyone.'

'What do you mean?'

Laura hesitated before replying. 'I dealt with a lot of bad people back then, love. I don't really want to go into details. I put you through enough as it is.'

Candice heard the tremble in her mother's voice, so she didn't press her. Instead, she said, 'Will you promise to tell me if anything else happens?'

'I'd rather I didn't have to,' Laura retorted.

'But, Mum, how can I be on my guard if I don't know what's going on?'

'I know, I get your point,' said her mother, holding up her hand in a conciliatory gesture. 'OK, I'll tell you. But I don't want you worrying. Like I say, the police are all over this now. They've even assigned that detective inspector to the case so I'm sure they'll come up with something soon.'

Candice smiled. 'OK.' Then she thought for a moment before speaking again. 'Now that we're being honest with each other, Mum, there's something I need to tell you.'

'Go on.'

'Right. Well, there's this boy at uni called Ethan...'

Candice filled her mother in on the conversation that had taken place with Ethan on her university night out before adding, 'Do you think we should let the police know?'

'Definitely.'

'But what if there are repercussions at uni?'

'That's something you'll have to face, Candice. I know you don't want to get him into trouble, but interrogating you like that was suspicious especially in view of how much he knew. And after what happened to Haley, we can't afford to take any chances. It wasn't easy for me to tell the police I used to be on the beat, but I did it because you wanted me to. And because I knew it was the right thing.'

Her tone wasn't hostile, just firm, but she must have seen the concern in Candice's face because she closed the gap between them then said, 'Come here,' before hugging her. 'Let's work together on this, Candice. I don't want us to fall out like that again.'

'Me neither.'

After a while her mother released her then, still holding her by the arms, she said. 'I tell you what – why don't you go and get yourself ready and I'll give that inspector a call? And try not to worry. It'll all work out, you'll see.'

But, despite her mother's reassuring words, Candice *was* worried. Her mother might not have told her all the details about her former life, but she remembered enough of it. Her mother's drunken nights. The drug taking. Her neglectful father. She also remembered the time she had been kidnapped and right now that was haunting her memories more than anything.

★

2012

It was Candice's second night in the barn. Her stomach was rumbling and she felt chilly. She was lying on top of a rotten pile of hay. It smelt offensive but it was more comfortable than the hard concrete floor.

Since the first day when the men had brought her here, the feeling of dread was ever-present, putting her senses on high alert. But that feeling intensified at certain times. Like now, when the barn was filled with strange noises as the rain hammered relentlessly on the roof and the wind whistled through the rafters.

Darkness was fast approaching, and Candice knew that she would feel even more afraid as gloom descended on the barn. Its windows were boarded up and the only source of light came from a hole in the roof, which let in the wind and rain.

When Candice heard a scampering, she sat up in alarm and searched around. Then she spotted the source of the noise. The rats were back, and she hated rats. This time, they didn't go away. They were heading towards her, one of them stopping to sniff at bits on the floor but the other one continuing towards the hay.

Candice pulled the thin shabby blanket tightly around herself. For a few moments she sat rigid with terror, watching the mangy rat as it approached. Then she began shivering and her teeth were chattering as cold and fear assailed her.

The rat was huge but thin, its matted fur forming oily streaks along its emaciated body. And its beady eyes had an intensity that was terrifying. As it drew closer Candice's heart was thundering inside her chest. Then she realised what its intentions were. It was after the empty sandwich packet, which she had discarded to one side of her.

She shifted away but continued watching it feed hungrily on the leftover crumbs inside the plastic sandwich carton, her body tense with fear. Candice heard squeaking noises as it battled with the carton, trying to get to the food, its long sharp incisors exposed. They were manky-looking but nonetheless lethal, like rusty razor blades.

Eventually the rat gave up, discarding the food carton and scampering away. Candice let out a sigh of relief. Then she hurled the empty packet across the barn floor, scared in case the rat returned. Once she was confident that the rats had gone, she settled back down on the pile of hay.

13

When she arrived for her first day at the offices of Foster's Motors, Candice was surprised to find that they were no more than a group of interconnected portacabins next to the main car lot. But inside she found them no different than any other offices she had seen with their banks of desks, computer terminals and busy clerks.

She reported to Thomas's father, Mr Foster, when she arrived. It felt weird to see him dressed formally in a suit and acting official. He took her through to the main office and introduced her to the staff before handing her over to an older lady, Carol, who was a supervisor. She would be looking after Candice and sharing a desk with her. Carol seemed welcoming, and Candice began to relax as they made general chit-chat.

Once Carol had shown Candice where the kitchen and toilets were, she got her started with some filing. After an hour she gave her a break from that, sending her to do some photocopying instead. Candice was glad of the break because the filing was becoming mind-numbingly boring.

The highlight of the day seemed to be at lunchtime when a van pulled up outside and the staff rushed out to buy sandwiches. Then they all trundled into the kitchen to eat them.

The rest of her colleagues were friendly and keen to find out what she thought of her first morning there. Candice obliged them by saying repeatedly that she found it alright even though in reality she would much rather have been working at the shop.

She enjoyed fashion and was at home in her mum's shops. But maybe working for Thomas's father would give her some insight into the business world, which might come in handy in the future. Her plan when she finished university was to work for one of the top fashion houses, maybe as a buyer or a merchandiser.

Candice had ten minutes of her lunch break to go when one of the girls rushed into the kitchen looking agitated. 'He's only just pulled me for smoking on my fuckin' lunch break!' she complained.

'Who has?' asked Carol.

'Who d'you think? Fuckin' Foster. I told him it was my lunch break, but he still didn't like it. He said it was creating a bad impression to the customers and that if I really needed to do it then I should go somewhere out of sight.'

'Ah, take no notice,' said Carol. 'You know what the moody bastard's like. You can't do right for doing wrong in this place.'

Candice was surprised to hear them talk so disparagingly about Thomas's father and was tempted to put them straight about what a nice guy he was out of work. But then she thought better of it. If they knew she was connected to the boss who they didn't seem to like then they might give her a hard time, and she had enough problems in her life without adding anything else.

Not wanting to hear any more derogatory remarks, Candice finished her lunch break early. 'You're keen,' said Carol as Candice left the kitchen and headed towards her desk.

'She's new,' said the other woman. 'She'll soon learn.'

Candice tried not to let their opinion of Mr Foster bother her. Maybe that's what it was like in the workplace. She supposed there would always be rebellious types who resented anyone in authority. She decided the best way to handle the remarks would be to ignore them.

Candice was glad when the day came to an end. The only break she'd had from filing and photocopying had been when she'd been shown how to work the franking machine. She consoled herself with the fact that at least it was a way of earning her own money during the summer holidays.

She'd kept her phone switched off all day and had only looked at it during her lunch break. That way she wouldn't be tempted to answer any calls and texts when she should have been working.

As she walked to her car, she checked her phone for any activity since lunchtime. Apart from two missed calls from Emma, there was a message from Ethan. It put her on edge as it dawned on it must be in connection with her mum giving his name to the police as a suspect. Candice opened it and quickly read the text.

What a nasty thing to do just because I commented about the graffiti on your mother's shop. Is that the way you get your revenge when you don't like what someone says? Thanks to you I was stuck at the police station for three hours yesterday. Please don't bother speaking to me when we're back at uni. I want nothing to do with you.

Candice felt guilty. She'd been reluctant to give her mum his name as she doubted he had anything to do with the vandalism, but she couldn't help thinking he might know more than he was letting on. And she knew the police would want to cover all bases. Now she felt even worse as it seemed more apparent that he was innocent, and he was obviously upset at being questioned by the police.

She guessed that the phone calls from Emma were probably about the same thing, but she put off ringing her straightaway. She preferred to get home first.

Her mum was waiting for her when she opened the door. 'How was your first day, love?'

'OK, I suppose.'

'Oh. Well, you don't seem too happy about it.'

'It was a bit boring to be honest.'

'Aw, give it chance, love. It'll get better once they've trained you up a bit.'

'I know. Don't worry. I'll stick it out and see how it goes.'

Candice was eager to get away so she could reply to Emma's phone calls. She left her mother standing in the hallway and dashed up to her room. Emma answered the phone on the second ring.

'Hi, Candice. What's going on? Have you seen all that stuff Dan's been putting on the group chat about Ethan getting taken in for questioning because you reported him to the police? He doesn't sound very happy.'

Candice hadn't seen anything on the group chat and hadn't had any notifications so this was news to her. It upset her to hear it, because Dan was one of their friend group. He was also the person who had set up the group chat. But Ethan was one of the boys who had shared their student house so she supposed he must feel a degree of loyalty towards him. He also seemed to get on better with Ethan than most of the others in the house. Maybe it was because of their mutual love of computer games.

'No, I haven't seen anything,' said Candice.

Emma continued to enlighten her: 'Dan says it's because he said something to you the other night. Was that while we were out?'

Candice replied reluctantly, wondering how to play this. 'Yeah, that's right.'

'Jesus! What did he say that was so bad it made you report him to the police and why didn't you tell us about it on Thursday if you were so frightened?'

'It's not so much what he said, it's the fact that he knew about the graffiti on the shutters at one of my mum's shops.'

'Yeah…and?'

'Well, it's not just that shop. Someone's been targeting two of my mum's shops and Ethan seemed very interested in my mum's business. In fact, he wouldn't shut up about it, so I had no choice but to tell the police.'

'Jesus, Candice! You don't think Ethan did it, do you? I mean, I know he's a dick, but surely he wouldn't do that.'

'No, I don't, not really. But the police asked my mum if anyone had been acting suspiciously and, well, he was a bit too interested in the graffiti and he knew what it said word for word. Not only that, but he was asking weird questions.'

'Right, so you reported him for asking weird questions?'

Candice could hear the sarcasm in Emma's voice and for a while there was an awkward silence between them until Emma spoke again.

'I feel sorry for you and your mum if that's what's been happening, but I really think you're barking up the wrong tree if you're blaming Ethan. It's no wonder him and Dan are annoyed.'

'I'm sorry, I didn't mean to upset anyone. I'll apologise to Ethan.'

'No, I think you should leave it for now, Candice. The damage has already been done. Look, I'll catch up with you soon. I've got to go.'

The line went dead, and Candice stared at the phone in her hand. What had she done?

It seemed to her that Dan and Ethan weren't the only ones she had upset, and she hoped her uni friends weren't going to hold it against her. She dreaded to think what she might have to face when she returned in September.

Curious, she decided to check the group chat and see what was being said. She knew she shouldn't as it might upset her more. But she had to know so she went through her phone and tried to find the group. Unfortunately, it was no longer there, and Candice came to the devastating conclusion that Dan had removed her from it.

14

It was only a few days since Laura had heard the news of Haley's attack, so she was still feeling stressed. But work was important to her, so, remembering Caitlin's bad attitude when she had called in at the shop, Laura decided to go round there to check on her. It would do Caitlin no harm to remind her who was the boss.

What Laura saw in the window made her hackles rise. Instead of showcasing the latest arrivals, it was full of cut-price items with a gigantic 'Sale' banner on display. And when she walked inside, she noticed all the cheaper garments at the front of the shop, packed onto rails that also had gory red 'Sale' signs attached to them.

Laura marched through the shop in search of Caitlin who she found sitting in the office drinking coffee and chatting on the phone. Her melodic tone and smiling face suggested it was a personal call.

'What the hell is going on?' demanded Laura, glaring at Caitlin who terminated the call then stared back.

'Do you mind? That was important!'

'Well, it didn't sound important from where I'm standing. And now you've finished whispering sweet nothings down the fuckin' phone, perhaps you'll tell me just what the hell is going on out there.' As Laura spoke, she pointed her hand forcefully towards the shop floor.

Caitlin looked shocked at her aggressive body language and use of bad language, and Laura felt a sense of satisfaction knowing her display of temper had unsettled the cheeky bitch.

'What you on about?' asked Caitlin, going on the defensive.

'I'm on about all those sale items out front. Where's the latest designer stock?'

'What do you mean? The Baudelaire dresses?'

'Yes, those, and the other designer items.'

'Oh, don't worry, they're still out, just not at the front of the shop.'

'Don't fuckin' patronise me! I'm not worried. I just want the display organising the way it should be. And you've no right to go switching things around. Aside from overstepping the mark, it's completely disrespectful. It's only a few days since Haley was viciously attacked and you're acting as though she never existed!'

'But aren't I supposed to be managing this shop? And managers are supposed to make decisions, aren't they?'

Her attitude did nothing to quell Laura's temper, but she tried to hold things together knowing how much she needed Caitlin's cooperation.

'Within reason, yes, but you're also supposed to act within company guidelines. When Haley trained you up as assistant manager, she told you what those guidelines are, and all the staff have a company handbook setting out the requirements. Even you!'

'Well, I thought it was best to put the sale items at front

of shop. After all, you want them shifting, don't you? All the shops do it; I don't know what the problem is.'

'The problem is this isn't a tacky little high street chain shop! This is an upmarket independent fashion shop, and you're creating the wrong impression to our customers. How are the latest designer outfits supposed to tempt the most affluent shoppers inside if they can't see them? All our shops are arranged the same. It's the way we do things at Crystals.'

Defeated, Caitlin kept her mouth shut but her expression was pure venom. Laura continued berating her. 'I want the whole shop putting back to how it was by the end of today.'

'But… but… that's impossible…'

'I want no arguments. I don't care what devious plans you had for the rest of today. This takes priority. Because every minute those high-value items are hidden from the public is lost revenue. And you might have thought yourself smart in negotiating a crafty pay rise but if takings are down then I'll be dropping your salary to recover the profits. And I'll be back to check on you, so make sure it's done!'

Once she'd had the last word Laura sped out of the office. She left the shop and strode to the car park. Caitlin had really annoyed her, and she wasn't prepared to listen to any more of her nonsense. It took her a while to calm down. Something about Caitlin always had that effect on her but with her new position she had become even cockier than ever.

Once her temper had diminished, Laura regretted her lack of control. She wouldn't normally have reacted so angrily but, apart from Caitlin's impudence, the whole situation with the vandalism was getting to her. It might have been gratifying to have put the little bitch in her place, but Laura knew that Caitlin wouldn't take kindly to a dressing-down within hearing range of the staff. She just hoped that her display of temper wouldn't backfire.

15

Caitlin was having a day off. It hadn't been a good week at work. At the start of the week, she and the staff had worked hard to swap the shop around only to be told on Wednesday by that snotty cow Laura that she had to change everything back to the way it was.

Laura might have been the owner and her boss, but Caitlin resented it. Despite her nice clothes and her money, Caitlin could tell she was nothing but a scrubber, and the way she had spoken to her on Wednesday confirmed it. How could she know the first thing about running a shop when she wasn't even educated?

Caitlin still thought she was in the right. The sale goods had been flying off the rails when she had put them at the front of the shop, and they might not have fetched anywhere near as much as the latest designer items but at least she had been getting shut of them instead of having to sell them off cheaply to discount outlets.

But it was Friday now, and she had the whole weekend to look forward to. She had arranged for her new assistant manager to stand in for her on both Saturday and Sunday, and she was due to meet a friend for a meal at seven.

She'd decided to come into Manchester early so she could

do a bit of shopping first. After splashing out on cosmetics and new lingerie, Caitlin made her way up to Deansgate to check out the Manchester branch of Crystals. She wondered if the shops really were arranged similarly, but one step inside the shop confirmed to her that they were. In fact, the layout in this branch was freakily similar to the Altrincham shop. Her cow of a boss was obviously fuckin' anal!

But one thing that wasn't the same was the lack of Baudelaire dresses. There was the odd one here and there, but they didn't dominate the shopfront display as they usually did at Altrincham. Plenty of other designer brands were out front though.

As she walked around the shop, she spotted a woman with a name badge that read, *Gina – Manager*. Caitlin couldn't resist going over for a chat.

'Hi, I'm Caitlin, manager of the Altrincham branch.'

Gina looked confused for a moment. 'Oh, I thought she was called Haley.'

So, she obviously didn't know Haley had left the shop. Laura must have kept that to herself. But Caitlin was going to enjoy enlightening Gina. And if she decided to walk it might even open up a position in the Manchester shop, which was bigger and in a better location.

'She's left. She was attacked after she left work last Friday, so I've had to step up. It's pretty scary really when you consider what happened. Whoever it was had been watching her because he knew she had the shop keys and remote for the shutters in her handbag. And with that as well as the graffiti, I think it was just a step too much for poor Haley.'

'Hang on! What graffiti?'

'At the shop.'

'What did it say?'

Caitlin lowered her voice, pretending to be discreet. 'It said, "I'm onto you" only the "you" was in capitals.'

Gina raised her hand to her mouth and sucked in her breath.

'You alright?' asked Caitlin. She had expected Gina to be shocked but not this shocked, and something told her there was more to this.

'Yes, I, it's just…'

Caitlin could tell she was about to say something but then seemed to think better of it. She would love to know what it was so she kept the conversation going, hoping to draw her in so she might come out with it. 'It's weird how similar the layout is in both the shops, isn't it?'

'I don't know,' said Gina who still seemed to be in shock. 'I've never been to the Altrincham branch.'

'Maybe you could call next time you've got a day off. We could go for a coffee. It's similar to this one, like I say, only the shop's a bit smaller. Laura likes the expensive items out front, doesn't she? I notice there aren't as many Baudelaire dresses here though.'

'No, not since…' As Gina paused, she looked around her, noticing a few shoppers hovering nearby. 'I tell you what, why don't you come through to the back. We can talk better in there.'

Caitlin smiled and followed her to the office. She noticed the serious expression on Gina's face as she said, 'I'm a bit worried about what you told me, to be honest.'

'About Haley, you mean? Oh, don't be. Just because it's happened at Altrincham, doesn't mean it will happen here.

It's miles away, isn't it?' said Caitlin, pretending to reassure her.

'Yes but... it's the graffiti too.' She seemed to hesitate a moment but then said, 'This is just between the two of us, but I think you should know as you're in a similar position to me. We've had graffiti as well as you and what it said wasn't very nice.'

'Really?' asked Caitlin. 'Why, what did it say?'

Gina repeated the words the perpetrator had used. It was Caitlin's turn to be shocked. After Haley's attack, she hadn't been too worried but now she realised that it fitted in with the words that Haley's attacker had used. She hadn't connected the dots at the time, thinking it was just some random attack by a crazed misogynist.

And despite what she had said to Laura to squeeze a pay rise out of her, she had been convinced that the same thing wouldn't happen twice in the same place and that the graffiti probably wasn't connected. But what Haley was now telling her suggested that she had been right in assuming that there was more to this.'

'That's terrible!' she said. 'Who the hell is Crystal anyway?' she continued. 'And why has somebody got it in for her? And why would they attack Haley? It doesn't make sense.'

Gina shrugged. 'I don't know. But whoever's behind it, they mean business. You know the Baudelaire dresses you mentioned?'

'Yeah?'

'Well, somebody slit them. With a knife, it seems. We had to throw a load of them out and then we had a run on those that were left, which is why there aren't many on the rails now.'

'Shit!' said Caitlin. 'This is bad. It looks to me like someone's got it in for Laura, seeing as how she's the owner.'

'Yes, I must admit, it looks that way. I had no idea they'd been targeting the Altrincham shop too.'

Apart from feeling shocked, Caitlin was furious. Laura should have let them know all the details. They were obviously more at risk than she had thought, and Laura hadn't even bothered to tell them. To hell with it, she thought, it was about time Gina knew everything. 'That's not all,' she said. 'When Haley was attacked, the man who did it said something similar to what he wrote on your shop.'

Gina raised her hand to her mouth in shock again. 'Sorry,' said Caitlin. 'I know it's bad, but I thought it best to tell you. I think you'd best keep it to yourself though, otherwise we'll both lose our jobs.'

Caitlin left the shop soon after, still reeling from what Gina had told her. She wasn't happy that Laura was keeping secrets from her and the rest of the staff, not when it meant they were in danger. But she decided not to say anything to the staff for now. She'd already taken a risk telling Gina about Haley's attack.

She'd always known Laura was a bit of a rough arse by the way she spoke, her lack of education and the choice language she used. And now, animosity against her boss made Caitlin determined that she would find out exactly what it was that Laura was keeping from her. What she would do with that knowledge, she wasn't yet sure.

16

Candice was glad when the film finished. She had been watching it at Thomas's home with him, his dad and Pam. She looked expectantly across at Thomas and was relieved when he announced that they were going up to bed. It wasn't that she didn't like the older couple – on the contrary, she got along with them well. But there were things she needed to talk to Thomas about and she preferred to do it in private.

They plonked themselves down on the bed and Thomas put a playlist on his mobile. 'Come on then, what is it that's troubling you?' he asked.

Candice flashed a curious glance at him. 'How did you know?'

'It wasn't difficult to spot. You were twitchy all the way through the film. Are you still worrying over what's happening to your mum's shops?'

'Yeah, it's awful, and I can tell it's getting to her. She's trying her best not to be snappy ever since we fell out but she's getting irritated with everything: the car, the TV, even the bread bin. She nearly smashed it the other night when she couldn't shut it because a barm cake was sticking out.'

'Aw, like that is it?'

Candice nodded. 'She's really on edge and it's getting to me too.'

Thomas planted a comforting kiss on her cheek. 'Try not to worry, Candice. I know it's bad seeing your mother like that, but I don't think any harm will come to you personally. It seems to be the shops they're targeting. Maybe it's a business rival.'

At the mention of any potential harm coming her way she was tempted to tell him all about the time when she got kidnapped years previously. But she decided against it. Although she didn't know the full story of why she was taken, she knew it was somebody connected to her mother's dodgy past who was responsible, and she didn't want Thomas holding it against her mother. She'd already told him enough about her background and, that reminded her, he still hadn't told her his secret.

'Penny for them,' he said.

'Eh?'

'You were miles away.'

'Oh, sorry, I was just thinking... you never did tell me about that secret.'

Thomas looked uncomfortable. 'It's not so much a secret, just something I was going to tell you.'

'Yeah, and... go on.'

'No, I've decided not to. You've got enough on your plate as it is.'

'Why – is it that bad?'

'No! Let's leave it please, Candice. I'll tell you eventually, just not yet.'

She tried not to dwell on it. Like Thomas had said, she had enough going on in her life. Her mind shifted back to what Thomas had said before she became sidetracked. 'I don't think it's a business rival, y'know. If it was then why would he refer to her as a whore? And why would he beat Haley up?'

'Well, he mugged Haley as well as beating her up, didn't he? And you said he took the keys for the shop.'

'Yeah, and the remote control for the shutters but he's not done anything with them yet, although Mum's changed the locks anyway, so he'd find it hard to get in.'

'He's given your mum a lot of worry and inconvenience though, hasn't he? And as for what he called her, he's probably just being nasty. He could be a misogynist. Maybe that's how he views all women. Crystal isn't even your mum's name, anyway, is it?' Then a recollection hit him. 'Oh yeah, it's the name she used to use before, isn't it? Sorry, I forgot.'

Candice frowned. Even though she didn't hold her mother's past against her, she hated to be reminded of it. They'd both come so far since those days. She changed the subject slightly. 'I've been thinking about Ethan too. What if he did do it? The police have let him go but he could still be a danger.'

'I thought you said he wasn't the dangerous type.'

'I didn't think he was, but you never know, do you? Then again, what if he's been innocent all along? My friends are all going to hate me for going to the police.'

'Yes, but from what you told me, Emma doesn't know everything, does she? If she knew about your mother's past and what you've both been through, she might be more understanding. And only you can decide how much to tell her.'

'I don't know what to do, Thomas. It's been nearly a week and I haven't heard from her or any of the others.'

'Come here,' he said, and she shuffled nearer to him on the bed.

He turned her around and started massaging the backs of her shoulders.

'Ooh, that feels good,' she said.

Thomas leant forward till she could see his face. 'Well, when I've finished this, I know something else that will make you feel good.' He smiled mischievously. 'And it will definitely take your mind off your problems.'

Candice smiled back. Despite what she was going through, she knew she wouldn't be able to resist his charms, so she tried to relax and enjoy the massage. She'd decide what to do about Emma tomorrow.

Student House Online Group

Ethan: *I can't believe it; the police have been round to question me again. And all because Candice has told them a load of crap about me. My dad's been going spare!*

Dan: *Are you alright, mate? I can't fuckin' believe it myself. What a nasty thing to do.*

Emma: *She must have had her reasons. What exactly did you say to her, Ethan?*

Ethan: *Nothing! I was just asking about her mum's shops, that's all. For fuck's sake!*

Dan: *Don't be blaming Ethan. We all know what this is about. Candice has obviously got it in for Ethan. If she's not interested in him, then why not just fuckin' tell him instead of going to the police with a load of false accusations.*

Emma: *They're not false. Candice and her mum are genuinely upset about all the graffiti and damage at her mum's shops.*

Dan: *That's still no reason to point the finger at Ethan though, is it?*

Emma: *Maybe not but you need to see things from her point of view. The police wanted to know if anyone had been acting suspiciously and you had been asking about the graffiti, Ethan.*

Ethan: *How the hell is that suspicious? I was just showing an interest, that's all. She's fuckin' paranoid.*

Dan: *Yeah, exactly! She's off her fuckin' head if she thinks that makes him guilty.*

Emma: *OK, let's just leave it at that shall we? Ethan, I'm really sorry about what's happened but us lot arguing amongst ourselves isn't going to solve anything.*

Ethan: *OK, suit yourself. I don't need this shit anyway. I'm already stressed enough thanks to your bitch of a mate.*

Caitlin was on the Internet trawling through anything she could find in the name of Laura Sharples. She was convinced that the attacks on the shops were aimed at her as the owner, and she wanted to find out why.

She had already checked her out on the two social media sites that had come up in the search results. One of them showed a few women named Laura Sharples, none of whom was the one she was searching for. On the other social media site, she thought she had struck lucky when she found her boss's account. There were various photographs of her with friends and her daughter but, unfortunately, she couldn't access her posts. The bitch had obviously put her settings on private.

Giving up on social media, Caitlin was now in the process of scrolling through the pages that came up in the search engines under the search term, *Laura Sharples + Manchester*. By the time she got to page seven, she had found nothing other than a couple of announcements relating to new branches of Crystals that had opened previously.

The news reports said very little other than the shops' locations, the fact that there were already other shops dotted around Greater Manchester and that they were owned by successful businesswoman Laura Sharples. Then there had been a smug quotation from Laura about how proud she was to be opening another shop following on from the success of the others.

Reading about Laura's achievements made Caitlin even more angry. Her resentment was bordering on obsession, and she doggedly continued searching the net in the hope of finding some useful information. It wasn't until she reached page ten that she finally spotted something that looked promising. There was an excerpt from the article with the name *Laura Sharples* emphasised in bold. But it was the heading that drew Caitlin's interest.

She clicked 'Manchester sex worker fined for soliciting'

and quickly scanned the brief article from 2012, wondering how she could tell whether it was the same Laura Sharples. Then she read the words 'Laura Sharples who goes by the street name of Crystal'. Bingo!

It all made sense. Caitlin realised that the perpetrators didn't just think Crystal was the owner's name: they knew. Caitlin had suspected Laura wasn't the respectable businesswoman she tried to pass herself off as, and it seemed she was right.

She was thrilled to have found something on the snooty bitch and wondered how she could use it to her advantage. Then a thought occurred to her, and she entered another search term into the Internet. Caitlin found what she was looking for along with a phone number to get in touch. She wasted no time in keying the number into her phone, grinning with satisfaction as she waited for someone to pick up the call.

17

Candice still hadn't heard from Emma, Alicia or any of her other university friends in almost two weeks. After her chat with Thomas, she had deliberated over what to do. Then finally, on the Wednesday, she had plucked up the courage to ring Emma.

Her friend had seemed cool towards her, but Candice had already decided that it would be difficult to talk on the phone. So, she had proposed a visit, telling Emma that there were things she needed to tell her face to face. Thankfully, Emma had agreed to see her at the weekend.

During their conversation Emma had also divulged that Alicia had come to visit for a few days so she would be there too. Candice had visited Emma in the past during university holidays. As Emma lived in Stoke, Alicia just outside Birmingham and Candice in Manchester, Emma's house was the obvious central location for them all to meet up. And Emma's parents were always very accommodating. But this time Candice hadn't been invited.

Candice had always been one of the stronger members of the group, and a natural leader. She was more mature than the other girls who'd had a more sheltered upbringing.

But now, since the events involving Ethan, it seemed to her that the group dynamics had changed.

She had opted for public transport and as the train chugged towards her destination, Candice felt trepidatious. This meeting could go either way. But she wasn't happy with the status quo so she felt it was the only way she could change things.

When Candice walked inside the Locomotion, she spotted her two friends already seated. She felt her heart speed up as she approached their table and received a lukewarm reception. Undeterred, Candice offered them both a drink, but they turned it down.

'OK, well I'll just go and get myself one,' she said.

Making her way to the bar, she took deep breaths, trying to slow down her racing heart and telling herself everything would be OK. Then she came back to the table and sat down. For a moment Emma and Alicia carried on talking amongst themselves. Candice felt daunted at the prospect of winning them round. Her future happiness depended on what was about to happen. And if they turned against her then everybody else would too.

When their conversation came to a natural close, Emma and Alicia stared at Candice, and she knew it was her cue to speak. She cleared her throat.

'I want you both to know everything. I know you hate the fact that I reported Ethan and I feel bad about it, but I had my reasons. You see, there's more been happening than I told you about. My mum's shops have been targeted by somebody who's got it in for her. This person, whoever it is, has even attacked and robbed one of the staff as well as leaving graffiti on two of the shops and damaging several of the high-value designer dresses.'

She noticed her friends were now paying rapt attention to her, and she took a sip of her drink to calm her nerves. 'The graffiti wasn't very nice, and the man who attacked one of the shop managers said something abusive too.'

'OK, but that man isn't Ethan,' said Emma. 'Surely you don't think he'd attack someone?'

'No, I don't.'

'Right, so why did you report him if you don't think he did it?' demanded Alicia.

'Well, I don't think he carried out the attack but then there's the graffiti.'

'But why? Why would he do that?' asked Emma.

'Well, if somebody put him up to it, he might, especially if he needed the money. Look, I don't know, he might have thought it was only a bit of graffiti and not realised what else was going on. My mum's been frantic with worry about it all and when Ethan was asking all about her the other night, it made me suspicious of him. So, I told her, and she insisted we reported him to the police.'

'Why, what was he asking?' said Emma.

Now that she had started, Candice was determined to carry on and before she knew it, she had told them everything including what Ethan had said, her mother's past and the fact that somebody associated with her mother's past might have been seeking vengeance.

'She dealt with a lot of bad people in those days,' she continued. 'One of them even kidnapped me and held me in a barn for two days.'

When she referred to the kidnap, Candice felt a lump come to her throat and she paused while she tried to calm herself. The recollection of what had happened still got to her after all this time. She had spent several months with a child psychiatrist afterwards and since then she had tried to block it from her memory. She and her mother hadn't discussed it since; it was an experience that neither of them wanted to revisit. But it was always there lurking in the depths of her mind.

Candice remembered the words her psychologist had often used, '*What's the worst thing that could happen?*' At the time, those words had helped because the worst had been behind her and she'd got through it all. But those words were of scant comfort now because the worst was maybe yet to come. And that didn't bear thinking about.

She noticed her friends still studying her with their mouths agape and wondered what they thought of her now. 'So that's it,' she said, to break the tense silence. 'I know you think badly of me for reporting Ethan, but I was up against a lot of pressure.'

Still, nobody spoke. 'OK,' said Candice. 'I'm going to go now. I've told you everything so I'm afraid there's nothing else I can do to explain myself. But, before I go, even if you can't forgive me, will you please promise me that you won't let what I've said go any further?'

'OK,' said Emma while Alicia nodded.

Candice got up and headed for the ladies'. Once inside the cubicle, she broke down, trying to stifle the sound when she heard someone enter, and grabbing chunks of toilet roll to stem her tears.

Then she heard Emma call her name. 'Candice, is that you in there?' she asked.

'Yes,' Candice sobbed.

'Can you come out? We want to talk to you.'

Candice didn't really want her friends to see her like this, but she worried that her refusal would be taken as a snub and might make matters worse. She slid the bolt and pulled the door open to find Emma outside, her face full of concern. She flung her arms around Candice, saying, 'I'm so sorry you had to go through all that.'

'Yeah, me too,' said Alicia, stepping forward and stroking her back.

Their sympathy caused renewed tears to flow, and Candice fought to contain them. 'It's OK,' said Emma, pulling away. 'You take a few minutes for yourself then come back and join us. Let me buy you a drink. After all, you've come a long way just to have one.'

Candice smiled weakly, nodded, and went back into the cubicle. She hadn't been comfortable telling them all about her traumatic past but at least she had brought them round to her way of thinking. And Candice knew that, as things stood, she needed all the allies she could find.

For the first time in ages, Candice was in a relaxed mood when she returned home that evening. She had stayed out with Emma and Alicia, going for a meal once evening arrived then having a couple more drinks before getting the train back to Manchester. It had almost felt like the incident with Ethan hadn't stood between them and she was relieved.

But her mood soon changed when she saw her mother. She was often in a glum mood these days but something about her demeanour told Candice things had just got worse. She was sitting on the sofa staring into space even though *Housewives of Cheshire* was playing on catch-up. And when Candice walked inside the room, Laura's greeting was half-hearted. Apart from that, she had a bottle of wine in front of her, which was almost empty, and Candice noticed that her speech was slurred.

'What is it? What's happened?' asked Candice.

Laura let out a heavy sigh. 'Come here, look at this,' she said, picking up her phone and flicking through the screens till she located an item on the Internet.

When Candice read through the article a feeling of dread shook her. Not only had the article reported the various attacks on Laura's shops but it had also delved into her past. It seemed that the reporter had taken delight in detailing Laura's life as a street sex worker as well as listing her various soliciting offences.

Candice's first thought was that Emma and Alicia might have betrayed her. But then she realised that, as they had only just found out about her mother's past, it would be too early for the information to be published even if they had reported it.

'Oh my God!' she uttered. 'That's terrible! Who do you think is behind it?'

'I've no idea. That's what I've been racking my brains trying to figure out for the last couple of hours. Who else knows other than us? Trina. Plus, a couple of my managers but they don't know all the details, and certainly not everything that's been written there.'

Candice felt herself flush. 'Well, I did tell Thomas, but he wouldn't say anything. And I told Emma and Alicia but that was only this afternoon and I made them promise not to tell anyone.'

'Jesus Christ, Candice! What did you have to do that for? Anyone would think you wanted people to know all about my seedy bloody past. I can understand you telling Thomas. He is your boyfriend when all's said and done. But why did you have to go and tell your uni friends?' As she spoke, she grabbed the phone back off Candice and slammed it down on the coffee table.

'Because I was getting shit for reporting Ethan!' Candice snapped. 'Which you told me to do. And I needed to have someone on my side, otherwise it's going to be hell when I go back to uni. They won't tell anyone. They've promised.'

Her words seemed to get through to Laura who relented. 'OK, OK, I suppose I can understand.'

'It's not them that's reported it anyway. They've only just found out.'

'I know. I'm just...' Laura then held up her hands, running them through her hair and massaging her temples. 'Things are just getting to me a bit, that's all.'

Candice grew concerned. For the last few years, her mother had been so busy trying to make things up to Candice that she rarely put any of her stresses on her. Whatever she was going through, she usually kept it to herself. So, for her to react in this way, she must have been feeling the pressure.

Without speaking, Candice went over to her mother and flung her arms around her. There was nothing she could say to comfort her because Candice was frightened too. But it was her mother who offered reassurance when she said, 'At least the reporter hasn't given our address out. I suppose we should be grateful for that really.'

But rather than her mother's words bringing her comfort, instead it emphasised to Candice the danger they were in. If he had found the shops, then what was to stop him finding out where they lived too?

Once Candice had spent a bit of time with her mother, her thoughts drifted to Thomas. She went up to her room where she decided to call him even though it was late.

'Hi, babes, you alright?' he asked. 'Did your meeting with your friends go OK?'

Candice could hear the concern in his voice, and she felt guilty for bringing all her problems to him. But she needed someone to confide in. And Thomas had been really supportive.

'Yeah, that went OK,' she said. 'I've told them everything, but they were alright about it. In fact, they were really good, which was a relief. But something else has happened.'

'What?' he asked.

Candice quickly told him about the news report then added, 'I'm worried about what your dad and Pam will think.'

'Don't you worry about that,' he said. 'I'll smooth things over. They'll be fine, honestly.'

'Are you sure?'

'Yeah, my dad is pretty broad-minded. And they think a lot of you. I don't think that will change just because your mum made a few mistakes in the past. After all, that's not your fault, is it?'

'Aw thanks, Thomas. What would I do without you?' she said, hoping that he was right.

What she didn't mention to Thomas was her other concern about her mother. The fact that she was sitting in the house on her own knocking back the wine wasn't a good sign. The heavy drinking might be just a blip and Candice could understand it under the circumstances. Hopefully, she'd bring it under control again once things were back to normal. But what about drugs? Candice prayed her mother wouldn't touch them again because she couldn't bear to even think about the consequences if she did.

18

Caitlin was online again but this time she was checking her bank statement. She was pleased to find that a sum of £500 had been credited and she thought about how she was going to treat herself with the money.

After discovering all about Laura's past she had decided to sell the story to the newspapers. The attacks on the shops were newsworthy in themselves and she figured that the press would be interested in the connection to Laura's past too. She had been right.

She had no qualms about what she had done. In fact, she had been thrilled when she read the article. It felt good to get her revenge on Laura. Not only had she shown disrespect by the way she had spoken to her, but she had also put her at risk by keeping the attacks at the other shop a secret. And now the bitch could deal with the fallout!

It was Sunday and Candice was spending some time with Thomas at her mum's house. Laura was out, and they were chilling watching a film when Candice's phone rang. She reached for it to check who was calling.

'Sorry, Thomas. Do you mind? It's Emma,' she said, pausing the film.

'No, course not. Go ahead.'

'Hi, Emma,' she greeted her friend.

'Hi, Candice, I'm just checking you're OK. Have you seen the newspaper article about your mum?'

'Yeah, she showed it me last night when I got home. I couldn't believe somebody would do that.'

'I know – that's what I thought. Who do you think it is?'

'I've no idea.'

'How did your mum take it?'

'Not very well to be honest.'

'Aw, I'm sorry to hear that, Candice. I hope you're OK.'

'I'm not too bad but, well, y'know…'

'I know, but listen, I just want to let you know that me and Alicia have got your back. You might get a bit of shit over it and the Ethan thing when you get back to uni, but we'll be there for you.'

'Thanks, Emma. I appreciate that. And thanks for calling.'

Candice then made her excuses so she could get back to Thomas. But when she cut the call, she could feel the sting of tears as she thought about everything.

'Are you OK?' he asked, taking her in his arms and holding her tight.

While he held her, she managed to fight back her tears so that when she broke from the embrace her eyes were dry. 'It's not good is it, Thomas? I just wish it would all go away. I hate to see my mum so stressed and I'm really anxious about going back to uni. I'm worried about putting this on you too. God knows what your dad and Pam will think of me when they find out!'

'Eh, shush,' he said, putting a finger to her lips. 'I told you everything would be OK, didn't I? And it is. I told Dad this morning.'

'What? Why didn't you tell me? What did he say?'

'I was about to tell you before you got that call from Emma. Dad was a bit shocked at first but then he accepted it. Pam did too. I told you, they think a lot of you and they're not going to hold your mum's past against you. In fact, Pam felt sorry for you when she heard what you'd been through.'

'Phew, well at least that's out of the way,' she said.

But although Candice was relieved that she had the backing of Thomas, his dad and Pam as well as Emma and Alicia, she was still troubled. She just wished the police would find the culprit before he did any more damage.

19

When Candice arrived at work on Monday, the first person she saw was Thomas's dad. In fact, she literally bumped into him. As she walked through the door to the portacabin, he was on his way out. He looked at her and she felt herself flush, knowing that he was now aware of her background.

'Oh hello, Candice,' he greeted, smiling warmly at her.

Despite her embarrassment, Candice's eyes met his and she smiled back.

'Do you know,' he continued, 'I haven't mentioned before what a lovely name Candice is. French, isn't it?'

'Its origins are African actually, but it's used a lot in France as well as in the UK.'

'Well, I never knew that. Anyway, it's a lovely name, unusual too. You don't get many of them.'

He carried on walking towards the car lot. Candice felt lifted by his friendliness. He was obviously going out of his way to be extra nice to her since he had found out about her difficult childhood. She walked into the office, said good morning to the other staff and took her seat opposite Carol who was staring at her.

Midway through the morning, Carol left her desk.

Candice presumed she had gone round the back of the building for a smoke as usual. Taking advantage of the time while Carol was away, Candice put down the file she had been working on. Her mind switched to other matters as she gazed through the window and across to the car lot.

In the distance, there was a man standing by one of the cars. His stance made Candice curious as he didn't seem to be viewing the car. Instead, he was peering over to another area of the car lot, and he seemed to be waiting for something or someone. Then Mr Foster came into view, marching straight over to the man.

Candice couldn't hear what was being said but their greeting didn't look friendly. Both of their heads were thrust forward, and their mouths opened wide as though they were shouting at each other. As Mr Foster drew nearer to the man and began jabbing his finger at him while continuing to shout, the man shrank back. Then he said something else to the man, his body language hostile but expectant as though he was waiting for the answer to a demanding question.

The man didn't speak at first, but he shook his head vehemently. Candice was fascinated by this exchange and was so caught up in what was happening that she didn't notice Carol returning to her seat opposite. When Mr Foster lurched at the man, grabbed him by his shirt collars and pinned him down onto the bonnet of the car, Candice jumped with shock.

'What the hell's wrong with you?' asked Carol, drawing Candice's attention away from the window.

Without waiting for a reply, Carol leant forward, her

own eyes now fixed on the scene outside. 'Bloody hell,' she said. 'That poor bastard must have really upset Foster.'

Carol continued to look out of the window, so Candice did likewise. As she watched, Mr Foster let go of the man but then seemed to issue him with a final warning, his finger pointing aggressively again. The man finally walked away, his shoulders slumped.

'Jesus!' declared Carol at the top of her voice. 'We'd best stay on the right side of Foster today. He's just had a right go at a bloke outside.'

Two of the staff dashed towards the window but Carol stopped them. 'Don't let him see you, for Christ's sake!'

There were nervous mutterings amongst the staff and, once they'd calmed down a bit and returned to their own desks, Carol locked eyes with Candice. 'You look shocked,' she commented.

Candice suddenly felt very self-conscious. She hadn't realised her reaction was that obvious. 'Yeah... I... I didn't know he was like that.'

Carol lowered her voice. 'Oh, yeah. Foster can be a right nasty bastard at times. You just be glad you're in favour and hope it stays that way.'

Unsure how to respond, Candice lowered her head and returned to her filing.

That evening when Thomas rang her, Candice decided to mention what had happened at work but she stopped short of letting him know the staff's opinion of his father.

Thomas didn't react straightaway, and she assumed he

must have been as shocked as she was. Then he finally spoke.

'Dad's OK but he does have another side to him. I mean, only in business. He'll be fine with you, don't worry. Well, he has been up to now, hasn't he? From what he tells me, he has to be ruthless at times to stop people taking advantage. But that's what it's like in the business world; you have to be tough to survive.'

'OK. Maybe somebody had overstepped the mark then.'

'Yeah, that'll be what it was. He probably owes him money and Dad can't get him to pay up.'

Thomas soon switched subjects, telling her all about his day at work, which temporarily took Candice's mind off what had happened. But the shock at his father's behaviour remained, and she made a mental note never to get on the wrong side of him.

20

'Oh, thank God you're here,' said Laura when Candice got home from work the following day.

Candice noticed that her mother was dressed for outdoors and seemed even more on edge tonight. 'Why, what's wrong?' she asked, alarmed.

'That inspector has been on the phone. He wants us to go down to the station.'

'Aw, Mum, I'm starving. Can't he come here?'

'No, apparently he wants to show us something they've found on CCTV.'

'Oh, right. What is it?'

'I don't know; he wouldn't say on the phone.'

'And he wants me to come too?'

'Yep, that's what he said.'

Shortly afterwards they were sitting in an interview room at the police station with DI Carson and DS Worrall sitting across from them. The younger officer had a laptop in front of him.

'We need you to look at some CCTV images,' said DI Carson. He then addressed the other officer. 'Can we start with the Altrincham shop, please?'

DS Worrall pulled up an image on the screen then turned

the laptop around so that Candice and Laura could see it. 'This was taken on the night your manager was attacked,' he said. 'Do either of you recognise the man shown?'

Candice and her mum both stared at the image, but it was grainy and therefore difficult to pick out any detail. All Candice could make out was that it was a man who looked slim and tall and was wearing jeans and a dark blue hoody. The hoody was pulled up so she couldn't see much of his face, but his fringe stuck out at the front. From what she could see he was dark-haired.

'By comparing him to the surrounding objects we put him at around five foot ten,' said the DI and his stance indicates that he's a young man, possibly in his twenties but, unfortunately, as we can't see his face in detail, it's difficult to tell for sure.'

Laura shook her head. 'No, he doesn't look like anyone I know.'

The DI turned his attention to Candice. 'What about you? Could it be the young man you reported – Ethan Smart?'

Candice shrugged. 'I don't know.'

'OK, let's see if this other image will help.'

On this cue, the DS took the laptop and pressed a few keys till another image appeared on the screen, then he turned the laptop to face Candice and Laura again, saying, 'This one was taken outside the shop on Deansgate in the centre of Manchester on the night of the graffiti incident.'

Candice and Laura both looked at the screen. This time the man was wearing a different hoody, a light grey one, and it was difficult to tell whether it was the same person as he had his back to the camera. Candice noticed that although he wasn't facing the shop, he was carrying a can of spray.

'This was possibly shortly after he had graffitied the shutters,' DI Carson pointed out. 'Unfortunately, the CCTV wasn't close enough to show him in the act, but this seems to be when he was walking away afterwards. Does he look familiar at all?'

This image, although not as grainy as the previous one, didn't show his face at all. Again, Laura didn't recognise him, but Candice said, 'I don't know. It could be anyone. I mean, Ethan is around that size but then so are a lot of the guys at uni.'

'And he's dark-haired too,' said DS Worrall.'

'Yeah, but a lot of guys are,' said Candice.

The images weren't clear enough to say for sure whether it was Ethan and Candice really didn't want to land him in it if it wasn't him. She'd done enough damage already by reporting him. As she sat there staring at the screen, she said, 'Can I have a look at the first one again please?'

DS Worrall obliged by pulling up the other image and Candice stared at it again. But she still couldn't say for certain whether it was Ethan. Then something occurred to her. 'Actually, I think Ethan may be taller than five foot ten.'

'What makes you say that?' asked the DI.

'Well, my boyfriend's five foot eleven and I think Ethan's even taller than him. It's hard to say though because I haven't seen them together so I'm going on my height compared to theirs. And that depends on whether I'm wearing heels or flats.'

'Very well,' said the DI.

Just then DS Worrall chipped in. 'Is your boyfriend slim and dark-haired too?'

'Yeah but, it's not him.'

He turned to Laura. 'Would you say you get along well with your daughter's boyfriend?'

'Yeah, course I do. Thomas is a lovely lad.'

'And do you think he'd have any reason to attack your business?'

'Would he heck!' Candice raged. 'Thomas would never do anything like that.'

'Alright,' said the DI, before the ambitious young DS had chance to speak again. 'Thanks for your help. Leave it with us. We'll be in touch again if we have anything further to tell you.'

Before they went, Laura asked, 'What about the graffiti at the Altrincham shop and the torn dresses at Deansgate?'

'I'm afraid we don't have anything on CCTV for those,' said the DI. There were so many people near to the shop on the day the dresses were torn that it's difficult to pick out just one individual and there's certainly no one wearing either a dark blue or a grey hoody. Likewise, the cameras haven't picked up anything near the Altrincham shop relating to the graffiti. The cameras don't focus on the shopfront, and it was through another camera that we spotted the assailant following your manager.'

Candice saw the pained expression on her mother's face and knew what she was thinking. If only she had installed cameras inside the shops instead of having to rely on the street ones. Laura had previously explained to her that when she opened her first shop the set-up costs had taken her by surprise, so she'd cut down on a few things. Candice assumed that the longer her mother managed without the cameras, the less they had become a priority – until now.

★

Candice was glad to get home, but all thoughts of food had now left her. Her stomach was churning, and she felt sick. Somehow, seeing the culprit on camera made it even more real. She wished the images had been clearer so that she or her mother could have pinpointed who it was. Candice wondered what the police would do next, and she wished she'd asked.

'Are you OK?' asked Laura.

'Yeah, I'm just…'

'I know,' said Laura, putting her arms around her. 'It's not easy, is it?'

'No. I just wish we knew who it was. Do you think it's someone from your past, Mum?'

Laura held her at arm's length and replied. 'I don't know, love. I thought so at first but, like the police said, the man in them images is only in his twenties. Think about it, I gave up that life nearly ten years ago, which would have made him a teenager at the time. So, he'd have been too young to have been a client.'

'Oh, yeah. I didn't think of that,' said Candice. 'I wonder why someone that age would want to attack Haley and frighten us like this.' She thought of Ethan again. 'Unless it's someone nasty who's found out about you.'

But she wasn't too sure about him. Surely Ethan wouldn't do all this just because she'd rejected his advances. Then again, maybe he might have done the graffiti but not the attack on Haley. Unless he was doing it on somebody else's instructions. And then there was the fact that her mum was the target, not her, so it had to be someone connected to her mum somehow.

21

The man hadn't been given any more orders for some time. The original plan once he had got hold of the keys to the Altrincham shop was to return in disguise and let himself in then cause some damage. But the locks had been changed before he got a chance. So now his boss had decided to take a different approach and given him new instructions.

Currently, he was sitting inside his car in the car park near to Altrincham shopping centre. He had his eye on a silver Ford Focus, waiting for the driver to arrive. She would be easy to spot because of her hairstyle and demeanour. Caitlin's hair was in a trendy, shaped bob and was obviously dyed as it was copper-coloured, and she walked with a confident gait, her head held high and shoulders pulled back.

He was glad his boss hadn't insisted on him returning to the shop again and attempting a break-in because he didn't want to risk being spotted. He'd been extra careful since the attack on Haley almost three weeks ago, knowing he was probably on CCTV by now. After what was about to happen this evening, there was a chance that the police would be checking the CCTV again. But they wouldn't find him outside Crystals because he'd already tracked Caitlin's movements on previous occasions from a safe distance.

Thursday night was late closing, but Caitlin didn't finish work as soon as the shop shut like the rest of the staff. He imagined she would have other duties as the acting manager. Her new position was something else he had found out about.

It was therefore almost nine o'clock when Caitlin reached the car park. That suited him. There were fewer people about and it would be dark when he made his move.

As she approached her car, he didn't intercept her. Instead, he started his engine then followed as soon as she moved off. He knew the direction Caitlin was going to take. He'd also tracked her going home previously, so he knew that she lived in an apartment block in Stockport, which was surrounded by a large car park. But he'd chosen not to wait for her outside the apartments; that would have been too suspicious. It was far better to arrive just after her.

He had a relatively uneventful journey to Caitlin's home. As there was less traffic on the roads at this time, he had managed to keep her in sight, at the same time making sure there were always one or two cars between them so there was less risk of him being spotted.

The fact that the car park of the apartment block wasn't barrier-controlled worked to his advantage. He simply followed Caitlin straight through the entrance then took another direction close by while he watched her through his rear-view mirror circling around in search of a space.

She drove to a secluded area at the back of the building where there were several vacant spaces and where the lighting wasn't so good. The man followed after her, pleased that she had chosen this particular area of the car park. Then he quickly slid his car in beside hers.

Caitlin didn't seem to notice anything amiss as she stepped out of her car and began to walk. She was too busy scrolling through messages on her mobile phone to pay heed to what was going on around her.

Caitlin saw the car that parked next to hers, but she didn't take much notice. After stepping out of her Ford Focus, she locked it up and slipped the keys inside her handbag then took out her phone. She'd put up a post on social media that afternoon boasting about her forthcoming night out and wanted to check how much attention it had attracted. Too impatient to wait till she got indoors, she thought she'd have a look while she was walking across the car park.

The feel of someone behind her took Caitlin completely by surprise. Before she had chance to check who it was, she felt a sweaty hand clamped over her mouth and something sharp digging viciously into her back. A feeling of terror pulsed through her, making her heart quicken.

Caitlin was unable to see the man, but she could smell his bad breath as his face moved towards her. The fact that she was dealing with an unknown quantity intensified her fear. Then he hissed into her ear, 'Keep fuckin' moving and don't say a thing else I'll ram this fuckin' knife right through you.'

She felt a renewed tremor of fear and did as the man ordered while he led her through the gap between a van and another car until they reached the building. Then he nudged her into the area behind the van and next to the wall. She was alarmed to notice that there were no windows nearby, which meant they would be out of view.

'Right, I'm gonna take my hand away,' he said. 'But you'd better not start fuckin' screaming or shouting if you know what's good for yer.'

She shook her head to indicate her compliance then felt his hand drop away. Caitlin turned to face the man who was still pointing the knife at her. He was wearing a mask covering his mouth and nose, but she noticed the colour of his eyes. They were brown.

Because of the mask anyone who might have passed him in the car wouldn't recognise him. Caitlin also noticed the way it distorted his voice slightly.

'I'm not gonna hurt you,' he said. 'As long as you give me what I want.' The menace in those words made Caitlin so afraid that tears rushed to her eyes. 'I want some information about your boss,' he quickly added. 'I want you to give me her address.'

Straightaway Caitlin realised it was the same man who had attacked Haley and her fear intensified. She didn't see why she should put herself in danger to protect Laura so she chose to comply.

'I don't have it,' she said. 'But I can get it for you.'

'OK. You find it out. I'll be back to get it. But don't think of wriggling out of it, because I know where you live and work. And don't tell the cops. I'll be round when you least expect it and if I see the hint of a copper, you'll have serious fuckin' problems.'

In her desperation to avoid another encounter, Caitlin recalled coming across the address when she'd entered Candice on the payroll during a previous university holiday. She'd even checked out the house on Google Maps out of curiosity. What was it? Wood something. Then she remembered.

'Woodlea. It's called Woodlea. In Altrincham. I don't know the number though.'

'It's OK. That's enough. I can find out the rest.'

Then his hand dropped away although he was still holding the knife. 'Don't forget, I know where you live. You'd better not fuckin' tell the cops or I'll be back for you, and I won't just point the fuckin' knife this time either.'

'I won't, I won't, I promise. My boss is a bitch anyway. I don't even like her.'

The man walked away leaving her shaking and numbed with shock. Although she didn't like her boss, Caitlin had a sudden attack of guilt knowing that if anything bad happened to Laura or her daughter she would have to live with the consequences for the rest of her life.

22

Ethan could hear a commotion coming from the hallway of his parents' home, so he peeked over the banister to see what was happening. Downstairs, a police detective was having a discussion with his father and waving a document at him while several uniformed officers waited outside. Then they bounded into the house and Ethan dashed up to his room.

But there was no refuge there. Within seconds two officers had arrived at his bedroom door and burst into the room without asking.

'It might be best if you wait in another room while we carry out a search,' said one of them.

Ethan walked out of his room with his head hung low. He could feel panic stirring inside his body. His stomach growled and he knew he needed the bathroom. Thank God none of the officers were in there!

He dashed inside, anxious to do what he needed to do. But before he could even finish, they were banging on the bathroom door.

'Come on out. We need to search this room.'

Ethan's stomach cramps persisted, and the fierce manner of the officers wasn't helping. He tried to finish as quickly as he could, flushing the toilet and hoping once was enough to shift the contents of his stomach.

When he opened the door, he felt embarrassed by the offensive stench he had left but the officers seemed more intent on the search. One of them patted him down while another started rifling through the contents of the bathroom cabinet. It was evident they thought he might have hidden something in there.

Ethan walked down the landing, catching a disturbing glimpse of the officers ransacking his bedroom on his way to the stairs. He met his parents in the hallway and felt a rush of guilt when he saw their troubled faces.

'Are they in all the other rooms?' asked Ethan.

'Yes,' his father replied solemnly.

His mother didn't speak. Neither did his father after that first word. While the search continued, they waited in the hall, each of them silenced by worry. Ethan felt culpable. His parents shouldn't have to go through this.

The time dragged and his legs ached with tension. After what seemed like an age, the officers left their home without saying a word. Only the senior detective spoke as he walked out carrying one of Ethan's hoodies.

'We'll have to send this to forensics for examination. We'll be in touch.'

He gave Ethan a pointed stare then walked out the door.

'I'm so sorry,' Ethan said to his parents, then he dashed upstairs, hoping to find solace.

But the state of his bedroom reduced him to tears. The police had rummaged through everything. His bed resembled a jumbled mess where they had emptied the contents of his wardrobe. Added to the clutter were his computer games and other valuable possessions, carelessly slung on top of the pile.

His drawers were hanging out of the chest with underwear spilling out of them. The T-shirts his mother had carefully ironed and folded were now creased up. And they'd taken his hoody. What the fuck? He'd thought he could handle this.

But now he realised that he couldn't.

Ethan had only been up there two minutes when he heard a knock on the door. His mother walked into the room to find him lying amongst the chaos.

'Are you alright?'

He felt embarrassed, angry, ashamed. 'Leave me alone!' he yelled, instantly feeling bad once she had left the room.

He realised he was being unfair. But he didn't want to talk to her. He couldn't. Nothing she said could put things right. The way he was feeling now, he didn't want to talk to anyone. He needed some time to wallow in self-pity. Maybe when he was feeling a bit better, he'd speak to her.

Candice read the message on her phone screen. The words were so vitriolic that the breath caught in her throat. Hardly believing her eyes, she had to read them again before they sunk in. *You're nothing but scum just like your mother and I want nothing to do with you. How could you do that to one of us?* But what made them more alarming was that they had been written by someone she had previously thought of as a friend: Dan.

She already knew that she wasn't currently in Dan's favour, but this was a step too far. Refusing to be cowed,

Candice rang him. Perhaps if she could explain the reasons for her actions then he might be a bit more understanding.

It took Dan a while to answer the phone but when she finally heard his voice on the other end, it didn't sound too friendly.

'What do *you* want?'

'I need to speak to you about this message, Dan. It's not a nice thing to write, especially when you don't know the full facts.'

'Don't give me that, Candice. I know exactly what's happened. Someone's been giving your mum a hard time because of her dodgy past, and you've decided to pin the blame on Ethan just because you don't like him.'

'It isn't because I don't like him. Anyway, you don't like him either, so I don't know why you're getting so defensive over him.'

'I never said I didn't like him.'

'Yes, you did. You said he was a dick.'

'Being a dick is a bit fuckin' different from committing a criminal offence though, isn't it?'

'But I didn't say he committed a criminal offence.'

'Yes, you did, Candice. You reported him to the police, didn't you?'

'Well, I... I told the police what he had said.'

'What? When he asked about the graffiti on your mum's shop, do you mean?'

Candice could hear the sarcasm dripping off every syllable and she rushed to defend herself. 'It wasn't just that he was asking about the graffiti. He was asking all about my mum's past too, and after what had happened...'

'And that's what this is really about, isn't it, Candice?'

he cut in. 'You couldn't stand the fact that it's out in the open about your mother, so you decided to blame Ethan just because you were uncomfortable about him asking questions. And it wasn't even him who exposed her as a prostitute. It was in the press, for fuck's sake!'

Candice was becoming agitated by now. 'Don't you call her that!'

'Why not? That's what she is, isn't it?'

She didn't have an answer to that question and had become aware that this conversation wasn't turning out as she had planned. As she thought about how to change the tone so that she could explain her actions, Dan cut in again.

'Do you realise the fuckin' trouble you've caused, Candice? The police haven't left Ethan alone. They're putting pressure on him to confess to something he didn't do! They even searched his house yesterday and took one of his hoodies away for evidence just because it's like the one spotted on CCTV. He's getting all sorts of shit from his parents and he's going out of his mind with worry. He might be a bit of a dick, but he doesn't fuckin' deserve that!'

'But Dan, you don't know one hundred per cent that he is innocent.'

'Are you fuckin' serious? Haven't you been listening to a word I've said?'

Then Dan cut the call before she had a chance to say anything further. Once he was off the phone, the tears began to fall. Everything was a mess. Not only were she and her mother worried sick about the attacks but the situation with Ethan was casting doubts in her mind too.

Deep down, she couldn't see Ethan carrying out such a vicious attack on Haley but could she really be sure? He did have an overinflated opinion of himself and had hounded her for a date, refusing to take no for an answer. But would that make him the type of person who would resort to violence against women?

But then she thought again about the graffiti. Could Ethan perhaps have done it then regretted it? Maybe he had thought he could get away with it but hadn't bargained on such dire consequences, especially if he wasn't aware that the damage to the dresses and the attack on Haley would follow. And why were the police pursuing him so doggedly if he was innocent?

Then there was the hoody. Was it just coincidence or was there more to it? And Dan hadn't mentioned what colour it was. The light grey worn by the graffiti artist at Deansgate? Or the dark blue worn by Haley's attacker?

23

After such an upsetting finish to the weekend, Candice was almost glad to get back to her boring job on Monday. Aside from the distressing call with Dan, there was a tense atmosphere in the house. Her mother was still on edge, jumping every time one of their phones rang or beeped, and Candice was feeling the pressure too. After everything that had happened, it felt as though they were just waiting for the next piece of shocking news.

She walked out into the street where she had left her car parked so she could quickly be on her way to work. But when she got to the car a shock awaited her. The tyres were completely flat, all four of them. Knowing it couldn't be just a coincidence, Candice examined the tyres to see what the problem was. She was alarmed to find that they had all been slit.

'Mum, Mum!' she shouted, returning to the house.

Her mother met her halfway up the stairs. Candice could tell she had woken her, as her eyes were heavy with sleep and her hair was tousled. As she came down the stairs, she was still tying the belt on her dressing gown.

'What is it? What the hell's the matter?'

Candice noticed her face was also pale and her eyes

red-rimmed, and she wondered if she'd hit the drink again last night after she'd left her alone downstairs. A whiff of her breath told Candice that she had.

'It's my car, someone's slit the tyres,' Candice complained with a tremor in her voice.

'No! You're joking. Let's have a look.'

Laura walked up to the car and examined it. 'The bloody swines!' she yelled before pulling her dressing gown tighter around her middle and returning to the house.

'What am I gonna do, Mum? How am I gonna get to work? I'll be late if I get the bus.'

Laura sighed. 'Alright, alright. I'll take you. But I need to get ready first.'

'Can you be quick please, Mum? I don't want to be late.'

'OK, I'll be as quick as I can.'

Candice could hear the irritation in her mother's tone. Her first thought was that maybe she was feeling a bit rough because of the alcohol she had drunk last night, and her feeling of irritation mirrored her mother's. But then she realised that her mother might be feeling irascible for another reason. Not only had the perpetrator just made his next move, but he had also found out where they lived.

It took ages for her mother to get ready. As Candice heard the shower running, she tried to contain her impatience. She would have thought her mother could have taken a shower when she got back home but she could hardly complain when she was doing her a favour.

By the time Laura came downstairs, worries about the increased threat were dominating Candice's mind. 'Will you be OK here?' she asked her mum once she was ready to go.

'Yes, don't worry!' she snapped. 'I'll get straight on to the police once I've got back home. We'll see what they have to say, then we'll take it from there.'

'OK. Thanks, Mum.'

Her mother dropped her off at the car showrooms, and she raced across the forecourt. She dashed into the office twenty minutes late to find all eyes on her. Her heart plummeted when she noticed that Mr Foster was there too. He stopped near to her desk.

'I'm so sorry,' she said. 'I couldn't get the car to start.'

'Have you rung the garage to look at it?' he asked.

'No, erm…' She faltered for a moment, wondering how much to divulge before adding, 'My mum's going to sort it out for me.'

'OK, don't worry. Let me know how you go on.'

He waltzed out of the office and Candice pulled out her chair and apologised once again to Carol who stared at her, incredulous. 'You're obviously in favour,' she quipped. 'Linda got in five minutes ago and he went ballistic at her and told her she'd have to make the time up.'

Candice didn't say anything. Instead, she looked at the pile of filing on her desk.

'That's just for starters,' said Carol, following her eyes. 'There's plenty more where that came from.'

Candice wondered if she was being punished for some reason, but she ignored the barbed comment and got on with her work.

As Laura made the journey back home, she regretted being so sharp with Candice again. She couldn't seem to help herself lately and knew the booze didn't help. This morning she was so shaky that she shouldn't really have been driving. But how could she have turned Candice down, especially when the damage to her car was probably the result of her own sordid past?

But even as she thought about the problem the drink was causing, she knew she'd probably turn to the bottle again tonight. This latest development gave her even more cause to be anxious. Could this person really be targeting Candice now? Surely not!

But, thinking about it, whoever this person was, they might not have known it was Candice's car. And it would have been difficult for them to get to hers because it was locked away in the garage. Maybe that would be the next goal as the perpetrator stepped up his actions. Or maybe he would go to even greater lengths to get at her. She hoped not.

Laura could have got carried away in trying to second-guess what was going to happen next. But she couldn't afford to go down that route. Things were bad enough. So, she tried to focus on her driving until she got back home. But as she parked her car and put her key in the lock, she couldn't help but feel anxious when she anticipated what might be waiting for her on the other side of the door.

24

Reluctant to ask her mother for a lift again, Candice caught the bus home from work. When she arrived at the garden gate, she had mixed feelings: glad to be away from the boredom of work but nervous because she no longer felt safe at home.

As she approached the house, Candice noticed there was something strange. Unaware at first of what exactly it was, she stopped on the driveway and examined the frontage in greater detail. Then she realised what it was.

'I've stepped up the security,' said Laura without preamble as soon as Candice walked indoors.

'I noticed the alarm and security light outside,' said Candice.

Her mother was standing in the hall as though she had been awaiting her return so she could impart more bad news. It gave Candice an eerie feeling.

'Yeah, that old alarm hasn't worked for years,' Laura continued. 'It's about time I got it bloody changed. I'll show you how to work it later. I've had more locks put on the windows and doors too and there's another security light at the back.'

'Wow! You have been busy. I'm amazed you managed to get it all done today.'

'I told them it was urgent.'

Her mother's words impacted Candice and Laura must have noticed her unease as she quickly backtracked. 'I just want us to feel safe in our own home. Don't be worrying though. The slit tyres might have nothing to do with what's been happening at the shops, but I thought it best to be on the safe side. Oh and, by the way, I'll have your tyres replaced tomorrow. How did you go on at work anyway? Were they alright with you being late?'

'Yeah, Thomas's dad was OK.'

As she spoke, Candice noticed how on edge her mother was. She was waffling and her jitteriness was there again. She might have tried to play down the fact that she'd had extra security installed, but Candice wasn't fooled.

'Right,' said Laura, switching topics. 'Tea's nearly ready. You go and sit yourself down, love, while I check on it.'

'Thanks, Mum.'

It wasn't long until they were seated at the dining table tucking into home-made lasagne. Laura placed a bottle of wine on the table. 'Do you wanna glass?' she asked, pouring a large one for herself.

'No, I've got work tomorrow,' Candice replied, unhappy that her mother was drinking again.

Laura didn't say anything, but Candice noticed the guilty expression on her face. Deciding to ignore it for now, she said, 'I've been thinking, I don't like leaving you when I stay at Thomas's so, if you want, I can see him here instead until all this is over.'

'No, it's fine. You stay at Thomas's whenever you want.

You'll be safer there. Not that I think you're not safe here. But, well, what I'm trying to say is that you shouldn't put your life on hold because of what's been happening. Anyway, I can always stay at Trina's, can't I?'

'OK, as long as you're sure.' Candice put a forkful of lasagne into her mouth and savoured the taste before swallowing it down. Then she came to her next point. 'I've decided not to go back into student digs in September. I'm going to stay here instead.'

'Why? You don't have to do that, love!'

Candice noticed her mother's assumption that she was doing it to support her: another sign that the imminent threat was on her mind. 'I do. Things will be difficult in the house now that the police have questioned Ethan.'

'But that's not your bloody fault. If he's innocent then he's got nothing to worry about, has he?'

'It's not as simple as that, Mum. The police have been giving him a really hard time apparently.'

Laura put down her fork and eyed Candice intently. 'Maybe they've got reason to suspect him.'

'I don't know. I can't see him attacking someone.'

'But what about the criminal damage?'

Candice shrugged. 'I don't know. Maybe. The police have taken a hoody from his house.'

'Really? And who told you this? One of your friends?'

'Yeah, well, ex-friend. It was Dan.'

'What d'you mean ex-friend?'

'He's not happy about me accusing Ethan. He said Ethan's getting all sorts of shit from his parents about it.'

'He wants to be in our bloody shoes. It's not exactly been a walk in the park for us either.'

'Do you think you could think about somebody else but yourself for once?' Candice snapped. 'What if Ethan is innocent? Imagine what it's doing to him and his family while he's under suspicion.'

'He should have thought about that before he started to poke his nose into our business then, shouldn't he?'

Then Laura poured herself another large glass of wine. Candice could see the alcohol getting to her, making her increasingly belligerent, and she guessed that the bottle of wine may not have been the first drink she'd had that day.

'For God's sake, Mum! Will you look at yourself? You're so busy getting hammered every night that you can't even see anyone else's point of view.'

'Don't you dare speak to me like that!'

'Why not? Are you frightened that you might learn some home truths?' Candice saw the look of shock on her mother's face, but she wasn't finished yet. 'Don't you think I remember how it was when I was a kid? When you were pissed all the time and high on drugs? There's no way I'm letting you put me through that again, so you'd better get your fuckin' act together!'

To Candice's surprise, her mother didn't retaliate. Instead, she sat in silence, a fat tear rolling down her face. That was worse in a way because it made Candice feel guilty for having a go at her. Obviously, her mother was finding things difficult. She just wished she didn't have to resort to booze to deal with her problems.

'Mum, I'm sorry but I really think you need to cut down on the drink,' she said, relenting a little. 'It's only Monday and you're drunk again.'

'I'm not drunk, I'm just merry. Anyway, how else do you

expect me to sleep with everything that's going on in my head?'

'You could get something from the doctor instead.'

'Candice, you know I have a bad relationship with drugs, and I don't want to go down that road again.'

'But alcohol's just as bad!' Candice snapped. 'And at least if you were on tablets from the doctor, it would be monitored.'

'Stop bloody lecturing me, Candice. I'll deal with this in my own way.'

Her mother was becoming irate, and Candice didn't want this going any further. She'd said her piece, but it seemed she was wasting her time. 'I'm going upstairs,' she said. 'I need to get my things ready for work tomorrow. Goodnight.'

Candice stormed out of the room and went up to her bedroom where she busied herself putting some clothes together for the following day. Then, after ringing Thomas, she watched some programmes on her phone, switching from series to series, but unable to concentrate on anything.

Eventually she got ready for bed. When she lay down to sleep, she could hear the soft, distant hum of the TV. She assumed her mother was either still watching something or she had fallen into an alcohol-induced sleep.

Candice's mind began to wander, and she wished *she* could find a way to sleep. Everything was going over in her head, flipping from scene to scene like those changing programmes on the streaming channels. Her damaged car. Concerns over her mother. Dan's hostility. And the ever-present danger that now loomed closer than ever.

25

It had been another dull day of filing and photocopying and, wanting a break from the monotony, Candice had decided to go to Thomas's place after work. She was determined not to stay though, knowing her mother needed her home even if she was too proud to admit it. And, despite their row, Candice still cared what happened to her.

She had told Thomas all about her latest troubles on the phone the previous evening and now she just wanted to escape from all the worry for a few hours. Seeing the beaming smile on his handsome, friendly face cheered her up straightaway.

He leant into her and planted a kiss on her cheek. 'Hi, babes, have you had a good day?'

'OK,' she said. 'What about you?'

'Yeah, good. Listen, I've got something to tell you,' he announced.

Candice's mind flashed back to a few weeks previously when Thomas had also had something to tell her but had then backed out of it. She wondered if it might be the same thing. 'Alright. Should we go upstairs?' she asked.

'No, it's OK.' He nodded towards the living room. 'They know what I'm going to tell you. In fact, it was my dad's suggestion. I told him about what had happened with your car, and he suggested you come to live here for a while.'

'Oh, right. Well, that's good of him. But... no. Sorry, I can't. I can't leave my mum on her own.'

'But you said she could stay with a friend.'

'She won't though, not full-time anyway. She likes her own space and she'd be worried she was cramping Trina's style. Anyway...' She then lowered her voice to a whisper. 'I prefer to keep my eye on her. She's drinking too much.'

Thomas nodded in acknowledgement. Just at that moment, his father strode out of the living room. 'Oh hello, Candice. I thought it was you. Come in, don't just stand out there.' He held out his arm in a welcoming gesture, beckoning her into the lounge. 'Sit yourself down. Let Thomas get you a drink.'

Inside she found Pam with a compassionate smile on her lips. 'Hi, Candice. How are you?' she greeted as Candice took a seat on the sofa and Thomas went through to the kitchen. 'I believe you've been having a tough time of it lately.'

Candice flushed, unsure that she wanted to discuss the unsavoury aspects of her life and that of her mother with someone she didn't know so well.

'Oh, don't mind us,' Thomas's father interjected in his usual self-assured manner. 'You're not to blame for what's been going on. We sympathise. You and your mother must be worried out of your minds.'

Candice spoke quietly, still uncomfortable with their candidness. 'Yes, we are.'

'Well, as Thomas has probably already told you, you're welcome to stay here with us.'

'I… thank you, but I don't want to leave my mum.'

'Oh, that's alright. I understand. She must be finding it really tough Still, I suppose the police will be keeping an eye on things, so I shouldn't worry too much.'

'Yeah, we've reported everything to them,' Candice offered.

'Good, so you should. I hope they're doing all they can to find out who's behind all these attacks. I can't believe they slit your tyres right outside your home.'

Candice noticed the quick flash of Pam's eyes, gesturing for him to be more subtle. But it didn't make any difference to Candice. No matter how much people tried to pussyfoot around her, they couldn't hide the facts.'

'Yeah, I couldn't believe it either,' said Candice, their compassion helping her to feel more relaxed.

'I don't suppose you've managed to capture anything on CCTV, have you?' he asked.

'No. We don't have any at home.'

'You would think there'd be CCTV near the shops though, wouldn't you?'

'Oh, there is but the images are too grainy to be able to tell who they are.'

'Pity,' he said.

Thomas then came back into the lounge carrying a drink for himself and Candice. His father and Pam already had theirs. He sidled up to Candice on the sofa and put his hand on her arm.

'You OK?' he asked.

She nodded but felt unable to say anything. All this pity had brought on a surge of emotion, and she worried her voice might crack if she spoke.

'I feel like having a word with that Dan myself. He's no right to talk to you like that!'

Candice wanted to respond, to tell Thomas she didn't blame Dan for how he felt if the police harassment of Ethan was true. But she still felt shaky.

'You sure you're OK?' he asked, noticing how distraught she appeared.

'Yeah,' said Candice and, to her embarrassment, she burst into tears.

'Aw, you poor thing,' said Pam, slipping into the seat beside Candice and putting her arms around her. 'Come here,' she said, pulling Candice's head into her bosom, and muttering reassuring words.

Candice tried to control her weeping, but Pam's sympathy was too much. As she held her tight, Candice's tears flowed freely, her shoulders shuddered with the loud sobs that engulfed her body, and she was unable to stop the mucus that dribbled down her nose and onto Pam's expensive-looking top.

Candice had been so preoccupied with trying to stay strong for her mother that she hadn't realised how much things had been getting to *her* until she was confronted with the situation from somebody else's viewpoint.

This was what she had needed, a mother figure to hold her tight and tell her everything would be alright. But, as things stood, it seemed that her mother was too overwhelmed with troubles of her own to offer Candice the comfort she craved.

Later Candice and Thomas went up to his room. Feeling ashamed of her emotional outburst, she was glad to get away. She couldn't blame Thomas's dad and Pam for their kindness though. In fact, she was bowled over by it and told Thomas so once they were alone.

'See,' he said, smiling. 'I told you Dad's alright really.'

Candice smiled back. Thomas was right. His dad was a lovely man. He might not have been liked by the staff at work, but outside of work, he was very caring. And Pam was really nice.

Candice felt grateful. Things might be tough at home but at least she had the support of Thomas and his family to help her get through.

26

It had started like any other evening for Laura. A glass of wine with her evening meal, a habit she had got into lately, then finishing the bottle while she watched TV. But tonight, she was getting through the drink more quickly than usual. Maybe it was because Candice wasn't at home, so she felt less restrained.

As the drink kicked in so did her imagination and she found herself questioning who could be behind the vendetta against her. She had already decided that it was connected to her past as a sex worker. But there had been so many clients that it was difficult to guess which one of them might have been responsible.

Thoughts of her past conjured up recollections of the nights she had spent in the Rose and Crown having a few drinks before work with the girls for a bit of Dutch courage. It was a backstreet pub in the centre of Manchester frequented by sex workers, thieves, fences, drug dealers and anyone else who operated on the wrong side of the law.

The Rose and Crown! That was it, she realised. It had to be her starting point to finding out who was targeting her. *Sod waiting around for the police!* she thought, feeling emboldened by the booze. She needed to get to the bottom of this and quick before things escalated to another level.

Twenty minutes later Laura was tumbling out of a taxi outside the Rose and Crown. She hadn't been there for years, and from the outside it looked no different. Bottle-green tiles clung to the exterior, framing narrow windows and a small porticoed entrance. And above the windows the old signage remained together with faded images of a rose and a crown to either side of the text.

Despite the fresh lick of paint on the pillars and door surround, Laura felt as though she was entering a time warp. But once inside, she was surprised to see that the pub had changed. It looked as though it had been recently painted in modern shades of dove grey and slate blue. The dingy old carpet had been replaced and the tables and chairs were new.

As she gazed around the Rose and Crown, Laura noticed that the clientele were different too. Although there were a few dubious characters hanging about, the majority were young professional types. In fact, they were no different from most people who now frequented the Northern Quarter since it had been redeveloped years previously. It looked like the old pub had finally succumbed.

Despite the alcohol she had consumed, Laura felt uneasy as she walked to the bar. She had expected a warm welcome inside the Rose and Crown but now she felt a bit self-conscious and out of place. Even the bar staff had changed, Laura realised as a young attractive woman rushed to serve her. She surmised that they must have finally pensioned Moira off, the barmaid of yesteryear and one of the pub's stalwarts.

Laura had made up her mind to have only the one drink at the bar and then grab a taxi home. Knowing there was fat chance of a table in the crowded lounge, she stood at the bar downing her drink till she noticed somebody in her peripheral vision. She looked up to see a man studying her then quickly looked back down again. *Oh no! Not Ron the pimp*, she thought recognising him from years previously.

A particular recollection sprang to mind from around ten years ago. It was not long after she had lost her lover, Gilly, and she was on the streets trying to do some business. Unfortunately, she had taken the news of Gilly's death badly and was so drunk and drugged up that the punters weren't interested. Ron had approached her suggesting she come to work for him, and she had told him where to stick it. Then he'd humiliated her by pushing her over, knowing she was already unsteady.

'Fuckin' hell, I thought it was you!' he said, inching up to her at the bar. 'I nearly didn't recognise you. Fuckin' hell, Crystal, you haven't half changed.'

'It's Laura actually. I don't use that name anymore,' she said, trying to disguise the slur in her voice so she didn't come over as vulnerable. She thought he had changed as well but not for the better. He was now going bald and had developed a paunch.

'Since when?' he asked.

'Since I came off the beat.'

'Ah, right. I heard something about you going into business. You running the brothel now with Ruby?' he asked, referring to her friend Trina by her street name.

'It's not a brothel, it's a massage parlour,' she snapped

even though she knew it was just a glorified name for the brothel. 'And no, I'm not. I'm in another line of business.'

She didn't trust Ron and was reluctant to tell him what her line of business was, but she realised that he might be useful to her in gathering information. And, seeing as how she didn't recognise anybody else in the pub, it was Ron or no one, so she'd best start being more friendly towards him.

'You're looking good,' he said, making it a bit easier for her to be nice. 'Proper classy, not like, well... y'know.'

She laughed. 'You can say it if you want; not like I was before, you mean.'

Ron held up his hands in supplication. 'Hey, you said it, not me.' Then, after a pause, he added, 'What brings you to this neck of the woods anyway?'

'I'm after some information. You might be able to help me actually seeing as how you've always got your wits about you.' She nearly choked on her words. Sucking up to seedy Ron the pimp went against all her instincts.

A smile played on his withered lips, and she could almost see his brain operating as he tried to think of ways in which this could benefit him. Some people never changed.

'Might be. It depends.'

'On what?'

'Well...' He was lost in thought for a while then he spoke again. 'I tell you what, I'll answer your questions if you agree to answer mine later.'

Laura sighed. 'OK, I will do, but you might not like the answers.'

Ron grinned then nodded over to a table that had just become free. 'Quick, grab them seats while I get us a drink. Red wine, is it?'

'Yeah,' Laura shouted back while she staggered across to the table.

She plonked herself down on a seat, placed her handbag on another then adjusted her clothing, too preoccupied to notice the brandy that Ron ordered and surreptitiously poured into her large glass of red wine.

'Fuckin' hell, Ron,' she said when she tasted her drink. 'This is strong.'

'Well, it's a bit different now to what it was in your day. It's not like the nine-per-cent plonk you might have drunk years ago; some of these new wines are fourteen fuckin' per cent. It's a decent wine though, not like the shite they used to stock.' Then he seemed to think of something. 'Which one did you have before, the Shiraz or the Merlot?'

'I dunno, I just asked for a red wine.'

'That'll be it then. You probably had the shitty stuff but, seeing as how we're old mates, I got you summat decent.'

Laura cringed but thanked him anyway, careful to keep him sweet till she got what she wanted. 'I'm wondering if you've heard anything about any dodgy clients,' she said. 'Not a youngster though, someone older, someone who would have been about in my day, a nasty, vindictive piece of stuff.'

Ron rubbed his chin, thinking. 'Yeah, a couple of the girls did mention someone a couple of weeks ago. Some guy who was getting rough with them. One of them recognised him from years before but said he hadn't been around for a while.'

'Might have been inside for a few years,' said Laura.

'Could have been.'

'And what did he look like, this client?'

'Big guy, chubby as well as tall. Older too so that would fit in with what you said. Why do you want to know anyway?'

'Never mind that. Did you get a name or anything?'

'Nah, they said he never gave it to them.'

'OK, so is that all?'

'Well, it's as much as I know.' He grinned. 'My turn now.'

Laura braced herself knowing this wasn't going to be good, whatever it was.

'I'm opening a new place,' Ron said. 'Upmarket to cater for men with plenty of dosh to splash around. And with this classy new image of yours you'd probably fit in nicely. I mean, you're a bit older than the rest of the girls but…'

'Fuck right off!' Laura snapped before he had chance to finish. Then she stood up and downed the rest of her wine before setting off in search of a taxi.

Ron shouted after her. 'I meant running the place with you being a businesswoman. It's a big earner.'

But Laura wasn't interested. Her days involved in the sex trade were well in the past.

As she made her way unsteadily to Piccadilly, she reflected on what a wasted journey she'd had. Knowing Ron, he had probably made up the story about the dodgy punter and had been stringing her along to get what he wanted out of their meeting. And even if such a client had existed, without a name or description, the information was of limited use. She'd had quite a few nasty clients during her time on the beat so how did you pin it down to just one man?

27

The driver of the blue Astra parked across the road from Laura and Candice's home on Woodlea. From his vantage point the man could see the black mini parked on the drive. The tyres were fully inflated now so he assumed she must have had them replaced. He wondered if that meant the owner was at home.

Perhaps the daughter was at home too, assuming that there was a second car in the garage. But all seemed quiet. There was no sign of activity coming from the house and, although it was late evening, there were no lights switched on.

He decided to go and check it out. At this point his intentions weren't to attack the owner, just to shake her up. And he had so many other things planned for her. If she were inside, he would settle for a brick lobbed through the window. But if she were out then it would be a great opportunity to sneak inside and inflict more damage.

He crossed the road and noticed that a new alarm box and security light had been fitted since his last visit. He scanned the house to see if there was also a camera but, thankfully, there was no sign of one.

After passing the Mini, he approached the front door and

knocked loudly then waited. He wasn't worried about her answering because he already had a cover story. Again, there was no sign of life but, to be on the safe side, he knocked again. No answer.

He came back out of the drive and crossed the road, flicking the remote control to his car. Inside the boot he had a carrier bag readily packed with the tools he would need to gain access to the house and disable the alarm. Checking there was nobody about, he grabbed the bag, locked the car, and crossed back over the road again. He was just about to enter the driveway when he saw a car turn in to the road and head towards him.

The man carried on walking, prepared to turn back once the car was out of sight. But instead of driving by, the car stopped. A young couple stepped out of it and made their way up the drive. The girl fished a key from her bag and, once she had unlocked the front door, the couple made their way inside.

'Shit!' he cursed, returning to his car then starting his engine and driving away.

When Candice arrived home just after 10pm she was surprised to find the house quiet and all the lights off. She knew it was unusual for her mother not to tell her if she was going out, and an ominous feeling settled in the pit of her stomach. What if something had happened to her?

'I wonder where she is,' said Candice once she and Thomas were inside.

'Ring her,' he said.

Candice took her phone out of her bag and rang her

mother's number. The call was answered straightaway, and, in the background, Candice could hear music as well as the sound of an engine running.

'Mum, are you alright?'

'Yesss, sssure, I'm fine,' she slurred.

'For God's sake. You're not driving in that state, are you?' Candice demanded flashing Thomas a look of consternation.

'No, no, I'm in a taxi.'

'Why, where have you been?'

'Oh, nowhere much, just doing a bit of investi… gata… ti… tive work of my own.'

'You're joking!' Candice yelled. 'Where? What have you been up to?'

'Oh, nothing much. Just talking to sssomeone I used to know.'

'Do you realise how dangerous things are, Mum?'

'Courssse. Why do you think I'm trying to find sssummat out?'

'And did you find out anything?' Candice demanded.

'No, wassste of time.'

Candice cut the call without saying goodbye. She was furious not only because her mother was probably putting herself in danger but also because of the state she was in. Even without seeing her, Candice could tell that tonight she was worse than ever.

'She's on her way home,' Candice said to Thomas.

Thomas's expression was one of curiosity so Candice elaborated. 'She's been trying to find something out, apparently. God knows what that involves. She's bloody steaming as well!' Then she felt her lip tremble. 'I'm worried about her, Thomas.'

Thomas flung his arms around her and stroked the back of her head. 'I'll stay with you until she gets home.'

Candice pulled away from his embrace. 'No!' she said, more abruptly than she had intended as she didn't want him to see her mother at her worst. Then, moderating her voice, she continued. 'I'll be fine. She'll be home any minute.'

'You sure?'

'Yes, yes. Go, you've got work tomorrow.'

She ushered him out of the door, relieved when he went despite her other concerns. He'd only just gone when she heard her mother attempting to put her key in the lock. She could tell from the sounds alone that she was struggling. When the scraping of key against door continued for a few seconds, Candice strode to the door and wrenched it open. Her mother wobbled forwards with the force but managed to steady herself. Candice could see a look of alarm on her face, but she didn't care.

'Just look at the state of you!' she raged, turning on her heel and storming back into the lounge.

She could hear her mother retaliating from out in the hallway. 'Don't fuckin' talk to me like that!'

Candice stood and waited for her mother's slow, unsteady entrance into the lounge. As Laura pushed the door ajar, Candice felt a draught sweep into the room. She stomped past her mother, flashing a look of contempt as she stepped back out into the hall. As she suspected, Laura had left the front door wide open. She slammed it shut before marching back into the lounge.

'No! Don't you talk to *me* like that. I don't appreciate being sworn at and I'm not having you going back to how you used to be. The drinking has got to stop, Mum. It isn't doing either of us any good.'

'It'sss not my fault,' Laura countered. 'It'sss that bloody Ron. I think he laced my drink.'

'Who the hell is Ron?'

'Oh nobody... jussst somebody... from the past. You don't need to know.'

'But I do need to know, Mother, because it seems as though you're not capable of taking care of yourself. Just what the hell you've been up to I don't know! Why would you be visiting somebody from the past? I thought you'd put that life behind you. And how do you think you're gonna defend yourself against a madman when you're in that state?'

'I needed to investi... gate.'

'Listen to you. You can't even get your words out properly. You don't NEED to investigate. That's what the police are for.'

'Aah, but they don't know what I know.' Laura tapped her nose conspiratorially. It was a drunken, exaggerated motion, which irritated Candice.

'What? What have you found out?' she asked.

'Bad men, Candice. There's bad men out there. It's one of them. I'm sure of it.'

'For God's sake!' Candice cursed, beginning to realise that she wasn't going to get any sense out of her mother while she was in this state. 'Do you not realise the worry that you're putting me through? You're so wrapped up in your own world that you don't even think about me anymore.' She heard her mother trying to retaliate but she cut in quick, not giving her chance.

'Thank God I've got Thomas!' she yelled. 'At least he's bothered about me; and his dad and Pam are too. Do you know they even offered for me to move in with them tonight because they were so concerned about me? But I turned them down. And do you know why?' Without waiting for her mother to respond, she carried on, 'Because I was worried about you.' She spluttered. 'What a joke! It should be the other way round. You're my mother.'

Candice was no longer yelling. She knew she'd upset her mother and she suddenly felt guilty for being so aggressive with her. She could understand her behaviour in a way. Her mother was obviously struggling with everything and, as a reformed addict, it was too easy for her to slip back into old habits.

But Laura soon recovered. 'Right, go and bloody live with them if that's what you want!'

A feeling of sadness washed over Candice. How had it come to this? She and her mother had got along fine for years. And now this person was hounding them; not only damaging her mother's businesses but destroying their relationship too.

'I don't want to live with them,' she said, trying to stay calm. 'I want to live with you. You're my mother. I just want things back to how they were.'

But by the looks of her mother Candice recognised that things weren't going back to how they were before the vendetta. Instead, they were going back to how they were before her mother got herself clean. And that was one of her biggest fears.

★

Late 2011

Laura had been crying again. And drinking. Eleven-year-old Candice didn't know what to do because her mum wasn't nice when she was drunk. She'd snap at her and use foul language.

Candice was worried. This had been going on for days and last night her mum hadn't gone to bed. Candice tiptoed into the living room where she found her on the sofa asleep and fully dressed. Empty bottles, a glass and other debris littered the coffee table as well as smudges of white powder.

She needed to get ready for school so she decided to leave her mum while she got dressed and searched for something to eat. Her stomach growled at the thought of food, and she hoped the kitchen cupboards weren't still empty.

As she was about to walk out of the room her mother stirred, and Candice stood motionless as she watched her come to. Laura swung her legs off the sofa and looked around her. There was a glazed expression on her face as she gazed around the room trying to refamiliarise herself with her surroundings. Candice recognised her look of confusion; Laura was trying to recall where she had been when she'd passed out.

Candice noticed that her eyes were like slits, the eyelids red and puffy. Her face was tear-stained and the hair was plastered to her cheek on one side where she had rested her head on a mangy cushion.

Then Laura focused on her daughter, and they locked eyes. To Candice it appeared as though a curtain of sorrow had crossed her mother's face. She was obviously remembering her misery of the previous day. And the tears started to flow again.

'Oh, Candice, love,' she wailed. 'I don't know what I'm gonna do. Gilly's dead.'

It was the first time Candice had been confronted with the reason for her mother's sorrow and, even though she had never personally liked Gilly, she felt sorry for her.

Laura's cries were becoming more forceful now, her words punctuated by a cacophony of heart-rending shrieks. Candice still stood watching, tempted to comfort her mother but afraid of a rebuff. It had happened before when Candice had felt like a verbal target for all her mother's anger and despair.

After a few seconds, Laura seemed to pull herself together. She wiped her eyes with the back of her hand and looked intently at Candice. Then she took a deep steadying breath before she spoke again with a tremor in her voice. 'He's dead, Candice. Your father's dead.'

Her words hit Candice like a sucker punch. She had never been told before that her mother's lover, the man who had never acknowledged her, had actually been her father. And as she grew older, a further shock was to come when her mother finally confided in her that Gilly had died of a drugs overdose.

28

For Candice it was another tedious day at work, and she was also tired and preoccupied. Carol had just gone for a cigarette break and as she sat there alone Candice found her mind wandering.

She hadn't seen her mother that morning as she had still been in bed when Candice got up for work. She was glad in a way because she felt bad about the way she had spoken to her the previous night. These days she couldn't seem to help herself where her mother was concerned and was constantly flying into a rage. But she knew that it was because of worries about the danger they were in as well as the danger her mother was to herself.

She was so lost in her thoughts that she hadn't realised she had stopped work until she became aware of Carol returning to her desk. 'Hey, daydreamer,' she said. 'How are you doing with that filing?'

Sitting in the seat opposite, Carol leant over the desk and looked at the pile of filing in front of Candice. 'Bloody hell! You've hardly touched it. What's wrong with you today?'

'Oh, sorry,' said Candice, grabbing hold of a bunch of papers and sorting them into alphabetical order.

For the next ten minutes she tried to concentrate on

what she was doing, hoping it would take her mind off her troubles. But it was difficult when the job was so mundane. She heard a door opening and looked up to see Mr Foster walking towards them.

He addressed Carol. 'Can you bring the Millgate file into my office please? There's something I need to discuss with you.'

'Sure,' said Carol, standing up then heading towards the filing cabinet.

He turned to Candice, smiling. 'And how are you today?'

She managed a thin smile back. 'Not too bad thanks.'

As she spoke, she could feel some of the other girls in the office watching her. When Mr Foster left the office, Candice looked across the room and several pairs of eyes quickly shifted back to the work in front of them.

Carol came back with the file and flicked through it before going through to Mr Foster's office. Before she walked away, she made a comment. 'I tell you what, I wish I was in as much favour as you.'

Candice felt herself blush. She didn't like being seen as colluding with the enemy. She dreaded to think how easily their feelings towards her could turn sour if they knew of her connection.

Candice was glad when it was time to go home. But as soon as she got into the car all her worries came flooding back. She had arranged to have tea at Thomas's again on the agreement that she didn't stay too long, and she should have been looking forward to it. Instead, she was thinking about her mother as well as all her other concerns.

Candice felt guilty that she wouldn't be back home till later, but she didn't want to face being sat across the dining table from her mother with a stifling atmosphere between them.

Then a thought occurred to her. She knew someone who would be able to help. Feeling more upbeat, she took out her phone and dialled a number. The voice on the other end was unmistakable.

'Hi, girl, how are you?'

Candice smiled as she prepared to unburden herself.

When Laura woke up it was late morning and she felt dreadful. Her head was throbbing, her heart racing and her mouth dry and raw. She knew she'd overdone it last night with the booze and, although Ron was partly to blame, she was also responsible. Lately, drinking was the only way she could shut her mind off from all the troubling thoughts.

Laura was worried sick about the attacks on her shops and staff. She was also worried about herself and Candice. This attacker was too close to home for her liking, and she was terrified that he'd do something to harm one of them. She couldn't bear it if something happened to Candice who was her world, and she was anxious about how Candice would cope.

Although Candice had inherited her mother's inner strength, it had taken a long time for Candice to recover from her ordeal of being kidnapped when she was just under twelve years of age. An ex-client was responsible for it, but Laura knew she had played her part. He was one of several clients she had tried to blackmail when she had come off the beat, and it had backfired when his goons had snatched Candice.

Thankfully, Laura, with help from her friends, had rescued her daughter. Candice had been relatively unharmed physically, but it had affected her mentally and emotionally. Laura had lived with the guilt of it ever since. And now that her past had caught up with her once more, she was having difficulty handling it.

Laura went into the kitchen and flicked the switch on the kettle. Going over to the cupboard where she kept the crockery, she reached for a cup. As she grabbed hold of it, her hands were shaking so much that she almost dropped it.

Her nerves were shot. She would love to get rid of this feeling of anxiety and knew that the booze was only making it worse in the long run. Then something occurred to her: booze wasn't the only thing that could help her. Maybe a bit of weed or a few vallies would take the edge off it, and she knew how she could get hold of them.

For a moment she deliberated, knowing she really shouldn't go down that road again. But, if she were honest with herself, although she'd managed to stay clean for years, she had been craving something for days. She knew it was easier to relapse when times were hard, and she had tried to resist but, with the way she was feeling now, that battle was becoming increasingly difficult.

She managed to hold out for four agonising hours. She'd had a few glasses of wine to tide her over but, despite all that, her anxiety was escalating, and she knew she needed something more.

In the end, she decided to go ahead, promising herself she wouldn't overdo it. Just a bit of weed or a couple of vallies. That was all she wanted. And she'd avoid the hard stuff, knowing the damage it could do.

It wouldn't be difficult to obtain them. She could be in the city centre in less than half an hour and back inside the Rose and Crown. Hopefully, she'd see someone she knew this time and, surely, they would know who she could score from.

Now that her mind was made up, she rushed to get ready and was soon back inside the pub. It wasn't as crowded as the previous evening, which didn't surprise Laura as it was only four o'clock.

She walked to the bar, grabbed a stool, and ordered a double brandy and lemonade. While she was drinking, she scanned the pub. It was a different crowd today, not so many young hipsters and more of the old type of customers. There was still nobody she knew but she decided to stay at least till she'd finished her drink.

To her consternation it wasn't long before Ron waltzed inside and addressed her. 'Bloody hell, slumming it aren't you? Twice in as many days! You hit hard times or what?'

Despite her harsh words of the previous evening, Laura decided to be nice to him because, yet again, he was the only person there who could help her. 'No, I need summat,' she whispered.

'But I told you what I knew yesterday.'

'Not that kind of summat.'

A look of recognition flashed across Ron's face. 'Ha, you want a fix?'

'Shush,' warned Laura, checking to see if the barmaid was watching and relieved to spot her at the other end of the bar. She lowered her voice again. 'Can I still get it here?'

'Yeah, there's one or two of them come in. Mainly at night. What is it you're looking for?'

Laura whispered her requirements. 'Is that all?' he asked.

'Yeah, I gave up the other stuff a long time ago.'

'OK, well, there's a small-time dealer called Milo who sometimes comes in. Usually late afternoon or early evening.'

Laura pulled back her sleeve to check the time, causing Ron to whistle when he spotted her Rolex. She quickly pulled her sleeve down again. There were no doubt still plenty of thieves in the Rose and Crown judging by the looks of some of them and she didn't want to risk getting mugged on her way out.

It was still only four-twenty. 'Sod it!' she said. 'I'll hang on for a bit. Will you point him out if he comes in?'

'If I'm still here,' said Ron.

'OK, I'll stay then. And this time I'll get my own fuckin' drink. I'm not having you pulling the same stunt you did last night.'

'It's OK, I wasn't offering.'

Ron didn't stay in her company for long. After they had made small talk, he went to join two guys at another table. Laura figured there wasn't much reason for him to stay with her as she was no longer any use to him in his line of business.

She'd downed three double brandy and lemonades by the time she realised that Ron had left the pub along with the two guys he had been sitting with. And he hadn't even bothered saying goodbye.

Shit! she thought. Even if Milo did come in, there was no way of knowing who he was, and she didn't want to risk approaching random strangers and asking who they were. Sod Ron! The snidey bastard. Feeling defeated, she slid off her bar stool and left the pub once again.

29

This time Laura didn't go straight back home from the Rose and Crown. Something Ron had said the previous evening was playing on her mind, so she headed for the red-light district. It was strange being back in her old stomping ground. But not much had changed really. Scantily dressed girls lined the road despite the pandemic. They still had a living to make.

Laura approached three girls who were standing chatting. 'Hi, girls, can I have a word?' she asked.

They turned around and sized her up, taking in her expensive clothes and shoes. 'What the fuck do you want with us?' asked a hard-looking brunette.

Laura held out her hand unsteadily. 'Eh, easy, I only want a chat. I've been talking to Ron. D'you know him?'

'Never fuckin' heard of him,' said the brunette, and the other two girls sniggered.

'Maybe he doesn't work this stretch now. Anyway, he told me about a dodgy customer you were having a few problems with, and I wondered…'

'What if we were? What the fuck's it got to do with you?'

Just at that moment a car slowed down but it didn't

stop. The driver seemed to be assessing the situation before driving away.

'Look what you've just done!' yelled the brunette. 'We've just lost a fuckin' customer 'cos of you.'

'Eh, I didn't mean any harm,' said Laura. 'I just...'

'I don't give a shit what you meant. Who the fuck do you think you are coming here with your fancy clothes? We're not interested in no fuckin' reporters. They won't do anything to help us.'

Laura was just about to protest that she wasn't a reporter when the brunette stepped towards her waving her fist. 'Now fuckin' do one unless you want that.'

Then she lowered her fist and pushed Laura into the road. It took Laura all her time to remain upright and, once she had straightened herself up, she looked at the girls, considering her options. But it was obvious from the fierce expressions on their faces that she wasn't going to get anywhere with them.

So, she did the only thing she could do under the circumstances. She walked away. This was no longer her world.

Laura was back home and drinking her second glass of wine when she heard a heavy hammering on the front door. Still shaking from her encounter with the working girls, she tensed and was immediately on her guard, wondering who it might be. Laura crept to the window and peeped from behind the curtain. Thankfully, she saw the tall, dark frame of her friend, Trina, and she heaved a sigh of relief.

'Where the fuck have you been?' asked Trina when Laura let her in.

'Charming! That's no way to greet a friend, is it?'

'Well, I've been trying to get hold of you for the last hour. I've tried the house phone and your mobile, and I've texted. I thought summat had happened to you.'

They walked into the lounge and Laura noticed the disapproving look on Trina's face when she spotted the glass of wine on the coffee table. She strode over to it and lifted the glass.

'Right, this fuckin' stops here now!'

She marched out of the room, carrying the wine with her.

Laura trailed behind. 'What the fuck are you doing?' she asked.

'I'll tell you what I'm doing,' said Trina, pouring the wine down the sink. 'I'm stopping you from hitting the fuckin' self-destruct button again.'

'What d'you mean? It's only a glass.' Laura didn't mention the other wine and the three double brandy and lemonades she had already drunk. 'I just wanted a hair of the dog after last night, that's all.'

'Why? Were you pissed again, like you were last time I spoke to you? And the time before?'

Trina wrenched the fridge door open and grabbed the bottle of wine, which was half empty.

'Only a glass, my arse,' she raged, going to the sink, and emptying the bottle down it.

Laura knew better than to try to wrestle the bottle from her. Trina was fearsome when she was in one of these moods. Instead, she tried to cajole her.

'For God's sake, Trina. You know what I'm going through. That's the only reason I'm drinking so much.'

'Yes, but it's not fuckin' helping, is it? You keep drinking like that and you'll be back on the fuckin' drugs next! That's if you're not already.'

Laura felt riddled with guilt knowing how much she had been tempted lately, and a hot flush ran through her as she thought about her visit to the Rose and Crown that afternoon.

But Trina wasn't easily fooled. 'Oh no, for fuck's sake! Tell me you're not, please. Is that what you want to be, a fucked-up junkie again? Look at this place! Do you want to lose it all?' As she spoke, Trina waved her arms around, her hands pointing out the modern kitchen with high-tech gadgets. 'Your home? Your shops?' she continued. 'Not to mention your lovely daughter? You owe it to her at least to stay fuckin' sober, Laura!'

'No, no I'm not using, honestly.'

'Well, why is there guilt all over your fuckin' face then?'

Laura sighed. 'Alright, I admit I've been tempted. But you know what I've been going through, Trina.'

'Yeah, you said. But booze and drugs aren't the answer. Your daughter is going through it too. She's just fuckin' rang me in bits because she's so worried about you! But do you see her hitting the bottle?' Trina answered her own question. 'No, you don't! And she's only a young kid. If she can get through it then you need to find a way too.'

She stepped over to Laura and grabbed her by the wrists shaking her hands as she made her point. 'Think of her, Laura. If you can't do it for yourself then at least fuckin' do it for her.'

'I can't, Trina. I can't,' Laura cried. 'I don't know how much more I can fuckin' take. This is sending me over the top. I wanna do right by Candice and stay sober, I really do. But how can I when all this is happening? It's starting to feel like everything I've achieved has been a waste of time. 'Cos, at the end of the day, I've just been kidding myself. Pretending to be somebody when all I am is scum.'

'Eh, eh, stop that!' said Trina. 'You fuckin' deserve what you've got. You've worked bloody hard. So don't let anyone take it all from you.' Then, at the sight of her friend upset, Trina relented. 'Come on, let's go and have a sit-down. I'll make you a cuppa. Hopefully, that'll calm you down a bit.'

Trina led Laura to the lounge as though she was having difficulty finding her way around her own home. Then she went back to the kitchen to make the drinks. As soon as she was out of the room, Laura lay down on the sofa and wept bitter tears of worry and frustration. She needed to see an end to all this before it was too late.

30

It was another week before Laura's nemesis struck again, but this time he chose the shop in Wilmslow, an affluent area of Cheshire just outside the Greater Manchester boundary. The manager, Donna, had rung her to report some staining to various garments and, having told her to ring the police straightaway, Laura was now on her way there.

During the past week Laura hadn't been feeling quite as bad. After Trina had virtually dragged her to the doctor's, he had given her something to calm her down. He told her it would take a few weeks for the tablets to fully kick in, but they would help her to sleep in the meantime. Laura felt better that at least she was getting a good night's sleep at last and, even though she was still tempted by drink and drugs, she was finding it easier to resist.

When she arrived at the Wilmslow branch, one of the staff told her Donna was in the office so Laura went through. She found her sitting on one side of the office desk with DI Carson and DS Worrall facing her. It didn't escape Laura's notice that the police had sent the two detectives assigned to the case rather than a couple of constables. And they must have dropped everything to get there so soon.

DI Carson politely stood up and shook Laura's hand before Donna invited Laura to take her seat. She was an older woman with platinum-blonde hair, cut short and neat, and was very smart and well-groomed. Her accent screamed Wilmslow although Laura knew she was originally from the inner-city suburbs. Despite that, she was a hard-working, conscientious manager and Laura knew she could trust her with anything.

Laura sat down behind the desk. She was joined by Donna, who had brought another chair into the office. Then the police got down to business with DI Carson addressing Donna.

'Now that Miss Sharples has arrived, would you like to advise us what prompted your call today?'

'Yes,' said Donna. 'One of my staff brought this to my attention.'

She pulled out a dress from a box that had been placed at the side of the desk and held it up. Laura drew in a sharp breath when she caught sight of the garment. It was a smart button-through day dress in cream with a price tag of £249.95. Across the front of it was a bright red stain. It looked like some sort of dye, but the colour red made Laura think of blood and she wondered if that had been the deliberate intention of the culprit. On examining the item, she concluded that it was beyond repair.

'I checked all of the other garments on the rails,' Donna continued officiously. 'And found these.'

She pulled half a dozen other items out of the box, amongst which were two evening dresses valued at around four hundred pounds each. All of them had the same colour dye sprayed all over the material.

'Shit!' Laura cursed, raising a hand to her mouth.

The officers ran through a series of questions with Donna about when she discovered the items, what time she opened the shop, how many customers approximately had been in the shop that day et cetera. Then DI Carson said, 'I notice you have cameras in the shop.'

Laura was about to say that she'd had them installed since the other incidents but then she thought better of it. It was best if Donna didn't know about that as it would only add to Laura's problems.

'I presume they're fully operational,' said the inspector.

'Oh yes,' said Donna.

'OK, well we'll need to study the tapes.'

'Great,' said Laura. 'Hopefully, you'll be able to catch whoever did this.'

'Erm,' muttered DI Carson.

'What do you mean, erm? They'll show up on the CCTV, won't they?'

'Let me get my team onto it before we discuss the results,' he said, noncommittally.

'What do you mean?' Laura repeated. 'If those cameras are switched on then that destructive bugger will be on them. I hope you're going to make sure they do a thorough job of checking. I've not forked out all that money on cameras for nothing.'

The DI looked across at his sergeant willing him to speak. DS Worrall obliged. 'I had a quick look at the garments before you arrived, and my guess is that the perpetrator has used an ink sprayer.'

'OK,' said Laura, knowing there was more to come.

'I'm not talking about the large, industrial ones. Chances are it was the type used for art. The bottles are small, holding as little as fifty millilitres of ink. They're easily hidden inside the hand.

'I'm afraid we've come across this sort of thing before. They pull out the garment with one hand, as though admiring it, then reach behind with the hand holding the spray. Once their hand is hidden behind the garment, it's easy to spray it without anybody noticing.'

'Aw, no!' yelled Laura, shaking her head. 'Will you check the tapes anyway? You never know…'

The DI cut in, 'Of course. We'll make sure they're fully checked but it's best to be warned in advance that we might not come up with anything substantial.'

Laura nodded. 'OK. Can I have a word alone, please?'

Donna took the hint and left Laura with the two officers. Once she was gone, Laura didn't waste any time. 'Have you come up with anything else? From the other shops? Or any ideas who slit the tyres on my daughter's car?'

'I'm afraid we've got nothing concrete yet but we're still investigating,' said the DI. He stood up and the DS followed suit. 'My team are working extremely hard on this, and we'll let you know as soon as we have anything. Now, if we could have the tapes, we'll be on our way.'

Laura didn't hang around after the police had gone. This latest incident had shaken her badly, and she wasn't in the mood to stay and make small talk with Donna or any of the other staff. Neither did she want to discuss how they were going to deal with replacement of the garments. She needed time to think, so she told Donna she'd be in touch soon.

Somebody, somewhere had it in for her; targeting her shops, her goods, her home and attacking her staff. And it seemed that the police were still no nearer to finding the culprit.

If ever there was a time when she could have done with a drink, that time was now. But she had to resist. Trina's words came back to her, '*If you can't do it for yourself then at least fuckin' do it for her,*' the '*her*' being Candice. Trina was right. She owed it to Candice to stay on the straight and narrow. And from now on, every time she was tempted, she would replay Trina's words in her mind till the shame penetrated her consciousness and put a stop to all thoughts of drink and drugs.

When she arrived home, Laura was still upset but there was no point sharing what had happened with Candice. That would only upset her too, and Laura had already decided that from now on she would protect her daughter as much as she could. Candice had already been through enough and she didn't want to cause her any more distress.

That evening Ethan was sitting at his parents' dining table picking at his food, his parents at either end of the table with him in the middle. Ever since the first police questioning, he had lost his appetite. Worry dogged him constantly and every time he looked at his parents' pained expressions, the guilt tore at him.

He glanced at them both tucking into their evening meal. His mother was the nervous type but lately she was worse than ever, and he'd overheard her weeping a couple of nights ago while his father yelled at her to pull herself together because her tears weren't helping the situation. Ethan knew that 'the situation' referred to him and the continual haranguing by the police, who were after a confession.

His father was a proud man with a strong sense of right and wrong. He had always been the disciplinarian whereas his mother was more timid and generally acceded to his father's wishes. But she would spoil Ethan whenever his father was out of sight, letting him get away with things and telling him not to tell his father.

Ethan had learnt over the years that as long as he made his father proud and lived up to his high expectations for him, everything was fine. Both parents had heaped praise on him every time he aced a maths exam, and at every glowing school report and parents' evening. And when he'd gained his university place, they'd made him feel like he was the best son in the world. Ethan had lapped up their adulation. But now everything had changed. His mother was constantly upset and his father was perpetually angry.

As he sat toying with his food, his phone rang.

'For God's sake!' yelled his father. 'What have I told you about using your phone at the dining table?'

Ethan had already seen the caller's name on screen. 'Sorry, I need to take it,' he said sheepishly. 'It's Sergeant Worrall.'

His father tutted and stabbed at a potato while Ethan got up and left the table. When he returned, his parents both looked up at him, his mother's expression expectant, his father's hostile.

'Well?' demanded his father.

Ethan hung his head. 'I've got to go to the station for questioning again. Tomorrow afternoon.'

'Oh for God's sake!' yelled his father. 'When is all this going to bloody end?' Then he pushed his empty plate away from him. 'I think it's about time you and me had a proper talk. Sit down,' he ordered, nodding at the chair Ethan had left.

Ethan sat down and he too pushed his plate away. The food was beginning to cool and congeal, but the smell of meat and potato pie lingered, and it was making him feel nauseous. His father didn't waste any time in speaking out.

'I think it's about time you told us everything, Ethan.'

Ethan looked at him in shock. 'What do you mean? There's nothing to tell.'

'Well why the bloody hell have we got the police on the phone every five minutes? I'm sick to death of it. How do you think me and your mother felt when we had them traipsing through our home, turning everything upside down, treating us like bloody criminals? And all because of what you've done!'

'But I haven't done anything,' Ethan pleaded.

'Oh haven't you? Well that's not what the police seem to think. Why did they take your hoody away? Why, Ethan? Because that's what you were wearing when you committed these crimes, that's why.'

'Oh, I don't think...' began his mother till she was silenced by his father lifting his hand palm outwards.

'Do you realise the neighbours have been quizzing your mother?' he asked. 'She was stopped at the shops the other day by that bloody Mrs Garside asking questions. Imagine how your mother felt having the likes of her looking down her nose at us.'

'But it's not my fault,' Ethan persisted.

'Isn't it?' His father then raised his voice, making both Ethan and his mother squirm. 'Well why won't the bloody police leave you alone then?' He raised his shoulders then huffed. 'If you didn't do anything then what did you say to this girl to make her think you did? There's no smoke without fire, Ethan!'

'I don't know. I was just asking about the graffiti I'd seen at her mother's shop, that's all. I can't remember everything I said; I was a bit drunk.'

'Drunk? So is that why we're spending all this money on your education, so you can go out getting drunk, making an arse of yourself, harassing young girls, spraying graffiti on her mother's shop, vandalising properties, and God knows what else you've been getting up to?'

Ethan noticed how his father had become red in the face, spittle accompanying his angry words as he spat them at him. He tried to defend himself against his overbearing father. 'I haven't,' he said, his voice now shaking, while his mother sat with a pained expression, wringing her hands.

But Ethan's words were in vain as his father carried on, delivering his final blow. 'You know, me and your mother had such high hopes for you, Ethan. I always thought you'd do well in life. We brought you up to be a decent person, to be someone we would be proud of. But you've let us down. We'll never be able to hold our heads high again after this. And I'll never forgive you for what you've put me and your mother through.'

Ethan's jaw dropped in astonishment at his father's harsh words and the tears of disappointment that coursed down his mother's face. He tried to speak but before the words would come, his father stood and slammed his chair under the table before he left the room, giving Ethan a look of disgust on his way out.

31

At Foster's car showrooms the staff still weren't aware of Candice's connection to Mr Foster, and she preferred to keep it that way. Because of that, she often heard some unsavoury words used in reference to him and had decided not to tell Thomas most of what they said. Nobody wants to hear their father referred to as a 'slave-driving, sly old bastard'.

It was Thursday and the week was dragging. She decided to visit the ladies' then grab herself a coffee on the way back to her desk. Hopefully, that would wake her up a bit.

Candice was inside a cubicle when she heard two members of staff enter the ladies'. Their voices were recognisable as those of Carol and Linda. She smelt the aroma of cigarettes and frowned, knowing that it was against the rules to smoke indoors.

'Just a quick one,' said Linda. 'I can't be arsed going outside.'

'What's wrong?' asked Carol. 'You've got a face like a wet weekend.'

Linda lowered her voice and Candice had to strain to hear what she was saying. 'There's summat dodgy going on.'

'What do you mean?' asked Carol.

'Well, do you remember the other week when I told you about that car a mate bought from here and it turned out to be a ringer?'

'Oh, when Foster denied knowing anything about it?'

'Shush. Yes, that's right,' Linda whispered. 'Well, it got me thinking, so I've been checking out the cars in the car lot. I've seen a couple that aren't listed in the books.'

'You're joking!'

'No. One of them was a few weeks ago. I kept an eye on it but it fuckin' disappeared and there was never an entry in the books for it. So, when it happened again, I decided to ask him about it.'

'Was that when you were in his office this morning?'

'Yes, that's right. And he told me there'd be a good reason for it. I mentioned that it wasn't the first time it had happened, and he got right on his high horse. He said it would all be in hand and that I should pay attention to my own job instead of interfering in other people's business.'

'Really? Jesus, I think you're probably right. It sounds dodgy to me.'

Inside the cubicle, Candice was feeling increasingly uncomfortable. She had been in there much longer than necessary, but she didn't want to come out and have them think she had been eavesdropping. She hoped they would wind up their conversation and leave so she could come out. But there was no sign of that and, the longer she waited, the more awkward it became.

As if reading her thoughts, she then heard Linda say, 'Eh, is there someone in that end cubicle?'

Candice heard approaching footsteps then someone hammered on the door making her jump. She pressed the flush to make it convincing and stepped outside. She tried to act casual and didn't refer to the hushed conversation she had just overheard. 'It's only me,' she said, rubbing her stomach and feeling herself blush under their scrutiny. She hoped they'd interpret her awkwardness as embarrassment over a dicky tummy.

Then she slipped past the two women and left the ladies' with her heart racing. Carol and Linda followed shortly afterwards. As they returned to their desks, Carol glanced at her but didn't say anything. Nevertheless, Candice could still feel her heart pounding after what had taken place.

Now that she had a clearer mind, Laura had been doing a lot of thinking. She had been troubled about how the attacker had found out where she lived as well as where the shops were. If it were somebody connected to her past, then how would they know all those things?

Back when she was working the beat, she had lived in a different area and, once she'd turned her back on that life, she had stopped visiting her old haunts. She hadn't told many people about her new business venture either. She couldn't afford to. A lot of the people she knew back then would have gone to great lengths to part her from her newly acquired riches.

She supposed it would be possible to find out about the shops because they were called *Crystals*, the street name she had used on the beat. But what about her current address? How the hell had they found that out? Then there was that news article, which had detailed the attacks at the

Altrincham and Deansgate shops as well as her previous convictions.

If someone was interested enough then maybe they could find out about her past. But, as for the attacks, not everyone knew about them. Even the staff at the Altrincham and Deansgate shops would only know about the attacks at those particular branches unless, again, they had taken the trouble to find out more. But that still wouldn't answer how the attacker had found out her address.

She had thought long and hard about it the previous day. Which member of staff would know where she lived? It wasn't something she shared with them. They had her phone number in case they needed to get in touch with her, but not her address.

Then it had finally occurred to her. Her address wasn't listed in the internal records but what about Candice? As an employee, she had been paid through the company, and the Altrincham branch would have had full details for her including name, address and date of birth.

Therefore, the connection had to be Altrincham. And who would be vindictive enough to trawl through press reports from years ago to get something on her as well as using her address to her own advantage? Laura thought about Caitlin's cocky attitude and bristled. She certainly knew about the graffiti at the Altrincham shop as well as Haley's attack, and she had her address on record. But how had she found out about the graffiti at the Manchester shop? There was one way to find out.

Laura was meeting Trina and Tiffany later that day, but in the meantime she had time to kill. She therefore decided that there would be no harm in making a phone call. It wasn't long before Gina, the manager of the Deansgate shop, answered it.

'Hi, Gina, how's things?' Laura asked.

'Good. The sale items are selling well. I don't think we'll have that many left to supply the discount outlets.'

'That's great,' said Laura, knowing that they got much more for the sale items when they sold them in-house.

'Just as a matter of interest, Gina, have any of the staff from Altrincham branch been in to see you recently?'

Gina hesitated before answering, 'Erm, yeah.'

'And who was that?'

'Caitlin, the new manager.'

'And what did she want?'

'Oh, nothing really. She was just passing so she called in to say hello.'

'Right. And is that all she said?'

'Erm, yeah. Well, y'know, just general chit-chat about the shops.'

'And did that chit-chat involve you mentioning the graffiti and the damaged dresses?'

There was hesitation again and Laura could picture Gina blushing furiously.

'I might have mentioned it, yeah.'

'Did you or didn't you, Gina? I need to know. This is really important.'

'Well, yeah. I'm sorry. Shouldn't I have told her? It was only because she was asking me about things.'

'Don't worry, I'm not having a go at you, Gina. I can imagine how persuasive she was.'

Gina apologised again before Laura gave her final assurances then terminated the call. Her suspicions had proved correct. But would Caitlin have been devious enough to have slit Candice's tyres?

She suspected that the person responsible for the damage to Candice's tyres was more likely to be the man who had attacked Haley and carried out the damage at the shops. But Caitlin might have put him onto her. He might even have been her boyfriend.

Laura now had enough facts to be going on with. But, before she contacted the police with the information, she was going to confront Caitlin and see what she had to say for herself.

32

DS Worrall was young and ambitious. He'd heard rumours about Carson's imminent transfer out of the department. A DCI on another team was due to retire and Carson was hotly tipped to fill the post. And if he were to leave the department, then Worrall wanted to take up the newly vacant position of DI. So, all he had to do now was make sure he proved himself.

DS Worrall was feeling frustrated. They had had the forensic results back from the grey hoody taken from Ethan's house but there was nothing. He was working on the assumption that Ethan wasn't working alone. There was every possibility that he was responsible for the graffiti at the Deansgate shop. The fact that he had been asking Candice so many questions about it made DS Worrall suspicious and the culprit had worn a grey hoody like the one Ethan owned.

But he didn't think he was guilty of the attack on Haley. For one thing, he didn't possess a dark blue hoody; although that alone wouldn't have put him in the clear as he could have stashed it somewhere. It was a gut feeling. His character didn't seem to fit the crime and he had no history of violence.

Worrall's guess was that the kid had bitten off more than he could chew and now he was regretting it. But that was more reason to crank up the pressure. The lad was about to crack and, when he did, Worrall would make sure he got all the answers he needed to help him solve the case. Unless, of course, the lad had been acting entirely separately from the other perpetrator in which case he would still do him for vandalism.

He continued to stare at the lad who sat across the table from him in the interview room. It was obvious from his body language that he had worked himself up into a state. His shoulders and arms were tense, he was fidgeting, and his breathing was shallow. But Worrall carried on relentlessly.

'Right, Ethan, I'm going to ask you again, and this time I want a truthful answer: where were you on the night of Tuesday 22nd June?'

Laura marched into the Altrincham shop with her head held high; she was determined not to show any sign of weakness. She locked eyes with Caitlin who was working on the till. Caitlin's jaw tightened and her nostrils flared as she flashed a glance towards her, then quickly gazed back at the customer she was serving.

Breezing past the shop counter, Laura ordered, 'Office, NOW!' then carried on walking.

Staff and customers looked at her with their mouths agape as she strode past them. Once Laura reached the office, Caitlin typically kept her waiting. But Laura wasn't worried. She would make sure she gained the upper hand.

She glanced at Caitlin's handbag on the floor beside the desk and, acting on impulse, reached inside it, grabbing Caitlin's phone, and secreting it inside her own handbag. Laura had just placed Caitlin's bag back on the floor when she sauntered inside the office, appearing relaxed with a smirk on her face. But Laura had spotted her reaction when she'd entered the shop and knew it was a front. How she was looking forward to wiping away that fake smile!

'We're busy out there, y'know!' she complained.

Laura forced herself not to rise to it and to focus instead on what she was here for. 'Shut the door and sit down.'

Caitlin did as she was told, her smirk now replaced by a puzzled frown.

'Right,' began Laura. 'Now I've got your attention, I want you to tell me why you saw fit to sell a story to the press about the attacks on my businesses and certain aspects of my past.'

Caitlin frowned as if in shock. 'What are you talking about?'

'You know what I'm talking about, Caitlin, so don't play games. You reported the attack on Haley to the press and the vandalism to this shop and the Deansgate one.'

'Attacks on Deansgate? I didn't even know about any attacks at Deansgate!'

Although Caitlin denied Laura's accusations, her face blanched and Laura knew she had her.

Trying to switch emphasis, Caitlin went into attack mode. 'Why weren't we told about these attacks? You should be warning the staff if they're in danger.'

Laura ignored her questions. 'Gina at Deansgate has confirmed that you went to see her. While you were there, you told her what had happened at this shop and managed to find out about the damage there too.'

Caitlin seemed to realise that denial was now futile. 'So what?!' she snarled. 'You can't blame me for that. Like I said, we should have been informed, then I wouldn't have had to find out from Gina. Haley's already been attacked. The staff should be on their guard. And anyway, it doesn't mean I reported it to the press. And I don't know anything about your past. You kept that a secret, didn't you?'

Laura noticed the sly smirk on her face again and she tried to contain her temper. There was no way she was going to answer to this slimy little bitch for her past mistakes. Caitlin was the one in the firing line, not her!

'I suppose you're going to deny giving my address out as well, aren't you?'

'I didn't give your...'

'Boyfriend, is it?' Laura cut in. 'The same guy who attacked Haley so you could get the job? Make a habit of attacking women, does he?'

'No! I haven't given your address to anyone. And I don't have a boyfriend.'

'OK, you can carry on denying it all you want, Caitlin, but you and I both know you were behind that press report, and I also think you gave out my address. So, we'll see what the police have to say when I report it all to them, shall we?'

Laura stood up, picked up her own handbag from the desk and made as if to leave.

'You won't be able to prove anything, and neither will the police,' Caitlin hissed, her sly smirk spreading across her face now.

'Won't they?' asked Laura, drawing level with Caitlin.

Then she patted her handbag. 'Maybe they won't get the truth out of you, but I'm sure your phone will tell them all they need to know. Calls, text messages, Internet browsing history, it's all on there.' It was her turn to smirk.

'You can't do that!' yelled Caitlin, swinging out her arm and making a grab for Laura's handbag.

Laura gripped it tightly. 'Just you fuckin' dare!' she yelled, raising a fist. 'And I'll scream so loudly that all the staff will come running. Would you like to add assault to your list of crimes?'

'You can't fuckin' take my phone! That's stealing.'

'I'm not stealing it, Caitlin. I'm helping the police out by handing it over to them before you manage to delete anything.' She had reached the door by now but, before she left, she turned to see the hangdog expression on Caitlin's face. 'Oh, and by the way,' she added. 'You're sacked!'

To hell with the consequences, she thought. She didn't want a snake like Caitlin working for her a minute longer. They'd just have to manage as best they could.

She walked away from the office to the sound of Caitlin yelling in anger. 'You fuckin' bitch! I hope you get everything that's coming to you.'

33

Candice and Thomas were inside his bedroom chatting. He was sitting on the bed, propped up against the wall while Candice was lying stretched out, her head resting on his lap. As she lay there, he caressed her, tracing the outline of her face with his fingers then running them down her body. She sighed with pleasure as he stroked her breasts.

'Who was your best friend when you were a kid?' he asked.

'Oh, that's easy,' said Candice. 'Sarah Baker.'

'What happened to her?'

'She went to a different secondary school, and I didn't really see her after that. What about you? Who was yours?'

'No one in particular. I hung out with a group of lads.'

'And what happened to them?'

'Well, some of them came to the same secondary school, but we were in different classes, so we hung out with different crowds,' said Thomas before asking, 'What sort of kid were you?'

'Confident, I suppose. Well, I was definitely the ringleader in my little group of friends anyway.'

Thomas spluttered. 'That doesn't surprise me. You are a bit of a bossy knickers.'

'Eh, cheeky!' said Candice, sitting up and whacking him playfully with his pillow.

'OK, my turn now,' she said. Then she stopped and thought for a moment. 'Erm… Ooh, I can't believe I've not already asked you this: what's your middle name?'

'You mean to say I haven't already told you that? I could have sworn I had.'

Candice shook her head. 'No.'

'It's John. Why what's yours?'

'I don't have one.' She smiled. 'A name like Candice speaks for itself.'

'Yeah, my dad commented on how unusual it was.'

They carried on probing. They'd reached that stage of their relationship where they wanted to know all the intimate details about each other and were happy to share.

She had come to Thomas's for tea straight from work, feeling happier now to leave her mum more often. There had been no incidents for a good two or three weeks and Laura seemed more relaxed. Candice hoped that whoever was behind the attacks had done their worst and had now grown tired of it.

When their chatter came to a natural end, she asked, 'What's a ringer, Thomas?'

'A ringer? In what context?'

'As in, a car.'

'Aah, right. Well, it's when they take the ID from a car that's been written off and use it for another one. Usually, the one they use it for has been stolen so they don't want it to be traced. Why do you ask?'

'Oh, nothing.'

'Come on, it must be something.'

Candice sighed. 'Well, it was just something I overheard at work today. Two of the staff were talking and one of them said that one of her friends bought a car from your dad's car lot, and it was a ringer.'

She noticed Thomas's shocked expression. 'No!' he said. 'Dad wouldn't do that. She must be lying.'

Candice forced a wry smile. 'Well, to be honest, they are a bit anti-management.'

'Why, what else have they said?'

Candice was curious regarding the cars, so she continued. 'She said that a couple of the cars in the car lot hadn't been entered in the books.'

Thomas's response was rapid. 'They've probably just got a backlog of paperwork and haven't got round to entering them in the books yet.'

Candice could sense that the mood had shifted, and she noticed the stress lines that had now formed on Thomas's face. She hated upsetting him, so she didn't mention Linda's comment about one of the cars disappearing without any entry ever being made for it in the books. Instead, she smoothed things over. 'Well, they are a pair of moaners, so I don't take too much notice of everything they say.'

'I'm glad you don't,' said Thomas, leaning over and kissing her, his mood now more relaxed.

It had been a busy day for Laura. After her confrontation with Caitlin, she had returned home where she had rung DI Carson and told him about her suspicions relating to her. She also told him she had Caitlin's phone, omitting to mention that she had taken it without her permission.

The inspector had seemed eager to get his hands on the phone, so she had waited in while an officer came to collect it. Then, once all that was dealt with, she set off for the city centre.

By the time Laura reached Piccadilly station in the city centre, she only had an hour in which to do some shopping before she was due to meet Trina and Tiffany. But she got carried away when a gold bracelet took her fancy at a jeweller's shop in the Royal Exchange.

Emerging onto Cross Street, Laura checked the time. She was meeting Trina and Tiffany on Deansgate so they could walk the rest of the way to The Ivy together, and she was already five minutes late.

Laura made her way to Albert Square before weaving her way through the narrow side streets that led to Deansgate. She wanted to avoid the busy thoroughfares, which were full of bustling restaurants and bars and would make progress slower.

She guessed that when the offices and businesses shut for the day, these side streets would be full of people taking the short cut to catch a bus, tram, or train home. But it was now nearly eight o'clock, and the street she had just walked into was deserted. In fact, it was more of an alleyway than a street with no inviting shopfronts, just the back doors flanked by industrial waste bins.

Suddenly she felt transported away from the city. She was still dwelling on the events of the day and felt unsettled. Somebody out there had it in for her and whoever it was, they knew too much. Her past. Where her shops were. Where she lived.

It felt as though they were watching her every move, and

an eerie feeling suddenly took hold of her. They could be watching her now. Waiting for a chance to get her alone. Wanting to pounce like they had done with Haley.

Laura tried to ignore such thoughts, telling herself she was being silly. Back in the day, she'd have thought nothing of walking down an alley like this much later at night and now here she was acting like a total wimp.

But back in the day she'd usually been so drugged up that she was oblivious to danger. And nowadays, she was a different prospect altogether. Laura now had items worth stealing. In fact, her shoes alone cost over five hundred quid. Heeding her own instincts, she speeded up, anxious to reach the end of the alley.

34

The man could hardly believe his eyes when he spotted Laura Sharples in Manchester city centre. He'd been meeting a mate on Albert Square to discuss a bit of business when he saw her rush past. Finalising the deal with his friend, he decided to follow her.

He reflected on the latest instructions he had received from the man he now regarded as his boss, telling him, 'I want her scared shitless'. He had been planning to return to her home to see what damage he could inflict. If he was honest with himself, this whole situation was getting out of hand. It had started out as repayment for a debt, but that had been settled long ago and even though he was now getting paid for his services, he would have preferred to earn his money another way.

The problem was that it was all so unpredictable. He didn't have a clue what he would be asked to do next or how extreme it would be, and he couldn't see an end to it. But he knew he'd be in deep shit if he didn't do as he was told. It didn't pay to cross some people.

He followed her through the maze of side streets. She was already a distance in front of him and was obviously in a hurry. Trying not to appear too obvious, he stepped up his pace. Meanwhile, he thought about what he was planning to do. Give her a good thumping? Knock her to the ground? Snatch her bag?

He emerged from a short side street into an alleyway and could see her ahead of him in the distance. A quick check told him there were no cameras here and it was also deserted. He decided to take advantage of that. He just needed to reach her before she got away.

He had shortened the gap between them when she looked over her shoulder and he ducked down behind a bin just in time. Being extra careful now, he stepped back out from behind the bin. But his caution was slowing him down and she soon reached the end of the alley.

Now that he was out of view, he sped up, anxious to trail her into the next street before she disappeared. The next street was wider but shorter and it opened onto the main drag of Deansgate. She had already reached the end of it, and as he watched he saw her shouting to somebody.

His eyes followed her until he saw two other women emerge into the side street. Again, he ducked out of view, taking refuge in the doorway of a shop. Peeking out, he sized up the two women. One was blonde, slim and of average height. But the other was a tall black girl, Amazonian in stature, and fierce-looking.

As Laura said something to her, the black girl gazed towards him and he ducked back quickly, his heart pounding. He didn't fancy grappling with three of them, especially the big one. For a moment he thought the game was up but then they walked away. He had no choice but to do likewise. There was no way he'd be able to get at Laura Sharples tonight. He'd have to wait till another day.

As Candice had decided not to stay the night, Thomas saw her to the door then went into the living room where his father was sitting watching the ten o'clock news. He was glad Pam wasn't with him this evening because he needed to speak to him alone.

'What's wrong?' asked his father, picking up on Thomas's unease.

Thomas came straight to the point. 'Candice overheard something at work. Some of the staff are saying that one of the cars was a ringer and that there are cars on the forecourt that aren't listed in the books.'

His father sighed. 'Let me guess... Linda Bartlett.'

'I don't know who they were. Candice didn't say.'

'Ah, so there are more than one of them?'

'Two. Candice said there were two of them talking. One of them was telling the other one about the cars.'

His father's face clouded over. 'Yeah, it'll be Linda Bartlett. She's a bolshie little bitch who should keep her opinions to herself. I hope Candice didn't take much notice.'

'No, she didn't, but you really need to be careful, Dad. If Candice has heard it then God knows how many other people have. You need to remember that there are other things at stake here. And I don't want anything to jeopardise my relationship with Candice.'

'Thomas, you worry too much. Leave it with me. I'll have a word with Linda Bartlett and stop this going any further. We can't have people casting aspersions about my character, can we?'

Thomas noted the hint of sarcasm in his voice and hoped he was taking this seriously. His father might not be overly concerned about the staff suspecting him of dodgy dealing, but he was.

35

Laura was pleased to get a call from DS Worrall the following day and relieved that they had quickly acted on her information.

'Yes, what have you got for me?' she asked. 'Has she admitted it?'

'Well, Caitlin Percival has admitted giving out your address but…'

'I knew it, I bloody well knew it!' she cursed before the sergeant had chance to say anything further. She thought about what a nasty piece of stuff Caitlin was. 'Have you charged her?'

'No, I'm afraid we can't do that.'

'Why not?' she snapped.

'Well, I'm afraid she gave out your address under duress.'

'What do you mean?'

'She was threatened by a man wielding a knife who demanded to know where you lived.'

'Really? Well, how come she didn't report it then?'

'She was afraid of repercussions apparently, which is understandable. From the description she has given us, it sounds like the same man who attacked Haley Parlow.'

Laura still wasn't convinced. And, still feeling betrayed

by Caitlin, she was finding it hard to be sympathetic. 'What about the story in the press? Can you charge her for that?'

'No, we can't. She hasn't committed a crime. If the press want to publish a story about you then they're free to do so and giving them information isn't an arrestable offence.'

Laura tried to make sense of his words. 'OK, so you can't arrest her for anything?'

'No, like I say, she hasn't committed a crime. But, if it's any consolation, she was very helpful to us with our inquiries. We believe that the man who attacked Haley Parlow and threatened Caitlin Percival is the same man that we've got on CCTV.'

Laura still didn't believe that Caitlin was completely innocent but what could she do? 'Right, so what happens now?' she asked.

'Well, we've had to let Miss Percival go. But I can assure you, we'll be pulling out all the stops to try to catch the man behind all this.'

Laura sighed. 'OK, thank you.' Then she terminated the call. She didn't know how to feel about what the sergeant had said. She was too preoccupied with thinking that Caitlin was somehow involved. But what if Caitlin had been speaking the truth? She might well have been confronted by the same man who had attacked Haley. Laura shuddered at the frightening thought.

The man's hands were shaking when he made the call to his boss the following day. After his near miss with Laura Sharples, he had noticed CCTV in the street where he had lost her. He hadn't expected to see cameras in a small side street and had been so intent on carrying out his orders that he had got sloppy.

He couldn't afford to make a mistake like that again, not with the record he had. The police would soon connect him to all the other attacks and the courts would throw the book at him.

He'd been so worked up that he'd gone on a massive binge afterwards, taking far more drugs than normal. And now he was a quivering wreck. He knew he couldn't carry on like this so, without preamble, he came straight to the point of his call.

'I want out.'

'You what?' his boss boomed.

'I said I want out. I can't do this no more.'

'You'll do as you're fuckin' told if you know what's good for you!'

'Look, I nearly cocked it up last night. The pressure's getting to me. I swear, if you make me carry on with this then we'll both be in the shit.'

'Are you threatening me?'

'No, no, I'm just saying... If they catch me, then they might trace things back to you.'

'They'll only do that if you give the game away.'

'Well, I wouldn't on purpose, would I? But you know what the cops are like with their questions. They tie you in fuckin' knots, have you confessing to all kinds of stuff.'

'OK, stop snivelling. Tell me what went wrong last night.'

The man explained what had happened the previous evening when he had intended to attack Laura Sharples.

He could hear a hint of laughter in his boss's voice when

he spoke to him again. 'I didn't tell you to attack Laura Sharples, you fuckin' dimwit.'

'You said you wanted her scared shitless.'

'Yes, but you don't have to go the whole fuckin' way! I want there to be a progression. I want her to *feel* the escalation. I want the bitch wondering what's going to happen next. Watching her back every time she walks out the fuckin' door. Shaking at every creak of the floorboards when she's sitting at home. Lying in bed awake at nights. Dreading another call about one of her precious shops.'

'OK, OK, I get the picture.'

'Good, I'm glad you do. Because here's what I want you to do next…'

'No, hang on. I've said I'm not doing anymore. You can't fuckin' make me!'

'Can't I? Right, well I'm giving you a choice. You can do it the easy way and I'll up your money into the bargain. Or you can do it the hard way. And you know what that entails, don't you?'

He thought about the other man's reputation. The last person to stand up to him had ended up in a wheelchair. Then there were the shattered kneecaps, missing digits, and other callous beatings. He shivered. 'OK, I'll do it.'

'Good. I thought that might get your attention. Now, here's what I want you to do…'

36

DS Worrall had come in on a Saturday specially to work on the Laura Sharples case and currently he was going through the CCTV from outside both the Altrincham and Deansgate branches of Crystals. The sergeant was convinced that the man who Haley Parlow and Caitlin Percival had encountered was the same man as the one on all the CCTV images. He was therefore looking for similarities that matched their descriptions although, admittedly, the description given by Haley Parlow had been sketchy. She had been too traumatised by the attack to notice anything much.

But it was no good; the images were too vague to draw up an accurate comparison. He sat for a while, mulling things over and wondering how to progress the case further. He couldn't rely on DNA or fingerprints. There would have been so many people touching the clothing in the shops that it would be impossible to isolate just one, and it was tricky obtaining fingerprints from clothing anyway.

There was another way to come up with a list of suspects, but it was slow and laborious. 'To hell with it,' he muttered. What alternative was there if he wanted to nail this guy?

DS Worrall began searching the database for all known

criminals in the Manchester area, looking for those whose height, frame and age group matched the man described by the two victims and shown on CCTV. He therefore restricted his search criteria to those who were Caucasian, slim, two inches either side of five foot ten, dark-haired and in their twenties or thirties. But that still left him a lot of data to sift through.

As he searched through the records, he ruled several of them out for various reasons. Some were currently serving time; others were deceased, and one had been left in a wheelchair due to a gang attack. Then there were several whose crimes didn't fit with the type committed by the perpetrator.

Finally, after several hours of painstakingly sifting through the records, he was still left with more than thirty names. It would be too many to justify the manpower needed to question all the suspects. But he did have two witnesses, so it might help him to narrow things down.

It was unfortunate that the culprit had worn a mask during both attacks, but then DS Worrall remembered something from the interview with one of the witnesses. Caitlin Percival had said she distinctly remembered the man having brown eyes.

He smiled to himself as he went through the records again and discarded any whose eyes weren't brown. Then he printed out the photos of the remaining suspects and collected them together ready to present his findings to the DI on Monday in the hope that he'd allow him to move the case further forward.

*

DS Worrall stared at the young woman across the desk from him: Caitlin Percival. She was confident, he'd give her that. But there was also something unpleasant about her, despite her obvious good looks.

The first time he'd interviewed her, she hadn't wanted to give any details about the man who had forced her to give him Laura Sharples' address. He presumed it was because she was scared of repercussions.

He had let her know that she was in danger while the perpetrator was at large. He knew where she worked, and there was nothing to stop him following her from work again and attacking her as he had done with the previous manager, Haley Parlow. It was only after this discussion that Caitlin Percival had co-operated.

Now he needed her co-operation again. After showing the DI his findings from over the weekend, he had instructed him to call in the two witnesses again and see if they recognised anybody from the photographs of the suspects.

The first witness, Haley Parlow, didn't have a lot of information to give. She couldn't recall much and even looking at the photographs of suspects was filling her with anxiety. When he spotted her panicked breathing on top of her already hunched shoulders, he stopped the interview and let her go.

He now passed the photographs to Caitlin, one by one, and told her to separate them into two piles. One of the piles was of people who didn't fit with her recollection of her attacker, and the other was of possible culprits.

But as he watched, the group of possible culprits grew bigger than the other group. He waited patiently while she continued to study the photographs. She seemed to spend an inordinate amount of time mulling over each one, and he got the feeling she was toying with him. Then, when she snatched a photo from the non-suspects pile, studied it, and placed it on the suspects pile, he began to despair.

He tapped his fingers on the desk, waiting for her to finish and was rewarded with a scornful look. Aware that she would only take longer, he excused himself and left the room to make a quick call. When he returned, she looked up at him and beamed a satisfied smile. He walked over to the desk and took in the two piles. The possible culprits one was double the size of the other.

Ethan had always thought of himself as strong, confident, self-assured. His parents had made him feel that he was something special because of his giftedness. He'd sailed through university up to now and was planning to go all the way. A top-notch career, big house in the suburbs, flash car, loving family and two holidays a year.

But he didn't feel strong now, all his hopes and ambitions were crushed and he had lost his parents' respect. Even his mother no longer tried to comfort him after one of his father's angry rants.

He was a police suspect, and he was putting his parents through hell. It was difficult to look at them without feeling intense guilt after everything they'd done for him. Even if he got through this he would be tarnished forever. The neighbours already knew about him being a police suspect so it was only a matter of time before the university found out too. They would put a black mark against his name. They might even throw him out.

Some of the other students already knew, Dan and the others from the house. They'd seemed supportive up to now. But that might change. Candice seemed to have the girls wrapped around her little finger. And there were plenty of others outside the house who would take Candice's side. She was a popular girl. Unlike him. He knew the other students had never liked him. Not really. It hadn't bothered him so much before but now it seemed like he was on his own against the world.

And what if the police found him guilty? Ethan knew he hadn't committed any crimes. But how did he prove it? He'd heard all about miscarriages of justice. What if he ended up in prison? How would he cope amongst all those murderers and rapists? And how would his father react? His parents would probably disown him. It was too dire to contemplate. He couldn't take it anymore!

The police questioning had continued, each time more relentless than the previous. Every time they called him in or visited the house, he had a feeling of dread. His nerves were shot. Sleepless nights, stomach cramps, panic attacks. And he'd dropped half a stone in the last few weeks.

He waited till his parents were out, but he'd had this in mind for a few days now. Inside the bathroom he ran the tap and waited for the bath to fill while he undressed. Then he stepped into the warm water and grabbed a razor from the side of the bath.

His hands were shaking as he held it over his wrist, and he almost backed out. But he forced himself on. This would be his last show of strength. Ethan regretted that his parents would have to find him like this. But at least then it would be over, and they wouldn't have the worry of it anymore. And he wouldn't have to live with the shame.

Taking a deep juddering breath, he swiped the blade across his wrist. Swift and deep. He let out a cry of alarm as he felt a sharp stab and saw the blood spray rising like a vermillion fountain. Then it touched down: puffy red clouds sinking slowly and colouring the water.

It was done. Ethan had found his way out.

37

Candice was having a night in with her mum. Ever since her call to Trina a couple of weeks ago, Candice had noticed a difference in Laura. It was a relief and, since then, she had tried to spend more time with her. They had patched up their differences and as, according to her mother, there had been no further incidents at the shops, Candice was feeling a bit more relaxed.

They were in the living room, having a cup of tea and watching a chick flick when her mobile rang. She looked at the screen and saw that Emma was the caller.

'Do you want me to pause it?' asked her mum, referring to the film.

'Please,' said Candice. 'I'll try not to be too long.'

She walked into the hallway and through to the kitchen so that she could talk to her friend in private. 'Hi, Emma,' she greeted enthusiastically.

But Emma's tone of voice didn't match her own. 'Hi, Candice. I'm ringing about Ethan,' she said.

Something about the way she spoke put Candice on her guard. 'What is it?'

When she heard Emma's words, her face drained of colour and, feeling light-headed, she grasped at the kitchen counter to steady herself. Candice didn't stay on the phone for long. There were a million questions she wanted to ask but she couldn't find her voice.

She cut the call and trudged back into the lounge. She didn't feel like watching the film anymore, but she couldn't leave her mum hanging. Laura would want to know what was wrong, and part of her wanted to confide in her mother about the shocking news she had just heard.

'You OK?' asked her mum.

When Candice didn't respond, she turned around and picked up on Candice's shocked state. 'Oh my God, Candice! What's the matter?'

Candice needed to sit down. Her legs were trembling, and she felt as though they were about to give way. Laura responded by wrapping her arm around her daughter and pulling her inwards. Candice thought randomly how relieved she was that her mother was no longer drinking because, right now, she needed her support.

Speaking almost in a whisper, her heart pounding and her voice shaky, she said, 'It's Ethan. He's killed himself.'

It took a while for Candice to get over the initial shock of Ethan's death. She had been in such a stupor when Emma had given her the news, so she had finished the call promising to ring back. Since then, she'd been inconsolable throughout the night, blaming herself for Ethan's suicide.

'If I hadn't have given his name to the police this would never have happened,' she had said to her mother.

'You can't go blaming yourself,' Laura had replied. 'You were doing what you had to do. What I told you to do.

The police have to cover every angle. It's the only chance we have of finding out who's behind all these attacks. I'm sorry it's come to this but it's not your fault if the police were too heavy-handed with him.' Then she had paused before adding, 'Anyway, we still don't know whether he was innocent.'

Her words had struck Candice. Her mother had a point. Just because he was dead it didn't mean he had been innocent. But, even if he had been guilty, he didn't deserve to die, and it didn't lessen her guilt.

Now, it was the following day, and Candice felt ready to talk to her friend. It turned out that Ethan's suicide had been a week ago, but her friends had only just found out. Emma, although just as shocked as Candice, was fine with her and reassured her that she wasn't blaming her for Ethan's death. Neither was Alicia.

'But what about the others?' asked Candice. 'I bet they're blaming me, aren't they?'

'Well, some of them, I suppose. But it's still raw. They'll be alright in time.'

'It's OK. I can understand them reacting like that,' said Candice.

She knew Emma was only trying to make her feel better, and she could well imagine what Dan and some of the others had been saying. But she didn't ask for details. She didn't think she could handle it at the moment.

Candice finished the call feeling no better than before she had made it. She had already been dreading returning to university at the end of the summer but now it was worse. And even though she had decided not to live in the student house, she still feared bumping into many of her peer group.

Before all this had happened, life at university had been good. She'd had a great group of friends and they had all enjoyed hanging out together. But, despite Emma's assurances, Candice knew that, after this, things would never be the same.

The next person Candice rang after she had spoken to Emma was Thomas.

'Hi, Candice. How's work?' he asked cheerily.

'I haven't gone,' she said with a catch in her voice.

Picking up on her upset, he asked, 'Why, what's the matter?'

Candice took a deep breath, and her words came tumbling out in a flood of emotion as she related what had happened before adding, 'I'm sorry but I just couldn't face work. I hope your dad doesn't mind.'

'I'm so sorry, Candice. And, of course, Dad won't mind. He already knows what you're going through. I'm sure he'll understand. Tell you what, let me ring him. I'll come straight back to you. I promise.'

It was ten minutes later when Thomas rang back but, for Candice in her highly charged state, it seemed to take forever. 'Right, I've spoken to him,' he said. 'He was fine, and he said you should take tomorrow and Friday off too considering what's happened. My dad will tell the staff you've taken the time off for personal reasons. Hopefully that'll stop them prying.'

'Oh, it's OK. I don't need…'

'Shush. Boss's orders. It'll be fine. In fact, I've just had a word with my boss and I'm going to take tomorrow and

Friday off too. We can go out somewhere, take your mind off it.'

'Aw, you don't need to do that, Thomas.'

'Too late, it's done. I had holidays that needed using anyway so it's no problem.'

'Thank you so much,' she said.

'OK, I must dash now. If I'm going to have the next two days off, then I need to do a bit of grovelling.'

Candice attempted a smile but as soon as the call was finished, she dissolved into tears. She hoped a couple of days with Thomas would help her to feel better, and she prayed that no more bad things were going to happen.

38

Candice had had a lovely day in Chester with Thomas. They'd taken a walk around the city walls and through its quaint streets with their galleried walkways and rows of shops. Then they'd visited the Roman Amphitheatre and Roman Gardens. Now they were seated inside an Italian restaurant, resting their aching legs, and enjoying the delicious cuisine.

While Candice had been busy taking in the attractions, she hadn't thought too much about her situation. But now that she wasn't so busy, it was difficult to relax. She couldn't help wondering if Ethan had been the man on the CCTV, or one of the men, assuming there might be two of them.

'Are you OK?' asked Thomas, picking up on her distraction.

Candice nodded but her focus was elsewhere. She cast her memory back to the CCTV footage. The image had been so vague and there were so many young men who could have matched it: Ethan, Dan, a stranger. Or even Thomas. She shut down the notion straightaway, feeling guilty for even considering him. Thomas was the most wonderful person she had ever met, and she knew he would never do anything to harm either her or her mother.

But then she remembered the secret he had been so unwilling to share several weeks ago when she'd confided in him about her mother's past. And when she'd attempted to find out about it again, he still wouldn't tell her. She'd been so preoccupied with other things since then that she hadn't asked again. But perhaps now was a good time.

'Thomas, do you remember a few weeks ago when I told you about my mum?'

'Yeah.'

'Well, you said you had something to tell me too. What was it?'

Within seconds he changed. He no longer appeared relaxed; now his shoulders were hunched, and his features strained. And when he replied his words were short and sharp. 'It's nothing. Forget about it.'

'But if it's nothing, then why can't you tell me?'

'You don't need to know. I'm sorry I mentioned it now.'

She raised an inquisitive eyebrow but remained silent.

'Look, Candice,' he said, filling the void. 'Let's not spoil a good night. I've brought you here to take your mind off things, so can we please just relax and enjoy ourselves?'

Candice didn't want to spoil the atmosphere, so she nodded. 'OK.'

It was apparent from his stern reaction that the conversation was over. But how could she just forget about it when Thomas, her lovely Thomas, was keeping secrets from her?

Two days later they were on their way back from Chester after a lovely break. It had been Thomas's idea to book the

Friday night at the B & B too, and now Candice was feeling more relaxed. As he drove, Thomas kept glancing across at her then swiftly focusing his eyes back on the road and Candice had a feeling there was still something on his mind.

'Are you OK?' he asked.

She smiled. 'Yeah, much better than when we came away on Thursday.'

But the nearer she got to home the more she thought about what had happened to Ethan. She still felt so guilty. And that wasn't her only concern. She hoped her mother had been alright while she had been away. She'd rung her that morning from the B & B, and Laura had confirmed that there had been no more incidents.

Candice prayed that the information Caitlin had provided would be of some use. She desperately wanted the police to catch the person responsible and for the whole situation to be behind them.

When they arrived at her home, Thomas glanced at her again. But this time he didn't look away. As his eyes remained fixed on her, he spoke, 'Candice, I've been thinking. Well, I know we haven't been together all that long and I know things haven't been so good for you lately, so I hope you're not offended by the timing but...'

He hesitated so she prompted him. 'But what?'

'Well, I was wondering, if I were to ask you to get engaged, what would you say?'

Candice was astonished. 'Bloody hell, Thomas!'

She felt bad when she saw his look of disappointment.

'Is it really such a bad idea?' he asked.

'No, but... I mean, we have only been together for just over eight months. It feels a bit soon, that's all.'

'I know it's only been eight months, but I feel as though I've known you forever and I couldn't imagine being with anyone else.'

'But it's different for you. You're older than me. Jesus, Thomas, I'm only twenty! I haven't even finished uni yet.'

'Nearly twenty-one.'

'In two months, yeah. But I've still got a year to go at uni, and I'm sorry but I've got too much shit going on in my life right now to even think about anything like an engagement.'

'I was thinking, maybe we could do it for your twenty-first.'

Candice thought about her imminent birthday in October. Not only would it be her twenty-first that month, but she'd also be returning to uni. And that was something she really wasn't looking forward to.

'I don't know,' she said. 'I need time.'

He leant in and kissed her on the cheek. 'Promise me you'll think about it then.'

She sighed. 'OK, I'll think about it. Now pop the boot open while I get my case. I want to get indoors and check Mum's alright.'

'OK.'

Once he had opened the boot, he came out of the car to kiss her goodbye before setting off home. They had agreed that he wouldn't be coming indoors as he had a few things to tend to at home.

Candice had a smile on her face when she walked through her front door. So that had been Thomas's big secret? It was just like him to be so considerate that he didn't want to raise it while she was under so much stress. Or perhaps he'd been nervous of rejection, knowing they hadn't been together all that long.

In fact, they had been together for such a short period that getting engaged had been the last thing on her mind. She regretted dismissing the notion so forcefully. Maybe it wasn't such a bad idea after all. Like Thomas, she couldn't imagine herself with anyone else. He was everything she could ever want in a fiancé and more. But she'd need to get her head around it first. And currently she had too many other things to think about.

39

The man drew up in a side street in the centre of Wilmslow a few blocks away from the shops. He wanted to make sure nobody spotted his car because, after what was about to take place, the police would pull out all the stops to find him.

As he made his way to Crystals on foot with his hood up and his head facing downwards, he could feel his heart thumping. His hands were so sweaty that it was difficult to keep hold of his carrier bag. He noticed that the streets were littered with people visiting the few restaurants and pubs dotted around the town centre.

It was the following Friday evening and any other evening during the week wouldn't have been quite as busy. But he had been ordered to do it on a Friday night to make the maximum impact because Saturday was the busiest shopping day of the week. Thank God there were no pubs or restaurants close to the shop.

He had been putting this job off ever since he had received his instructions almost three weeks ago. If he were honest with himself, he had lost his nerve ever since he'd almost been caught on CCTV when he had trailed Laura Sharples.

Thank God her friends had appeared, preventing him from carrying out the planned attack.

But he was coming under increasing pressure from his boss who was, in his opinion, holding all the cards. He was being well rewarded for what he was doing. And not only did he need the money, but he also knew what a nasty piece of work his boss could be. He replayed their recent conversation over in his head: *'Where's your balls? You'd better fuckin' find them or you won't have any left to find!'*

They weren't just empty words.

The crimes he had been ordered to carry out were becoming worse, and he dreaded being found out by the police. He didn't want to end up in the nick again. But, each time, he kept telling himself it would be the last and that hopefully he wouldn't have to do this again.

He spotted Crystals in the distance on the other side of the street, and he crossed the road. Passing a young couple, he kept his head down, but they were so wrapped up in each other that he doubted they would have noticed him anyway. Fortunately, he didn't pass anybody else on his way to the shop.

A few more paces and he was there. He gazed around him, making sure there was nobody nearby. Then he pulled down the front of his hood until it obscured most of his face. Checking his surroundings again, he turned to his side where the carrier bag was dangling from his right hand, and he rummaged inside it.

He was just about to take out the things he needed for the job when he heard the loud cooing of a bird overhead. His nerves were so jangled that he looked up instinctively, and as he turned his head upwards, his hood slipped, exposing his face.

'Shit!' he cursed, quickly pulling it back up.

It was a momentary lapse and he hoped it wasn't enough to capture on CCTV. But he was here now. And the pressure was on. He needed to see this through because, if he didn't, he would suffer the consequences. Beatings. Torture. Maybe even an agonising death. And the thought of that sent a cold chill through his body.

It was the middle of the night when Laura was awoken by the shrill ringing of her mobile. She reached across to the bedside cabinet where her hand groped around for her phone. Lifting it, she peered at the screen through bleary eyes and saw a number she didn't recognise.

At this time of night, she pictured a telesales person sitting in an office somewhere on the other side of the world. Curiosity made her answer the call, and she prepared herself to give them a piece of her mind. Then the caller spoke. It was DS Worrall.

'I'm afraid we've had reports of a fire at the Wilmslow branch of Crystals,' he said.

Laura soon came round. 'What! How bad is it?'

'We don't know at his stage. Someone reported it to one of our officers, but they didn't stay on the line. We're on our way there now to assess the damage.'

'OK, I'll be there as soon as I can.'

Laura was already out of bed and was just about to use her en-suite bathroom when there was a knock on the bedroom door.

'Can I come in?' asked Candice.

'Yeah.'

Candice looked concerned. 'I heard your phone. What is it?'

'The bloody swine's at it again. I thought it was too good to be true when it all went quiet for a while.'

'Why? What's happened?'

Laura inhaled sharply. 'Reports of a fire at the Wilmslow shop.'

'And did they say who it was?'

'No, the police just said they'd taken a call. I don't think they know much yet.'

'Then it might not be him,' said Candice.

She didn't expand on who the 'him' referred to; they both knew she meant the person behind the attacks.

'Oh, it's him alright.' Then Laura turned towards the wardrobe. 'I've got to get ready, love. I need to go and see how bad the damage is.'

'I'm coming with you.'

'No, you don't need to do that, love. It's the middle of the bloody night.'

'So? I don't have work tomorrow.'

'Yeah, but there's no point in us both going, is there? And I need to get there as soon as possible.'

'I'm not gonna let you go on your own. I'm going, Mum, and that's that! I'll be ready in five minutes.'

Thirty minutes later Candice and her mum arrived in Wilmslow and Laura parked up on one of the main streets in the town centre. As soon as Candice stepped out of the car, she could see smoke billowing above the shops, and her heart thudded inside her chest. Her mother had noticed too, and she dashed through the throng of people who had gathered to watch the spectacle despite the late hour. Candice rushed to keep up with her.

As they broke through the crowd, the extent of the blaze became more apparent. They could feel the heat from metres away and smell the smoke, the intensity of it causing an acrid burning sensation in Candice's throat.

'That's not a fire, that's a fuckin' inferno!' Laura yelled as they watched the flames shoot above the building.

The shutters on this shop weren't solid like the other branches, and Candice watched in despair as the flames soared through the latticework of the metal grille and engulfed the shop's frontage. She visualised rails of scorched clothing and burnt-out fixtures and fittings inside the shop. It was obvious that the emergency services had arrived too late. Everything would be ruined!

As firefighters tried to control the blaze, the police fought to hold the crowd back. Candice led her mother away, aware that the devastating scene was causing her distress. They hovered on the edge of the crowd while Candice gazed around, looking for DI Carson and DS Worrall in the hope that they could give them some answers.

She saw tears in her mother's eyes and heard her plead. 'Just who the fuck is doing this to me? Please God, let it stop!'

Then Laura dropped to her knees and howled.

40

'How's your mum?' asked Thomas.

'Not too bad, I suppose.'

'Jesus! I bet she's got shedloads to sort out, hasn't she, not to mention the expense?'

'Yeah, but she's going to claim on the insurance and Trina said she'd help her with things if she has to refurbish the shop. I'm not sure whether she'll bother though with the way she's feeling right now.'

'Well, it is only two days since it happened. I suppose she needs a bit of time to recover.'

'Yeah, definitely. And she's not sure whether she wants to go ahead with the refurbishment only to have the same thing happen again. But then she needs to think about the employees too. I just hope she'll be OK in herself. I'm glad she's got a mate like Trina. She's round at hers now having Sunday dinner.'

'Aw, that's good. And to be honest, it takes the pressure off you a bit too.'

'I don't mind,' said Candice, defensively. 'I want to be there for her.'

'I know,' said Thomas, putting his arm around her. 'I

can understand that but it's my job to look after you.' He smiled. 'And you've not had it easy either, y'know.'

Ethan's suicide flashed through Candice's mind, but she quashed the thought. She didn't want to focus on that right now. It would only upset her again.

'Candice?' Thomas said, his tone obsequious. When Candice looked up at him, he continued. 'I hope you don't think I'm being insensitive so soon after what's happened, and tell me to shut up if you don't want to discuss it, but I just wanted to say, well... have you thought any more about what I asked you a week ago?'

Candice smiled. 'You're joking!' His face dropped as though expecting a reproach, but his expression lifted again when she carried on speaking. 'I've thought about nothing else.' She smiled. 'Yeah, I think we should get engaged on my twenty-first birthday, but I think we should have a long engagement as I've still got a year left of uni.'

Thomas grabbed hold of her. 'That's brilliant, Candice,' he gushed.

'Hang on,' she said. 'Before you get carried away, I want to keep it from my mum for now. She's going through hell, and it might look a bit, well, insensitive, like you said. I'm going to keep it from my friends at uni too for the same reason. In fact, if things don't change, we might have to put it off even longer. Maybe a Christmas engagement? We'll have to see how it goes.'

'OK, that's great. Obviously, I'd prefer to do it when it's your twenty-first, but I can understand it if you want to wait a bit.'

Candice smiled. 'I'm just as keen as you, Thomas, and if it weren't for everything else, I'd do it tomorrow.

*

Candice left for home late in the evening, wanting to get back before her mother returned. Once he had seen her into her car, Thomas went into the living room to join his dad and Pam.

'You're looking happy with yourself,' his father commented on noticing Thomas's expression of joy.

'I am. Me and Candice are getting engaged.'

His dad's face bore a shocked expression and he sat there for a while in stunned silence.

Picking up on his reaction, Thomas elaborated, 'Oh, I know we've not been seeing each other all that long. We're not doing it straightaway. We're waiting till Candice's twenty-first probably, maybe longer.'

'And when's that?'

'Erm, next month actually.'

'Bloody hell, Thomas! It's a bit soon, isn't it?'

'How long have you been seeing each other?' Pam enquired.

'Nine months so it'll be ten months by the time we get engaged.'

'Well, if you know she's right for you then that's long enough in my view,' she said, looking at her partner for his agreement.

Thomas's father, who had been deep in thought, now seemed to recover from the shock announcement. 'Yes, yes, I suppose Pam's right. I mean, you're a grown man and you know your own mind.'

'And she is a lovely girl,' added Pam.

'Yes, quite right,' Thomas's father agreed. He then got up

from his chair, his face suddenly animated, as he declared in a booming voice. 'I suppose congratulations are in order.'

He walked over to his drinks cabinet and grabbed three crystal glasses and a bottle of his best malt, pouring a good measure for each of them and handing them out.

He smiled wryly and held up his glass. 'To Thomas and Candice. May you have a happy future together and may nothing ever spoil your happiness.'

41

Candice had been back at work for a week and a half. When she'd returned, the staff hadn't commented much about her absence. In fact, they'd carried on as normal: busying her with mundane tasks while they got on with their own work or chatted to each other, their discussions peppered with complaints about the workplace.

She was currently sitting at her desk glancing around the office when something suddenly occurred to her. She hadn't seen Linda for ages, and nobody had mentioned anything. It seemed a bit strange.

Her gaze shifted to Carol. 'Is Linda on holiday?' she asked.

Carol laughed sarcastically. 'Huh! Chance would be a fine thing.'

Hearing Carol's brusque manner, Candice didn't think she'd get anything more out of her, so she carried on with her work until she heard Carol say, 'Apparently her services are no longer required by the company. And guess which bloody mug has copped for part of her workload?'

'Oh,' muttered Candice. She knew she shouldn't have said anything more; it was obviously a touchy subject. But curiosity got the better of her. 'How come they don't want her working here anymore?'

Carol sniffed. 'Dunno. Perhaps you can tell me, seeing as how you're well in with the boss?'

Candice blushed then silently admonished herself. Why should she feel ashamed for being in a relationship with Mr Foster's son? But then, she supposed she had kept it a secret from the rest of the staff.

'You mean because of Thomas?' Candice asked.

'Yeah, that's right.' Then Carol raised her voice: 'If that's what you call him.' She looked around the room checking she had caught everyone's attention. 'You were seen in town all lovey-dovey with him, Foster's son.

But Candice wouldn't be intimidated. 'Just because I'm seeing Thomas doesn't mean I'm well in with the boss,' said Candice. 'I still do my work like everyone else.'

Carol snorted. 'Yeah, and you come in late whenever you feel like it and get days off for…' then she emphasised the last two words, forming quotation marks with her forefingers '…*personal reasons*.'

Candice noticed that all eyes were now on her, and the atmosphere had become decidedly chilly. She didn't want to get drawn into an argument, not when it felt like the whole office was against her. So, instead, she ignored Carol's last comment and glanced out of the window where she could see Mr Foster talking to another man on the forecourt.

She hoped that Carol would shut up if she ignored her, but instead she followed her line of vision. 'Oh look, talk of the *devil*.' Again, she emphasised the last word. 'It's your superhero.'

Candice gave her a sarcastic smirk then returned to the mundane task of sorting through the pile of documents on her desk.

Mr Foster was talking to one of his sales team when Rob Bennett strode towards him in that bumptious way of his.

'Hi, mate, how's things?'

Foster stared contemptuously at the short, stocky man. Just because he did business with him, didn't mean he had to like him. Why did the man always have to be so nauseatingly cheerful? 'It's fine, everything's fine,' he said abruptly.

'Wait till you see what I've got to show you!'

The man was even more upbeat than usual. In fact, he was buzzing with excitement – so much so that Foster couldn't resist indulging him. 'What's that?' he asked.

'Follow me.'

Rob turned and almost bounced along the rows of parked cars in his eagerness to reveal whatever had got him so excited. They had nearly reached the exit gate when Rob stopped.

'Here we go!'

He pointed at a high-spec Mercedes in a gleaming metallic blue then awaited Foster's reaction as he walked around the vehicle and examined it for several seconds.

Then Foster asked, 'Is that what I think it is?'

'A ringer? Yeah. It's had a respray, so it looks like new. Beauty, isn't it?'

'Shut the fuck up!' ordered Foster, checking around him.

'What have I told you about bringing them here? Get it off the forecourt. Now!'

Despite his gruff manner, the other man was bemused. 'I thought you'd be pleased. What's the big deal? No one will be able to trace it back. I've made sure of that.'

Foster got hold of him by his shirt collar, ramming his fist into his neck. 'The big deal is that one of the fuckin' accounts staff has been poking her nose in where it's not wanted. I've had to get rid of her. Why do you think I told you not to bring them here? Dickhead!' He was apoplectic with rage. 'You'll have to take it to one of the other car lots where there are no admin staff poking their fuckin' noses in.'

He saw the look of astonishment on Rob's face and released his hold. 'Try Salford,' he said, calmer now. 'Harry there is alright. He doesn't ask too many questions.'

Rob's demeanour soon changed. His enthusiastic grin had now been replaced by a grimace. 'I'm sorry, I didn't think.'

'No, you never fuckin' do! Now do what I ask and make it snappy. I'll be round there later to collect the paperwork, so you'd better make sure everything's in order.'

Then he walked away leaving the man quaking with fear.

42

There were two CCTV cameras located close to the Wilmslow branch of Crystals. One of them was two shops down on the other side of the road. It therefore had a limited angular view of the front of the shop. The other was located further down the street and to the right of the shop.

Ever since the police had been handed the footage after the torching, DS Worrall had been keen to examine it. He had started with the tape from the nearest camera first: the one situated across the road from Crystals. By sifting through it, he had spotted the culprit. Unfortunately, the view of him was from behind so there was no way of identifying him. But DS Worrall had no doubt that it was him.

Again, the man was wearing a hoody, although it was a dark green one this time, and DS Worrall was convinced it was the same man who had been picked up on CCTV from the previous incidents. He had watched the suspect as he stood back from the shop's frontage and took several items out of a bag he was carrying including what looked like a petrol can. For a second, he had looked up and the camera had caught his face at an angle when his hood slipped.

The man had quickly pulled the hood back up and carried

on removing items from his bag. Then he had stepped forward and unfortunately gone out of range of the camera.

DS Worrall had checked and rechecked the footage, freezing it at the point at which the man's hood had slipped. The image was slightly grainy but of better quality than that from the previous shops. The problem here was that the image was at an angle and from behind, giving him a limited view. He had checked it against the photos he had shown Caitlin Percival and there were a few possible matches, but he hadn't been able to pin it down to one.

Unfortunately, since this discovery DS Worrall had been unable to check through the footage from the other camera as he'd been assigned to another more urgent case a few days ago. He had been reluctant to hand the job to a more junior member of staff. If anybody was going to make a breakthrough on this case, then he wanted to make sure it was him.

Despite his eagerness, it was a week before he was able to get back to the task. And now he was analysing the footage from the second camera. He knew that the angle would have been perfect to capture the suspect's face. But what if the camera was too far away?

It took him a while, and two cups of coffee, before he came to the right point on the tape. He could have sped through it, familiar by now with the sequence of events leading up to the fire, but he didn't want to miss any details. So, he carried on studying it until he came to the point where the man was standing holding his carrier bag.

DS Worrall felt a surge of exhilaration as he peered intently at the video images on screen and then, there it was! A full image of the man's face was on the screen in front of him. He had then frozen it and zoomed in on the shot of his features. Again, it was a little grainy, but he felt sure it was sufficient to identify him.

With his excitement building, the sergeant fished in his desk drawer for the bunch of photographs that Caitlin Percival had picked out. He flicked through them in search of a likely match. And there it was. All he needed now was for Caitlin to confirm it was the same man who attacked her.

It was mid-afternoon when Laura received a call from DS Worrall telling her that Caitlin Percival had positively identified a man picked up on the CCTV at Wilmslow. He wanted her to come down to the station to see if she recognised him.

As she entered the station Laura was full of trepidation. For three months now this person had put her through hell and she dreaded seeing his face staring back at her from a photograph.

What if she recognised him from the past? The thought of some of the brutality she had endured during her time on the beat gave her an involuntary shudder. It was a part of her life that she had never wanted to revisit. And yet, here she was.

But then, could it be someone closer to her than that? Someone from the present who she dealt with regularly? A supplier, competitor, business associate, maybe even her solicitor or accountant? All those people had an insight into her business affairs. And any one of them could have had reason to target her, even if that reason was a misguided one such as jealousy or rivalry.

Laura went to the desk and asked for the sergeant then waited with a racing heart until a member of staff came to take her through to his office. When she walked inside both the sergeant and the DI were already seated. They got up to shake her hand and Laura realised with embarrassment that her palms were clammy. DI Carson motioned for her to sit down.

'OK, when you're ready, I would like you to have a look at the image on the screen and tell us if you recognise this man,' said the inspector.

She took a deep breath, trying to compose herself while DS Worrall pressed a few keys on the PC.

'It's OK, take your time,' the DI urged.

Laura looked at the image that the DS had brought up. She picked out the man's features, feeling a little calmer when they lacked familiarity. She shook her head. 'No, I don't know him.'

'You sure?' asked the DS.

'Yes, I'm sure.'

DI Carson nodded at the DS then turned to her. 'OK, we're going to ask you to have a look at a photograph next. Again, I want you to tell us whether you recognise the man in the photo.

DS Worrall placed a photograph on the desk in front of her. She bent forwards and reached for the photo so she could examine it in greater detail. It was a large picture with the features more defined and she could tell straightaway that it was the same man the police had captured on CCTV. But she still didn't recognise him. She turned to the DI, shook her head again, then returned the photo to the desk and tried to relax back in her chair.

'Very well,' said the DI. 'We believe that this is the man who set fire to your Wilmslow shop. He was also picked out today by Caitlin Percival from a group of known criminals we have on record. She identified him as the man who attacked her. In addition to this, we think he might be responsible for a lot of the other incidents that have occurred over the past few months in relation to your businesses.'

Laura nodded, trying to stay composed even though she could hear her heartbeat thundering inside her ears.

'This man goes by the name of Milo Swain. He has quite a lengthy criminal record, and his profile would fit with the sort of criminal who would have committed these crimes.'

As soon as she heard his name, Laura felt a ripple of fear run through her. The DI must have noticed her reaction because he then asked, 'Do you know him?'

'No, no,' said Laura but she could feel her face becoming heated on hearing her own half-truth.

This time it was the DS who asked, 'Are you sure?'

'Yeah, erm, yeah. I don't know him. I was just a bit shocked to put a face to the person who has been doing all those horrible things, that's all.'

As she spoke, the sergeant's phone rang, and he excused himself while he went out of the room to answer the call.

The DI gave Laura a reassuring nod. 'That's understandable. Just to set your mind at ease, we have officers visiting his last known address as we speak. As soon as they locate him, he will be placed under arrest.

'We'll keep you up to date with any developments and,

in the meantime, if you think of anything at all that might help, please get in touch.'

Laura could feel the interview coming to a close, and she was just about to stand up when DS Worrall came back into the room.

'That was DC Reid, sir. She's at the suspect's last known address now but I'm afraid it's boarded up and there's no sign of anybody having lived there for some time.'

43

When Laura got up to leave the station, she found her legs were trembling. Hearing the name Milo had been a shock. It was unlikely for her to come across two different criminals both with an unusual name like Milo.

She was convinced it was the same man she had almost tried to score drugs from in the Rose and Crown. Thank God he hadn't turned up! Anything could have happened, assuming that he knew what she looked like. But at least now she would recognise him too so she could make sure she was on her guard.

Her mind was in a jumble. Had she done the right thing in denying all knowledge of Milo? Could she risk telling the police about her visit to the Rose and Crown though? If they found out, then they might take the case less seriously under the presumption that it was somebody she might have upset.

Her other concern was that Candice would find out, which was something she wanted to avoid. She couldn't risk losing her daughter's trust when she'd worked so hard to rebuild things, not to mention the psychological damage it might do to Candice if she thought her mother was drifting back to her old ways.

Laura felt guilty for not coming clean to the police but, in a way, she hadn't lied. They had asked whether she knew Milo Swain, and she didn't. But he certainly knew her or knew about her. And she was puzzled as to why he was carrying out this vendetta.

As she drove through the streets of Manchester, her thoughts turned to home. Candice would be back not much later than her, so she needed to compose herself. She had already decided not to tell her daughter anything about her association with Milo, and she didn't want her to guess anything was amiss.

'Hi, Mum, how are you? asked Candice when she walked into the kitchen to find Laura preparing their evening meal.

'Not too bad thanks, love. I've not been home long myself. I've been to the station.' Candice's eyebrows rose in curiosity. 'The police have found a suspect. He's called Milo Swain and they're searching for him.'

'Milo Swain? I've never heard of him.'

'No, me neither.'

'Erm, strange. I wonder why he's targeting you.'

'No idea, but hopefully the police will find out if they ever manage to catch up with him.'

'Well, it's good that they know who he is. Hopefully, it won't take them too long.' She walked over to her mother and placed a hand on her shoulder. 'Then we'll both be able to relax, Mum.'

Laura spun around and Candice noticed her furrowed brow. 'They've already been to his last known address and the bugger wasn't there. From what they told me it looks as though he's done a bunk.'

'Oh right. Well, let's hope they find out where he's got to.'

Candice didn't say anything further. She was at a loss as to what else she could say to reassure her mother because she too had an uneasy feeling about this.

It was later that evening when Laura's phone rang. Candice could tell from her mother's responses that it was the police. She watched as Laura finished the call, then she waited for her to speak.

'That was DI Carson,' Laura said. 'They're going to put his name and description out through the media.'

'Oh, that's good. There must be plenty of people who know him. Surely one of them will know where he's got to.'

'I bloody hope so,' said Laura.

Candice walked over to her mother again and gave her a hug. 'I know so, Mum. There's no way he'll get away when his photo is splashed all over the papers and Internet. You watch, they'll have him inside in no time and then this nightmare will all be over.'

She let go of her mum and stared into her face. But something in her features told Candice that she wasn't so convinced.

44

'Boss,' said Milo, his breath ragged. He listened for some form of acknowledgement on the other end of the phone.

'What?'

Milo felt a rush of adrenalin as he prepared himself to stand up to his boss. 'I can't do it no more.'

'Oh yeah, and why's that?'

'The fuckin' cops are onto me. A mate of mine told me he's seen my photo on the Internet. They're saying I'm wanted for questioning, "in connection with a number of crimes including arson" it says. It's a fuckin' good job I don't still live at my old gaff, or they'd have had me by now.'

'Alright, take it easy for fuck's sake! Why don't you contact the cops and answer their questions? If you deny everything, they can't prove it.'

'It's not that easy.'

'What do you mean?'

'Well, I think I might have been caught on CCTV.'

'You fuckin' dimwit!'

'It wasn't my fault. My fuckin' hood fell down when I was on the Wilmslow job. That's probably why they've said arson in the news but not mentioned any of the other jobs.'

'Right, well you'll need to lie low for a bit. It shouldn't be long till things die down.'

'It's alright for you to fuckin' say that. You're not the one they're after. Anyway, that's it now. I can't risk doing any more, not even after the heat dies down, not with the record I've got. I'll be banged up for fuckin' years.'

Milo almost lost his grip of the phone, his hands were sweating and shaking so much. He was afraid he might have pushed his luck too far, speaking to his boss like that. But he had to tell him! The man's answer took him by surprise.

'Well, you might be relieved to know that I won't be needing your services anymore.'

'Really?'

'Yeah, really.' Then Milo heard the gloating tone of his boss's voice as he said, 'I've got something far bigger and better lined up for Laura Sharples, and I won't need any help from you whatsoever.'

Some of Milo's tension drained away. 'Oh, oh right. Erm, I was thinking, I've done everything you asked, and you said you'd pay me a bit extra. So, can I come to collect it?'

'Yeah sure. Where are you staying?'

'Just sofa-surfing at the moment.'

'OK, no worries. It's probably best if no one sees us together anyway. I tell you what, I know a nice little country pub out Lymm way. Why don't I meet you there? Can you make it tomorrow evening?'

'Yeah, sure,' said Milo. 'What time?'

'Well, let me see, let's make it about seven.'

'Yeah OK.'

His boss gave him details of the pub and then the line went dead.

Laura had decided to visit Trina and Tiffany on Saturday evening while Candice was out and about. She needed to offload about everything. Up to now, Laura had only given Trina sketchy details of the previous day's events.

'So, what happened at the cop shop?' asked Trina when Laura was settled down with a cuppa in Trina and Tiffany's front room.

Laura told them everything including the fact that the police had a suspect.

'What's his name?' Trina asked.

'Milo Swain.'

Trina shook her head. 'Doesn't mean anything to me. Do you recognise it?'

Laura shuffled uncomfortably before confessing to Trina about her trip to the Rose and Crown, and how she had almost met Milo. 'It's a bit of a coincidence, isn't it?' she added. 'I'm thinking it's probably the same guy. And, if it is, then maybe Ron could tell us something if we called in at the Rose and Crown.'

'No fuckin' way!' yelled Trina. 'You leave this to the police. They can deal with it.'

Laura was stunned into silence by Trina's extreme reaction, but her friend wasn't finished yet. 'Not only will you be putting yourself in danger if you come across this Milo, but you should keep away from that place anyway. I've told you before, Laura, that life is in the past now and

I don't want you tempted to go back on the drugs! Think what it would do to Candice.'

'Alright, alright, I'm not going back on the drugs. I just thought that someone might be able to tell us where he's hiding out.'

'And why can't the police do that? I take it you have told them he hangs out in the Rose and Crown, haven't you?'

Laura looked shamefaced. 'No, I haven't. Do you really think the police would take me seriously if they knew I'd gone there to score? They'd just think it was another junkie who had upset their dealer.'

'But they'd still have to look into it no matter what they thought. They have an obligation.'

'It's not just that, if I tell the police what I was up to then there's a chance Candice would find out.'

Trina didn't say anything straightaway, and Laura knew she understood. She and Tiffany had become like aunties to Candice, and they cared about what happened to her. It was Laura who eventually broke the silence.

'It's three days now since the police put out his details, Trina, and I'm beginning to worry they might never find him. And, until that man is caught, I can't rest easy in my bed knowing he could strike again at any minute.

45

It was only a couple of weeks before Candice was due back at university, and she decided she needed to get some textbooks ready for the new academic year. She and Thomas had travelled into Manchester late Saturday afternoon so they could go round the shops together before she went to the library. When it reached early evening, Thomas left her as he was meeting his friend Jamie at a bar in the Northern Quarter.

As she walked through the doors into the library, she was preoccupied thinking about which books would be available and which ones she'd have to buy. She wasn't expecting to bump into anyone she knew because it was still two weeks till term started and most of her friends didn't stay in Manchester during the holidays.

Candice was therefore taken by surprise when she saw Dan a few paces ahead. Of course, she thought, Dan was from Manchester too. Her first reaction was one of panic but there was no way she could turn and flee without him noticing. So, she had no option but to tough it out. Candice even hoped it might be a good chance to smooth things over with him.

'Hi, Dan,' she said, trying to be friendly.

As soon as he saw her, his facial expression changed to one of horror. He stopped next to her and hissed into her ear, 'You've got a fuckin' nerve, haven't you? How dare you act like nothing has happened!'

'I'm not... Look, I'm sorry about Ethan...' she began before Dan interrupted.

'Sorry doesn't fuckin' cut it! You killed him.'

'No, I, I...'

But Dan was already moving away. 'Fuckin' bitch!' he spat as he passed her.

Then he stormed out of the library leaving Candice standing there, her face scarlet with shame when she felt all eyes on her. It was obvious they had heard what Dan called her, and they were probably wondering what sort of person she was to warrant such a derogatory term.

She carried on walking, feeling better once she was behind the bookshelves and away from attentive eyes. But her limbs were shaking, and she still felt flushed. Dan's attack had been so venomous that it had shocked her. He hadn't even given her a chance to explain herself. It seemed he had already decided that she had deliberately targeted poor Ethan for some reason.

Never before had she seen that side of Dan. But she supposed she could understand it in a way. He must have been upset by Ethan's death just as she was. But she couldn't help thinking that there might be something more to Dan's violent reaction. Maybe this had been the true Dan all along. She just hadn't witnessed it yet. And if he could turn on her so viciously, it left her wondering what else he might be capable of.

★

Milo arrived early at the country pub in Lymm. It wasn't a pub he was familiar with, so he'd given himself plenty of time to find it and was there by a quarter to seven. But there was another reason he had arrived early. He was eager to receive his payment so that he could finally walk away and escape this man's clutches.

The time seemed to drag especially as the person he was due to meet didn't arrive till late. Milo was on his second drink by then. He was tempted to ring him and see where he had got to. Maybe he wasn't going to get paid after all.

In the end he decided to wait another ten minutes before making the call. He didn't want to upset him unnecessarily. Milo was glad he'd made that decision because it was only two minutes later when he arrived.

'Ah, I see you've already got a drink, Milo.'

'Yeah, I was wondering whether to get you one but well…'

'Don't worry,' his boss said. 'I'll grab myself a quick one while you're finishing that.'

He returned from the bar with a short and soon polished it off. They made polite chat while Milo supped at his pint. But the conversation was stilted. Milo felt awkward wondering at what point his boss was going to dispense with the small talk and pay him off so they could both be on their way.

As if reading his mind, his boss said, 'I'll give you the cash outside away from prying eyes. You never know who's watching even in a place like this and I can't afford to take any chances.'

'Sure,' said Milo, feeling obliged to rush his pint.

Outside they passed the pub car park. It was often full, so it was usual for patrons to park down a nearby side road like Milo had done. But when they walked past the side road, he glanced at his boss who responded to his look of surprise.

'I've parked in the next one along. I've not been round this area for a while, and I took the wrong turning. I didn't realise till I was out of the car and well on my way to the pub.'

Milo nodded and carried on following him till they reached the next turn. It was a narrow country lane, much narrower than the previous one and was lined with mature trees that overhung the road and formed a canopy. It was picturesque to look at although secluded, and despite it being a September evening, it was dark as the trees blocked out the light.

Milo noticed his boss's car parked further down, but it was the only car there. He couldn't see any other cars or properties lining the road either. A feeling of disquiet descended on him. Only now did it occur to him that it was strange to arrange a meeting this far away. At the time he'd assumed it was because he liked to be discreet about his nefarious affairs, and Milo had swallowed it. But now, he wasn't so sure.

'Why are you parked all the way down there?' he asked.

'I told you, I took the wrong turning.'

'OK, but why park all that way down the road?'

'What the fuck is this, the Spanish Inquisition?'

The fact that his boss was being aggressive as well as evasive made Milo even more uneasy. 'I think we should go back to the pub car park. We'll be alright there. No one will see us.'

He stopped and made to turn around. But his boss took him by surprise when he pulled a gun. Before Milo knew what was happening the barrel was up against his throat. He flicked his head back, but his boss kept the gun pressed tight till Milo's head was so far back that his neck ached.

He heard his boss chuckle manically. 'I thought that might grab your attention. Right, now you're going to do exactly what I tell you to. When I take this gun away, I want you to carry on walking to the car. Any funny business and I'll blow your fuckin' brains out.'

Milo obeyed his orders while his boss slipped behind him and prodded the gun into his back. He had a feeling of trepidation, wondering what he was going to do to him when they reached the car. None of the scenarios he came up with were good. But he daren't make a run for it, knowing that if he did so he'd be a dead man.

46

When Milo's boss reached his car, he took the gun away momentarily. It would have been a good opportunity for Milo to jump him. But he was too slow. By the time he realised what was happening, he had his arms wrenched behind his back. Milo struggled to break free. Then he felt the gun in his back again.

'Do you want me to pull the fuckin' trigger?' his boss yelled, jabbing the gun so hard that Milo felt himself break out into a sweat.

'No, no, please don't.'

'Right, well do as I fuckin' tell you then!'

Milo's shoulders slumped when he felt the gun being withdrawn again. He guessed that his boss was about to tie his hands together. This was his only chance. He raised his leg and aimed a backwards kick, catching him hard on the shin. Then Milo swung around and belted him on the side of the head.

He ran, trying to gain ground before his boss recovered. He had to get to the road. Where there were cars passing by. Where there were people milling about. And where he would have a chance of escape.

Milo heard a shot at the same time as he felt the impact

in his buttock. Then he dropped to the ground. The bullet ripped through his insides. Still desperate to escape, Milo forced himself to stand despite the agony. He managed a few paces, leaving a crimson trail. But he could hear his boss behind him, getting closer. Another shot. This time his arm. The excruciating feel of the bullet tearing through flesh. Then the fight left him.

When his boss wrenched his arms behind him again, Milo screamed with pain. But he felt too weak to resist. He bound his arms and legs before gagging him. And Milo became overwhelmed with despair.

His boss threw him inside the car. This time the gag prevented him from yelling as intense pain assailed his body. Once he had recovered a little, Milo was horrified to notice the polythene covers on all the seats. Was that to protect them from bloodstains? What the hell was the sick fuck planning to do to him?

The car was going at speed now. Milo surmised that he wanted to get away from the area. Somebody may have heard the gunshots. Or even Milo's screams. They travelled for some miles and Milo wondered where he was taking him. It took a while till he realised they were heading up to the Moors; a desolate open expanse of land where you could travel for miles without seeing another soul.

Throughout the journey, the other man talked, his tone a mix of accusation and excited animation.

'So, you think you can threaten me, do you? Telling me you couldn't do the job because the police might trace it back to me? Were you stupid enough to think I wouldn't recognise a veiled threat when I heard one?'

Milo remembered the conversation. It was about a month

ago and he couldn't believe his boss was now quoting it virtually word for word. He obviously held a grudge. Milo couldn't talk so he shook his head from side to side, sending stabbing sensations throughout his body. Regardless of Milo's meagre attempt to defend himself, his boss carried on.

'Then you go and get yourself captured on CCTV. You've become a fuckin' liability, Milo. And I don't carry liabilities around with me. I won't put up with insubordination either. You've served your purpose. When you started losing your bottle it made me nervous and I can only work with people I can rely on.'

Then he grinned before he said his next words. 'So, I'm afraid you'll have to go because I can't have the police tracing things back to me. And I tell you what, Milo, after you've dared to threaten me, I can't fuckin' wait to get rid of you!'

Milo shook his head more vigorously now, his panicked state overriding the intense pain from his injuries. They eventually arrived at the Moors, high up in the Peak District. He tore the gag out of Milo's mouth.

'We won't be needing that now, will we? And besides, I want to hear you squeal.'

He pushed him out of the car, and Milo shrieked as he landed on the barren ground with a thump. 'Please, please don't kill me,' he begged. 'I'll do anything you want – leave the country, anything, just name it.'

His boss stared at him, a gleeful smile spreading across his face as he reached into the car's glove compartment and withdrew a knife. Milo knew his pleas were a waste of time. The look on the other man's face, and the fact that he'd swapped the gun for a knife, told Milo he wasn't just going to kill him, he was going to enjoy himself while he was doing it.

Then he ran the knife along Milo's cheek and punctured the flesh, to check how sharp it was. Milo knew it was just the beginning. His only remaining hope now was that death would come soon.

The following day Candice decided to give Thomas a lie-in before she rang him. But the time dragged as she was anxious to confide in him about what had happened with Dan. It had been a horrible experience and even the desk staff had been cool towards her after Dan's verbal onslaught. It was as though her confrontation with him had alerted them to who she was: the girl who was responsible for another student's death.

'Hiya, babe, are you alright?' he said, when he answered the phone, but she could tell he was still a bit groggy.

'Hi, sleepyhead, did you have a good night?' she asked.

'Yeah, it was great. What about you? Are you alright?' He sounded concerned. 'Did you get what you needed at the library?'

Candice was amazed at how Thomas could pick up on her frame of mind even when she was trying her best to hide it. She sighed and told him what had happened with Dan, expecting sympathy. But his reaction surprised her.

'I suppose you can understand it in a way. I mean, death is a horrible thing, and it can cause all sorts of feelings to manifest themselves.'

Candice recalled that his mother had died when he was still young. 'Yeah, I know, but it's really not my fault.'

'That's not the way he sees it though, is it? And you've got to understand that. When my mum died, I hated everyone. And then when Dad went away too. Well, let's just say it was difficult.'

Candice wanted to plead her case, to argue that Ethan hadn't even really been a friend of Dan's. But she had to take Thomas's feelings into account. He had been through major trauma when he was only a boy. And his words had made her appreciate how death could do strange things to you.

47

DI Carson and DS Worrall had just returned from the Moors where they had been greeted by the sickening sight of a dead body. Not only was the body dead but evidence of torture was still apparent even though the body had been there for some time according to the pathologist. His initial estimation of time of death was more than a week ago, possibly two.

At the DI's insistence they didn't talk about the case in the car. He wanted them both in the office where they would be fully focused on the discussion. But DS Worrall guessed that, like himself, the DI had probably wanted some time to get his head around what they had just seen. Once they arrived, DS Worrall grabbed them both a strong coffee and pulled up a seat at the DI's desk.

'This is a bad one,' he said.

The DI nodded. 'One of the worst.'

For a moment they both reflected on the scene up on the Moors. There had been no attempt to hide the naked, exposed body of the deceased. It was as though the killer was making some kind of sordid statement.

The body was covered with multiple lacerations on the

torso, face and limbs, and a variety of maggots fed hungrily on the open wounds. Flies swarmed the corpse, attracted by the foul stench. DS Worrall gulped on his coffee as he recalled that the lobes of both of the victim's ears had also been severed.

Eventually DI Carson spoke. Switching on the PC, he said, 'Let's have a look at those images of Milo Swain.'

DS Worrall had recognised him as soon as they found the body, but in view of the state of decay it was best to be on the safe side.

'Yeah, that's definitely him,' confirmed Worrall as they both stared at the images on the screen.

'But why?' asked the DI.

DS Worrall shrugged. 'I dunno. Is it connected with the vendetta against Laura Sharples or is it something else?'

'Well, judging by his record, he was probably involved in all sorts of other crimes too. He's obviously upset someone at some point.'

'Yeah, and whoever it is has a taste for torture. He must be a right nasty bastard. I wonder if he's involved with the vendetta too.'

'I doubt it,' said the DI. 'My guess is that it's connected with drugs or gangs. He's probably got an outstanding debt. These sorts of people often like to make an example of someone.

'Anyway, assuming he and Ethan Smart were behind the vendetta against Laura Sharples, that's the case wrapped up as both suspects are now dead. I think you should call her and break the news.'

*

It was the day of Candice's return to university. Although she was glad to get away from the atmosphere of mistrust from the staff at the car showrooms, she couldn't help but wonder if she would have been better off staying there. Her experience when she'd bumped into Dan at the library was still fresh in her mind.

She had been full of trepidation for days and hadn't slept well for the past two nights. Fortunately, the morning had passed by uneventfully. There had been one or two pointed stares from people when she had attended lectures but no outright animosity.

However, Candice knew that the worst was yet to come. She hadn't yet seen Dan and the other boys who shared the house where both Candice and Ethan used to live. They weren't on the same course as her and she hadn't had the misfortune of bumping into them around campus.

Now she was spending her lunch break with her friends Emma and Alicia. The three of them took a table together.

'Well, it's not gone too bad so far,' said Alicia, and Candice immediately knew what she was talking about.

'No, thank God!' Then, realising her last comment might seem a bit self-absorbed, she quickly added, 'I mean, I feel bad about what happened to Ethan. And I would never have wished that on him but...'

'It's OK,' said Emma. 'We're not blaming you.'

'No, I know you're not. But what about Dan and the other boys? I'm dreading bumping into them.'

'Why don't you come round to the house after lectures then and get it out of the way?' suggested Emma.

'Oh, I don't know.'

'Look, Candice. You'll have to face them sooner or later.'

'I know but going to the house seems a bit... well, I dunno... like I'm rubbing their noses in it.'

'Listen, you're still paying rent so you've just as much right to be there as them,' said Alicia.

'Well, yeah but that's only because I haven't found a replacement to take over my room yet.' She then thought for a moment and added, 'Do you think they'll be alright?'

Alicia shrugged but Emma said, 'Probably not, to be honest. But we'll have your back. And apart from getting it out of the way, maybe they'll start to come to terms with things too.'

'OK, I'll come.'

As soon as she spoke the words, Candice felt a flutter in her stomach. But she'd said it now, so she felt she had to go through with it.

48

Laura was busy at the Wilmslow shop. Since the torching just over a month ago, she had decided to have it refurbished so that she could eventually reopen. She owed it to the staff. Not only that, but to throw in the towel would be admitting defeat and that wasn't who she was.

So now she was busy directing a team of interior designers and tradesmen as well as consulting with her branch manager on her vision for the shop. And she was going to make sure that when she did reopen, it would be spectacular. She would hold an opening day for all the local dignitaries with fizzy plonk and canapés laid on.

Laura had just taken a coffee break and she found her mind drifting to thoughts of Candice. She knew today was going to be a tough one for her daughter and she hoped Candice would be able to handle it.

In terms of her own life, refurbishing the Wilmslow shop was keeping her busy and taking her mind off any negatives. Fortunately, there had been no recent incidents and she dared to hope that it was over.

When her mobile phone rang, she was busy tucking into a chocolate biscuit. She quickly swallowed it down, licked her sticky fingers clean and pulled the phone out of her handbag. It was DS Worrall.

'Hello, Miss Sharples? We have some news.'

'Yeah?'

'Yes, we've found the body of a man. We believe it's the body of Milo Swain.'

The mention of his name sent a chill through her. 'Oh. Oh. Bloody hell! What happened?'

'I'm afraid it's not possible to say at this stage but we think it's probably connected to drugs debts or something similar. Obviously, we'll be carrying out inquiries to see if any of his acquaintances know anything.'

'Right,' she said, hesitantly, recalling her previous intention to score from Milo.

'I know it's come as a bit of a shock but, as he was our main suspect, hopefully it will mean an end to the attacks on your shops.'

'Yes. I hope so too. Thanks for letting me know.'

Laura cut the call and gazed ahead of her as if in a trance. Wow! It was hard to believe that the person behind the torment of the past three months was dead. She supposed she should have been thankful really or at least relieved. But hanging over her was the realisation of how close to danger she had come. And how close to danger Candice had come.

She still didn't know why she had been targeted by this person. And that thought worried her. But at least it was over. And now she hoped that she and Candice would be able to get their lives back on track.

*

Candice's heart felt as though it was doing summersaults when the time arrived for her to go to the house with Emma and Alicia. Even though the girls accompanied her up the garden path then led the way through the front door, she felt so nervous that she thought she was going to be sick.

Inside they could hear conversation from the back of the house, and she guessed the boys must have been in the kitchen.

'It's now or never,' said Emma, giving her an encouraging smile then leading the way.

Candice waited for Emma and Alicia to go through to the kitchen before she followed them. When Emma opened the door, Candice smelt the pungent aroma of cannabis drifting out of the room. She heard the effusive greetings when the boys spotted Emma and Alicia. But then they saw her standing nervously behind the two girls. And all conversation stopped.

The three boys were staring at her, wearing expressions of outrage. 'You've got to be fuckin' joking!' Dan yelled to Emma.

'Hear her out, Dan, at least.'

'No, I fuckin' won't. Nothing she can say will make me feel any different.' As he spoke, he glared at Candice and pointed his finger angrily.

'It's not her fault Ethan took his own life,' said Alicia.

'Course it's her fault,' shouted one of the other boys.

'Yes,' chipped in Dan. 'Stop fuckin' sucking up to her. It's Ethan's family you should be feeling sorry for. How do you think they'll be feeling now they've lost their son? And if *she*...' he pointed at Candice again so there was no mistaking who he was referring to '...hadn't gone running to the police then it would never have happened.'

'She didn't mean for it to happen,' Emma said. 'How was she to know how the police investigation was going to affect him? He always seemed so self-assured but obviously he must have been more fragile than any of us realised.'

Dan was beyond pacifying. He rounded on Candice, stepping towards her with menace. 'You should be fuckin' ashamed of yourself for doing that to an innocent man just because you couldn't stand anyone knowing about your mother's past. How fuckin' sick and twisted is that! And how do you think his poor fuckin' family feel now he's gone?'

Emma tried to hold him back, pleading with him to calm down, but Candice had heard enough. 'It's OK. I'll go.'

She turned and headed down the hallway. The encounter had been even more unpleasant than anticipated. The lads were like a pack of savage wolves baying for her blood, and she felt distressed by their anger.

Emma stayed in the kitchen trying to cajole Dan and the others while Alicia followed Candice down the hall. 'Come up to my room for a bit while they calm down,' she said.

Candice was about to do as Alicia suggested but then she heard Dan yelling angrily at Emma. 'I'm fuckin' disgusted with you for still hanging out with her!'

She couldn't take any more. 'I'm sorry, Alicia,' she said, her eyes filling with tears.

Then she fled out of the front door. Once inside her car, she started the engine and drove, blinking away the tears that were clouding her eyes. She had hoped that by now Dan might listen to her, and that with time she could talk him round. But judging by his attitude tonight, if anything his animosity towards her was growing rather than dissipating. And she realised with a feeling of despair that this thing wasn't over yet.

49

It had been Candice's toughest week yet since going back to university. After her encounter with the boys on Monday evening, it seemed that word of what had happened to Ethan was gradually getting around the campus. Now people stopped in the corridors to eye her warily then sped up again once she locked eyes with them.

Although none of them said anything, it was obvious to Candice what they were thinking. There she is. That girl. The one who drove Ethan to commit suicide.

Apart from Monday she had only bumped into Dan and his friends once. Thankfully, he hadn't said anything antagonistic to her. But his hateful glare when she passed him in the corridor had been bad enough.

The atmosphere around campus was so hostile that it was affecting her work and making it difficult to concentrate. Each evening Candice had confided in Thomas about the situation. She didn't feel able to speak to her mother about it as she was still dealing with the damage to her Wilmslow shop. Candice was therefore glad she had Thomas. He listened to her problems without judgement and seemed to have endless patience.

It was now Sunday, and she was with Thomas in his

room chatting. They had had a wonderful weekend, going out to Dunham Massey on Saturday before touring a few bars in Manchester in the evening. Even though Candice didn't relish the prospect of another week at university, she was feeling much more positive than she had done at the start of the week.

In fact, she had reached a resolution. Seeing how well her mother was recovering from what she had been through recently, Candice was no longer going to let things get to her. Although she couldn't do anything about Dan's feelings towards her, or those of his cohorts, she would try to ignore them and hope that in time things would change.

It wasn't her fault that Ethan had committed suicide or that the police had hounded him. She had seen it as her duty to report anything suspicious to the police, and Ethan *had* acted suspiciously when he had shown an undue interest in her mother's affairs. If he chose suicide as a way out, then she couldn't be held responsible for his actions. And she refused to carry the burden of it around any longer.

With that thought in mind, she had reached another decision. The way Thomas had been towards her this last week proved to her even more what a wonderful person he was, and she couldn't wait to let him know how much he meant to her.

'How are you feeling?' he asked.

Candice smiled. 'Not too bad.' She shared her thoughts with him about university then surprised him by adding, 'Thomas, you've been my rock this past week. I don't know how I would have got through it without you. I really love you and want to spend the rest of my life with you. So, I was thinking, now that things are a lot better for Mum, how do you fancy going ahead with our engagement on my twenty-first?'

Thomas was overjoyed. He picked her up and swung her around the room and, for the first time in ages, Candice felt dizzy with happiness.

'Let's tell Dad,' he gushed.

They rushed from the room, giggling like toddlers, to find his father and Pam sitting in the living room watching a film. 'I've got an announcement,' said Thomas, taking hold of Candice's hand and staring into her eyes as he said, 'Me and Candice are going to get engaged.'

'That's wonderful news,' said his father, getting up from his seat and vigorously shaking both their hands.

Then Pam came over for a hug. Candice noticed straightaway that neither of them seemed surprised. 'You knew, didn't you?' she said to Pam.

When Pam looked coyly across at Thomas, he admitted, 'I might have mentioned the possibility. But Dad did promise they'd keep it quiet till you were ready to make it official.'

Candice wasn't offended. In fact, she found it endearing that Thomas had been so anxious to share the news. She looked up and smiled. 'It's OK.'

Then she saw that Thomas's father was already delving into his drinks cabinet and brandishing a bottle of malt. As he began pulling out his crystal glasses, Candice chirped up, 'Oh, not for me, thanks. I've got to drive home.'

'Come on,' he encouraged. 'I'm sure you can manage a small one.'

Candice laughed. 'Not on top of what I had last night. Honestly, it wouldn't take much to put me over the limit.'

'When are you going for the ring?' asked Pam.

Thomas turned to Candice. 'Next Saturday?'

She smiled. 'Yeah, that would be good. It's my birthday the following Wednesday so it'll mean you can put it on my finger then.'

'Ooh, sounds like you've got a plan,' said Pam.

Thomas's father, who had seemed lost in thought since he'd poured out the drinks for himself, Pam, and Thomas, suddenly said, 'I tell you what, why don't we all celebrate the weekend after your birthday, Candice, on the Saturday night? I could call in a chef and we'll have a special celebratory engagement dinner party. Your mum's invited too. What do you think?'

After turning down the offer of a drink, Candice didn't like to say no. 'Yeah, why not? I'll check first that my mum wasn't planning anything, but I don't think it will be a problem. In fact, I'm sure she'll be overjoyed.'

'And we will be very pleased to meet the future mother of the bride too,' he said, looking across at Pam and raising his glass.

Laura was sitting at home in front of the TV trying to relax. Candice was due home from Thomas's any minute, and she was looking forward to seeing her. Even though she'd been busy at the Wilmslow shop for much of the weekend, she still missed Candice when she wasn't at home.

Although things were a lot better for her since the news of Milo's death, she still found her mind wandering during the quiet times. Laura was starting to come to terms with what had happened. She felt safer knowing he was dead, but she still couldn't understand why he had targeted her.

Maybe the police were right, and he was just a drug-ravaged nutcase who had got hold of her name from somewhere. And, considering his connection to the Rose and Crown, that was probably where he'd heard of her.

Her main concern now was Candice and how she was coping at university. During this past week she'd tried to ask her how she was getting on. Even though she'd insisted everything was fine, Laura had seen the strain in her features each time she had walked through the door.

Laura was therefore surprised to see Candice come bounding into the house with a beaming smile on her face. She was the happiest she had seen her for days, and Laura wondered what had caused it. Candice didn't keep her guessing for long as she announced, 'Me and Thomas are getting engaged.'

Laura leant forward in her chair, her eyes wide with surprise. 'Bloody hell! When did this happen?'

'Just now. Well, we've been thinking about it for a bit. But we've only just decided properly. Thomas is going to propose officially when he gives me the ring on my birthday,' Candice gushed, her words spilling over each other in her excitement.

'Bloody hell! That's a bit soon, isn't it? Your birthday's only a week and a half away.'

'I know it is. A week on Wednesday. That's when he's coming round. Oh, but he wants to do it in my bedroom, on our own. I'll show the ring to you as soon as it's on my finger though. I hope you don't mind.'

Laura laughed at her daughter's exuberance. 'No, I don't mind, love. I'm just a bit surprised, that's all. It just seems... well... a bit soon.'

A look of disappointment fell across Candice's face. 'I know we've not been together for all that long, but I know he's the right one, Mum.'

Laura immediately felt guilty. 'I'm sorry, love; I didn't mean to put a dampener on things. Thomas is a lovely lad, and I couldn't think of anyone better to be my son-in-law. I just thought you might wait till you've finished your degree, that's all.'

'Oh, we're having a long engagement. We're not going to get married till after I graduate.'

'Well, that's good,' said Laura, beginning to get over her initial shock. 'And, do you know, love, with everything you've been through lately, it's good to have something to celebrate. I'm happy for you. I really am.'

She stood up and walked over to her daughter. Then she flung her arms around her, holding her tightly and kissing her on the cheek. 'I'm sure you and Thomas will be very happy together.'

Candice looked up at her and smiled. 'Thanks, Mum. I'm glad you're pleased for me.' As Laura loosened her hold, she added, 'Oh, and Thomas's dad and Pam have invited us for a meal to celebrate.'

'Really, when's that?'

'The Saturday after my birthday. He knows this really good chef apparently and he uses him whenever they're having a celebratory meal. They can't wait to meet you.'

Saturday the 30th, Laura was thinking. That was the date when she had arranged a surprise twenty-first birthday meal at a top-notch restaurant in Manchester. She'd also booked them rooms at the Hilton, so they didn't have the trouble of finding a taxi home afterwards. Laura had invited Trina and

Tiffany and told Candice to put the date in her diary as she had a surprise outing planned for her.

It must have skipped Candice's mind. But, seeing her so excited, she didn't want to spoil things for her, and she could always rearrange her booking. Laura didn't want to upset Thomas's father and girlfriend by turning down the invitation either. It would look like a snub, and it was important for her to get along with them.

After all, Thomas's dad was going to be Candice's future father-in-law, so she needed to make a good first impression.

50

Laura twisted around, examining her pert behind in the changing room mirror. 'No,' she said. 'It's not right. It clings to my arse too much.'

'So fuckin' what!' said Trina. 'If you've got it, flaunt it, girl.'

'No, that's just what I don't want to do.'

Trina laughed. 'Why, what you worried about? Scared his dad might fancy you more than his girlfriend.'

Laura tutted. 'Trina! This is Candice's future father-in-law.'

Trina restrained her laughter a little. 'All right, keep your hair on. I was only having a laugh.'

It was the Saturday after Candice's surprise announcement. While Candice and Thomas were ring shopping, Laura was touring the upmarket designer shops in the Trafford Centre searching for the perfect outfit to wear to the celebratory engagement meal that Thomas's father had planned.

Normally she would have grabbed something from one of her own shops but such a special occasion gave her a great excuse to really go to town. She wanted her look to be just right, something that appeared effortlessly chic even if she had already spent three hours shopping and still wasn't happy with any of the outfits she had tried on.

'D'you know?' said Laura after a while, 'I think that blue dress would have been better after all.'

'What? You mean the one you tried on three shops ago and said was too frumpy?'

'It wasn't that bad.'

'Well, not for a sixty-year-old churchgoer. But you're not that, are you, Laura? You're a young attractive woman so why should you hide it?'

'Because I want to create the right impression.' She saw her friend's look of amusement. 'I'm serious, Trina. I want something understated and… well… classy. I don't want them thinking I'm some kind of…'

'Ah, now we're getting to the bottom of it,' said Trina. 'You think you're not good enough because of your past, don't you?'

Laura shrugged but her thoughts were speaking to her and making her flush with shame. She recalled the occasion only a few weeks ago when she and Candice had been at loggerheads because of her drinking. Candice had mentioned Thomas's dad suggesting she came to live at his home when she had been upset. Laura wondered just how much he and Pam knew about her past life. Did they think it was just the drinking or did they know about everything else as well?

At the time she had been so drunk that it had escaped her mind the next day. But now it was rushing back with startling clarity. She was tempted to ask Candice exactly what she had told them, but she didn't want to mar the occasion. So, she decided to keep her mouth shut in front of her daughter and after today she would try put it out of her mind. She owed it to Candice to make the dinner party a great success.

As if reading her thoughts, Trina said, 'Just be yourself, Laura. You're as good as anyone.'

'But what if they ask what I used to do before I got the shops?'

'You can tell them owt you like. Tell them you used to work in a shop till you decided you could make a better job of running one yourself and decided to buy your own chain. And if they still think they're too good for you then fuck 'em.'

It was the day of the engagement and Candice's twenty-first birthday. As it was a weekday, she'd had to go to university, but her mother had got up especially early to give her a lavish present and card before she went. Candice had been thrilled with the pendant necklace featuring her birth stone, an opal. It was set in white gold, surrounded by lots of tiny diamonds and hanging from a white-gold chain. She had also given her a five-hundred-pound gift voucher for Crystals.

Fortunately for Candice, she had no afternoon lectures on a Wednesday, so she'd spent a few merry hours in the student union bar with Emma and Alicia. They'd picked up on the fact that she was in a rush to get home, but she'd told them it was because she wanted to spend the evening of her twenty-first with Thomas and her mother.

She couldn't tell them it was because she was getting engaged. It would feel like she was being insensitive about

Ethan, and she didn't want her only university allies to turn against her.

The past few days hadn't been quite as bad as the first week back at university although it still wasn't wonderful. The curious stares weren't as blatant. Now that most people were aware of what had happened, it had ceased to be the wonder of the week. But Candice still felt a sense of shame. Thomas had told her that they'd soon find something else to gossip about and she was trying to hang on to that thought.

But the main problem lay with her own friend group. There was still an atmosphere when she bumped into Dan or any of Ethan's friends and she had noticed that Emma and Alicia weren't mixing with the others as much. It made her feel guilty as it meant they were missing out.

Candice tried to put all that out of her head and focus on the present. She was in her room with Thomas, and they were about to become engaged.

'Are you ready?' he asked.

'Yes, come on,' she encouraged.

Thomas then surprised her by getting down on one knee. 'Right, let's make this official then. Candice, will you marry me?'

She stifled a giggle. Seeing him get down on one knee felt weird. But it was just like Thomas to do things properly. 'Yes, course I will.'

When he slipped the ring on her finger, she yelped with delight. It looked even better than it had in the shop. The trio of diamonds were set in a white-gold band, and they sparkled under the bedroom light.

She smiled. 'Come on, let's go and show Mum.'

*

Laura couldn't believe she was feeling nervous. But then, it wasn't every day that her only child got engaged. It was hard to believe how quickly she had grown up. She hadn't really expected Candice to take such a big step so soon. Without even realising it, she'd had the course of her daughter's life all planned out in her head.

First, she would get her degree in business studies. Then she'd get a good job with prospects. After working for about five years, she should have reached a level where it would be easy to return to her career after having children, knowing that she had some good experience under her belt. But Laura had overlooked the fact that Candice had a mind of her own. And not only that: she was strong-willed like her mother.

When Laura heard a door opening upstairs amidst excited chatter, she knew it was time. Any second now Candice would come dashing into the room sporting an engagement ring. It happened sooner than she expected, and she could tell by the speed of footsteps on the stairs how eager Candice was to show it off.

'Oh wow!' said Laura when she saw the beautiful ring on her daughter's finger. 'It matches your necklace.'

'That's what I thought,' said Candice, smiling.

Seeing the look of joy on her daughter's face, Laura suddenly felt overcome with emotion. Before she could stop it, she sensed the dampness of a tear landing on her cheek. She felt such a fool and hoped Candice and Thomas hadn't noticed. If they did, they were polite enough not to draw attention to it.

Laura managed to contain any further tears. She told herself it was probably just the stress of the last few weeks. But there was also a strong chance that it was the thought of losing her little girl.

In recent years, she had done her best to protect Candice who had been through so much as a child. And now, Laura dreaded the thought that Candice would soon be fleeing the nest and her chances of shielding her from danger would be diminished.

51

It was the evening of the dinner party. Laura had spent two hours getting ready, and she still wasn't happy with her appearance. She'd opted for a baby pink sheath dress with ruffle sleeves in the end. It was a flattering fit, which graced her curves, but she still wasn't sure. Was baby pink appropriate for a woman not far off forty?

When Candice walked into her bedroom, she was examining her appearance in the mirror. 'Aw, you look gorgeous, Mum,' she said.

'Ooh, I'm not so sure, Candice. Do you think the black one would be better?' She grabbed a black dress and held it up in front of her.

'No, Mum. You look perfect just as you are. Honestly, stop worrying. You're only meeting Thomas's dad and Pam. They're great and really down to earth. You'll love them.'

Laura managed a smile for Candice's sake, but she was still worried. Thomas's family probably knew everything about her since the leak to the press: the drink, the drugs, her life as a working girl. And how could she expect them to feel overjoyed knowing Thomas was going to marry the daughter of a former prostitute?

It wasn't long before Thomas arrived to pick them up.

Laura was grateful that he'd offered them a lift so they could have a drink. Maybe a bit of wine with dinner would help her to relax. She took one last look in the mirror then quickly grabbed her handbag.

But all through the journey she still couldn't settle. It was more than just nerves at meeting Thomas's parents. There was something else. She couldn't put her finger on it but for some reason she had a very uneasy feeling about this evening.

By the time they arrived at Thomas's home, Laura's stomach was clenched tight with nerves. She willed herself to calm down. Why was she so anxious? Thomas's dad and Pam might have already known about her background but the fact that they had still invited her to dinner told her they were alright with it.

She walked up the drive with Candice and Thomas, who put his key in the lock. The grating of the key in the mechanism made Laura feel even more on edge. The hosts were already waiting in the hallway and Laura heard the jovial tones of a man's voice greeting Candice before she saw him. She relaxed slightly and smiled at the friendly welcome.

But the smile died on her lips when she caught sight of the man and realised she knew him. It had been years previously and a lot had changed during that time. But Laura would have recognised those evil features anywhere.

Please God, NO! her brain screamed. His face didn't mirror her surprise and she realised that he had planned this moment all along. The bastard!

Laura noticed that he had stepped forward and hugged Candice, all the while looking over his shoulder at her, his face full of smug satisfaction. The thought of him touching her daughter was anathema to Laura who was tempted to drag him off. Fortunately, he let go just then and Pam stepped forward, hugging Candice just as ebulliently.

Candice then swivelled around, her face glowing with happiness. Seeing her like that put Laura in a quandary. She wanted to yell at the man, to tell them all what he had done, unsure just how many of them were aware of his dirty deeds. The low-down, stinking, rotten bastard!

But how could she spoil her daughter's joy? So she took a breath and tried to stay calm. It was important to think about how to play this.

Candice smiled at her. She must have read Laura's strained expression as one of lingering self-doubt because she stepped back and took her mother's hand. 'Mum, this is Justin, and this is Pam,' she said.

They both smiled back, and Justin held out a slimy hand. 'Justin Foster at your service,' he said sarcastically. 'Pleased to meet you.'

The others laughed at his mock formality; Laura was the only one aware of the hidden torment in his words. She began to wonder, did Thomas know? Was he involved? Did he carry out some of the attacks on the shops; the ones that Ethan had previously been blamed for? Yes! That was it. That nasty bastard Justin had set this all up and used his son as bait to reel Candice in. Laura felt sickened.

And all those weeks since the attacks, Justin had been lulling her into a false sense of security. She had thought that it was all over once Milo had been found dead. But now she realised that Justin had just been building up to this moment. His main event.

They all trundled through to the dining room and Justin pointed out their seats. It didn't surprise Laura that he had seated her opposite him. He wanted to see her squirm. Laura made an impulse decision. She would keep schtum throughout the meal for Candice's sake then she'd deal with the fallout later.

'Now then, before we start eating, there's a little something I want to share,' Justin announced. He reached down by the side of the table and pulled out a plastic carrier bag then put his hand inside it, taking out two envelopes. He handed the larger one to Candice who opened it to find a twenty-first birthday card inside and a two-hundred-pound gift voucher for a fashion shop that wasn't Crystals.

'Aw, thanks, Justin; thanks, Pam,' she gushed.

'You're welcome,' he said. 'And we haven't finished yet.' He waved the other envelope. 'In this one we have your engagement present. Now, which one of you would like to open it? Or would you both like to open it together?'

'Thank you so much,' said Candice, turning and smiling at Thomas. 'Should we do it together?'

Thomas nodded and they awkwardly tore the envelope open between them. In his excitement Thomas grabbed hold of the contents. 'Oh wow!' he said. 'Flights to New York.'

'Yes, and a seven-night stay at a top-notch hotel,' added Justin. 'We thought it would be a great way to start your lives together.'

Thomas and Candice were both effusive in their thanks, making Laura feel uncomfortable and inadequate. She had been so busy thinking about Candice's twenty-first and preparing for tonight that it hadn't occurred to her to get an engagement present.

Justin swallowed down their gratitude feigning modesty as he said, 'Oh, it's the least we could do.' Then he looked at Laura, 'Candice is such a lovely young lady, and it will be a privilege to have her as part of this family.'

Laura smiled politely then everyone's focus turned to food. Pam helped Justin to serve up a starter. It looked delicious and he was happy to announce it, 'Scallops with chorizo and hazelnut picada.'

But Laura had lost her appetite. Resigned not to let her daughter know anything was amiss, she chewed on the food, willing it to go down. She had almost finished the starter when her stomach rebelled.

'Can I use the bathroom please?' she asked, getting up from her seat with her hand covering her mouth.

'Certainly, it's at the top of the stairs,' said Justin.

She raced to the bathroom, making it just in time. As she looked at the splashes of vomit around the top of the toilet basin, she felt ashamed. After grabbing at some toilet paper and flushing repeatedly, she cleaned it as best she could. Then she looked at her reflection in the mirror. Her eyes were bloodshot, her face ruddy and she had vomit stuck to the ends of her hair.

While Laura was rinsing herself with cold water, she heard Justin's voice at the bottom of the stairs. 'No, it's OK, I'll go and check on her. I wouldn't want any harm to come to our guest.'

Again, Laura felt the implication wrapped up in those

words: innocuous-sounding to everyone but her. Then she heard him tapping at the door, and her heart leapt in panic. She opened the door.

His face was a picture of menace as he quietly hissed, 'All that kept me going through those wasted years in prison was the thought of getting back at you. And now I'm gonna make your life a fuckin' misery! If you think the damage to your poxy shops was bad, I haven't even started yet. You'll be sorry you ever crossed me.'

'That's what you fuckin' think!' she hissed back, trying to keep her voice from trembling. 'You won't think you're so clever when I tell the police what you've been up to.'

'Prove it! There's nothing linking me to what's been happening. And do you really want to risk your daughter's happiness by making a load of false accusations?'

'They're not false though, are they? Just like when you assaulted me all those years ago even though you denied it in court.'

'Well, it's what Candice will think that's important, isn't it? And you, as the perfect mother, should know that.'

Then his voice adopted a more relaxed tone as he shouted downstairs, 'Yes, she's absolutely fine. Don't worry, Candice.'

Laura realised that Justin had been playing a sick game with her, not only in getting Milo involved in the vendetta but also in trying to turn her daughter against her. It was apparent to her now why he had invited Candice to live at his home.

She rejoined them at the table where a main course of lamb shanks in red wine with roasted vegetables was waiting for her. 'Are you OK?' asked Candice.

'Yes, I'll be fine now,' said Laura, pulling out her chair and staring at the sizeable meal with dismay.

As she struggled through the food, Justin asked, 'Have you lost your appetite?'

'No!' said Laura whose mind was on her daughter.

It was only last night that Candice had walked in from university, her face full of sorrow again. The contrast in her daughter between last night and now was palpable.

Laura knew Candice had been having a hard time. And now she knew that it was all her fault. Her foolish acts of the past had started this whole thing off: the vendetta, the police suspecting Ethan of being involved, the lad's suicide and the subsequent animosity aimed at Candice by her peers. But she couldn't afford to think of all that now. She had to act happy for her daughter's sake at least till they got through the meal.

But she couldn't do it. As she tried again to force the food down while Justin fuckin' Foster looked on with glee, she knew she'd had enough. She peered at Candice who was in animated conversation with her fiancé.

'I'm sorry, but I'm not feeling at all well. I need to go home. Will you come too, Candice?'

Justin stood up. 'Oh, we're terribly sorry to hear that. Not the food I hope.' He chuckled falsely. 'I ordered the best chef specially for the occasion.'

He then looked across to Candice. 'Oh, but I'm sure there's no need for Candice to go too. That is, if you're feeling well enough to go home alone. Let me call you a taxi. I'll charge it to my account.'

His insincerity was irritating and it irked Laura who was aware from everything Candice had said that she had been totally taken in by him: the nice guy who couldn't do enough for you.

Laura looked at Candice, her eyes pleading. But her daughter didn't pick up on the look of desperation on her face. 'Aw, Mum. I'm really sorry you'll have to miss the rest of the meal. Will you be OK if I stay here? I'll check on you when I get home. Promise.'

Four pairs of eyes stared at Laura, awaiting her response and making her feel pressured to agree. But she refused to make what she considered the wrong decision. How could she leave Candice alone here with them now that she knew who Justin really was?

'No, I want you to come home with me, Candice. I don't feel at all well, and I really don't want to be left alone tonight.'

As she looked around at the four of them, she could tell they were shocked at her extreme reaction, and Candice didn't look happy. But Candice knew her mother and she also knew that she wouldn't insist on her coming home for no good reason.

'OK,' she said reluctantly. 'I'll ring you when I get home, Thomas.'

All the way home there was a stifling atmosphere between them. 'What's really wrong?' asked Candice.

'I told you, I'm not well.'

Candice didn't say anything, but her face did the talking. Her mum had spoilt her engagement meal, and she wasn't at all happy about it.

They fell silent and Laura retreated into her own thoughts. She was tempted to tell her daughter everything, but she wasn't sure she was ready to do that yet. Why cause a problem between Candice and the man she loved just because of his father?

Laura wondered what to do when she got home. Should she ring the police and send them round there? But what would she tell them? Justin hadn't done anything wrong as far as Candice was concerned so to get the police involved would only cause her daughter more upset.

Laura knew he was behind the vendetta against her and her business but, as he had clearly said tonight, she had no way of proving it. And as for the crimes he had committed in the past, he'd already served his time for them.

When they arrived home, Candice stormed up to her room. 'Let me know if you start feeling *really* ill.'

Laura picked up on the sarcasm in her words, suggesting that she had dragged her home for nothing. But Laura wasn't going to argue with her. She preferred to be alone right now. Her mind had a lot to process.

It was only once Candice was out of the room that she could allow herself to think about what had happened all those years ago. But as the harrowing memories came rushing back, she felt her heart racing. Laura was clammy and gasping for breath. She needed a drink to calm her down.

Now that the thoughts had resurfaced, she tried to suppress them. She couldn't handle it, not when she thought of the connection to Candice, and the danger they might both be in. But the flashback refused to go away. So, she poured a glass of the strong stuff to give her courage while she began to relive the brutality of that time when this whole chain of events had begun.

52

Once she had reached her room, Candice rang Thomas.
'Is everything alright?' he asked.

'Yes, she's fine. Don't worry.'

'Aw, well I hope she'll be OK. I'm glad you've rung me actually. There's something I wanted to tell you tonight once the meal was finished and we could get some time alone.'

'Oh yeah?' said Candice, curious to hear what he had to say.

'Yeah. It's been eating at me for a bit. Do you remember a while ago when I said I had something to tell you?'

'Yeah, course I do. You kept me waiting ages till you told me it was the engagement, didn't you?' she asked playfully.

She noticed him hesitate. 'Erm, it wasn't the engagement actually.'

'Eh?'

'There was something else. You just assumed it was the engagement and I was happy to let you think that but now that we *are* engaged, I think it's only fair that I come clean with you.'

'What is it, Thomas? You're scaring me now.'

'Oh, there's no need to worry. It's not about us. It's… well, it's about my dad. And I know I should have told you when you told me about your mum, but I just found it so hard.'

He stopped and paused for breath, and she could tell he was gathering himself together before he continued, 'He's been in prison. I'm sorry but I lied when I said he'd worked abroad. He didn't; he was in prison.'

Candice took a sharp breath. 'Prison?' she asked, in shock. 'What for? What did he do?'

'It was on drugs charges.' He gave Candice a moment to take it in then added, 'Oh, but it wasn't for dealing in hard drugs. It was cannabis. A friend of his was growing some plants and Dad was in on it. Apparently, his business went through a rough patch, and it was an easy way to earn some fast money. But he regrets it and there's no way he would do anything like that now. Well, you've seen what he's like. He's a respectable businessman.'

He was rushing to get his words out as though he needed to convince her that his father was a reformed character.

'Thomas, it's OK. I understand,' she said. 'It's not easy to share something like that. I should know. I just wish you would have told me before, that's all. It doesn't seem fair that I went through the pain of telling you about my mum when you were holding all this inside. It might have made us both feel better if we had shared it together.'

'I know. And I'm so sorry, Candice. I almost told you so many times, but I kept backing out at the last minute.

Candice could sense his pain, it was evident in his tone of voice, and she empathised with him. 'It's alright. Don't worry. You've told me now, and that's all that matters. What happened after he went to prison?'

'Well, my mum died of a heart attack like I told you but,

to be honest, I don't think the shock of Dad being put inside helped. Then my grandparents brought me and my sister up; they're my mum's parents who you've met. They're great but, unfortunately, they don't get along with Dad. He told me it's because they've never forgiven him for being sent down and they blame him for my mum's death.'

'Aw, I'm so sorry, Thomas. But now that it's in the open, I'm glad. It means there'll be no more secrets between us, and we can concentrate on planning the rest of our lives.' Then she asked. 'What about Pam? Does she know?'

'I don't know,' he said. 'Dad hasn't said. He doesn't really like talking about it. So, it's probably best if you don't either just in case.'

'Of course, I won't say anything if your dad doesn't want her to know.'

'OK, thanks. Can I just ask, does it make you feel any different about Dad?'

'No, not at all. Like you said, he regrets what he did and he's not like that now. We all make mistakes and circumstances can push us to do things we wouldn't otherwise do. I mean, look at the mistakes Mum has made, and she's managed to turn her life around.'

'That's right,' said Thomas and she could picture his smile of relief.

'Would you mind if my mum knew?' she asked.

'It's up to you. Why do you want her to know?'

'Well, to be honest, I'm sure it will make her feel better. She was in a bit of a state about going to yours tonight because your dad and Pam know all about her past. I think that's why she wasn't well. I think it's because she'd got herself all worked up.'

'Aw, that's a shame.' Then he laughed, trying to make light of the situation. 'Yeah, go ahead and tell her my dad's got a dodgy past too if it makes her feel better.'

Candice smiled. 'I'm sure it will.'

53

When Laura had the flashback to that night, she felt every emotion that she'd felt during her ordeal. It might have been nine years ago, but the distress was so strong at times that she felt like it had taken place only recently.

Justin Foster had seemed like an average punter. They'd met in a hotel foyer where they'd had a drink and then gone up to a room he had booked. While talking to him she noticed that he was in fact more polite than most punters. Well, at least he was before he'd had a drink.

But once they reached the inside of that hotel room, his manner towards her changed. The more he drank, the worse it became, going from polite to abrupt to demanding. And then his nasty side came out.

A cocktail of alcohol and drugs had made Laura less alert to the signals, so he took her completely by surprise when he handcuffed her to the bed so that she was spreadeagled. And once he had her cuffed and gagged, he was free to carry out his perverse sexual fantasies involving pain and torture. As bad clients went, he was the worst. He brutalised her body with an intensity that she had never before experienced.

Eventually he released the handcuffs but only so that he could turn over and go to sleep. His intention had been to continue the following morning. But, after a while, when there was no sign of him waking up, Laura fled the room, convinced that she might not survive a repeat attack. By then her flesh was a mass of bruises and welts.

Once it was over, Laura's terror turned to anger, so she grabbed a wad of his cash and a credit card on her way out. That was the catalyst for her idea of revenge on not only him but on all her worst clients. She couldn't take the abuse anymore. Unfortunately, in the case of Justin Foster, her plan had backfired in the worst way imaginable. But she couldn't revisit that now. Reliving the assault had shaken her badly enough and what had happened after that was something she didn't want to think about.

And now Justin Foster was back and was exacting his revenge on Laura for all those years he had spent inside. In Laura's view he had got off far too easily, but she remembered that the prosecution hadn't been able to prove all the counts against him. He'd probably got time off for good behaviour too.

His poor wife had committed suicide after that, unable to bear the shame he had brought on the family as well as the realisation that she had been married to a monster. Laura thought about Thomas then. It must have been difficult for him losing both his mother and, in effect, his father too at such a young age.

She wondered again whether he was involved. The police had confirmed that Milo had carried out the attacks on her staff and set fire to the Wilmslow shop, but what about the other things such as the graffiti? They had previously assumed Ethan was responsible but maybe that wasn't the case.

Whether Thomas was involved or not, it would still break Candice's heart when she found out the truth about his father. With all these thoughts going around in her head Laura eventually drifted off to sleep, still unsure how she was going to tackle the situation the following day.

'Are you ready for bed, Justin?' asked Pam.

'I'll be up in a minute,' he said, as he sat in the lounge swirling whisky around in a glass.

He reflected on the evening and smiled. It couldn't have gone better. The look on Laura Sharples' face when she clocked him was priceless, and it was great seeing her get so worked up that she made herself ill.

He'd been dreaming of this day for so long. As he'd told the bitch tonight, the thought of getting back at her was all that had got him through his prison sentence. And if she thought tonight was bad, she'd seen nothing yet. Now that he had her where he wanted her, he could do what the fuck he liked. And it would be such fun dreaming of ways in which he could hurt Laura Sharples.

Targeting the shops had been fun. Of course, he'd had Milo doing his dirty work for him, and now that he was out of the way there was no way the police could trace any of it back to him. But now it was time to target her in a different way, and what better way than through her daughter? He knew how close Laura and Candice were. He could tell from the way the girl talked about her and the things Thomas had told him.

When his son had first mentioned Candice, Justin had recognised the name instantly. And it was such an unusual name that, surely, there couldn't have been that many of them. A bit of snooping around confirmed his suspicions as to who it was. Thomas had unwittingly played right into his hands by bringing her to him.

Justin was confident Laura wouldn't tell anyone that he was behind the vendetta. She'd be too frightened of her precious daughter finding out just who it was she was getting engaged to, knowing it would break her heart. So, she'd have to suck it up just like all tarts did.

Just who the fuck did she think she was anyway, accusing him of assault? Bollocks to that! That's what those whores were there for, wasn't it? And, for all her designer fashion shops and trying to create this new fancy life. For all the ways in which she tried to make it up to her daughter for being such a fuckin' waster in the past. At the end of the day, a common whore was all she was.

And now she was going to learn that there was no way a piece of scum like her could fuck up his life and get away with it.

54

'Hi, love, are you OK?' Laura asked when Candice got up the next day.

'Yeah, what about you? Are you still feeling ill?'

'I'm a lot better thanks. Are you seeing Thomas today?'

'No, I need to study. I've got a load of catching up to do. It's been a hectic few days with all the celebrations.'

Laura tried hard to hide her relief. That meant she wouldn't be worried about what would happen to Candice while she was under Justin's roof. It also meant she could put off deciding about what to do until the following day. She preferred to speak to Trina first and get her take on things.

'Y'know, Mum, I hope you don't mind me saying, but you were daft to get yourself so worked up last night. Like I say, Justin and Pam are great. I hope you liked them.' Fortunately for Laura, she carried on speaking without waiting for her response. 'Anyway, as it turns out, Thomas's dad has got a bit of a dodgy past too. Thomas told me on the phone last night.'

Laura's ears pricked up. 'Oh yeah?'

'Yeah, do you remember me telling you ages ago that Justin went to work abroad, and Thomas's grandparents brought him and his sister up?' Laura nodded. 'Well, he wasn't working at all. He was in prison. Oh, but please keep it to yourself. Thomas isn't sure whether Pam knows or not.'

Typical, thought Laura. *The poor cow probably doesn't know what she's let herself in for. Or maybe she does know by now. Unless he saves that sort of treatment for working girls.*

'Poor Thomas,' Candice continued, breaking Laura out of her reverie. 'It must have been terrible for him and his sister, especially when his mum had the heart attack too. It must have been like losing both parents at once.'

'Hang on,' said Laura, too quickly. 'What heart attack?'

'The heart attack that killed her. That's why Thomas was brought up by his grandparents. They reckoned it was the shock of Justin being sent to prison for dealing in cannabis that brought it on.'

Laura couldn't believe what she was hearing and was tempted to put her straight. It seemed that Thomas had lied to Candice. But why?

'So, you see,' said Candice, 'there was no need for you to feel so on edge about meeting them. Everyone does things they regret, Mum. And according to Thomas his dad feels really bad about it. He's a nice guy really. Well, you saw that for yourself last night, didn't you?'

'What? Oh, yeah. Pam's lovely too.'

The lie tasted bitter on Laura's tongue, but she still couldn't bring herself to tell her daughter the truth. She was so wrapped up in Thomas that she'd be devastated.

*

On Monday morning Laura rang Trina as soon as Candice had set off for university.

'Bloody hell, Laura! What's got into you? It's only half eight in the morning. I'm still in bed.'

'Sorry,' said Laura. I couldn't sleep.'

'Why, what's happened?'

Laura then brought Trina fully up to date about everything including who Thomas's father was and the threats he had made. She also told her about the conversation she had had with Candice the previous day.

'Shit,' Trina repeated. 'What are you gonna do?'

'I was hoping you could tell me.'

Trina paused and Laura could sense her mulling things over. 'Let's get this straight. Are you saying Candice doesn't know anything?'

'That's right. I wanted to tell her but how could I? She's so madly in love with Thomas that she would never hear a word against him. They're going to be married, for fuck's sake!'

'You can't let her go through with it, Laura. She needs to know.'

'But if I tell her everything, she'll know what I did. She'll know it was all my fault.'

'I thought she knew all about your past.'

'No, not everything. She knows I worked the beat and had a problem with drugs, but I didn't tell her everything. And she was so traumatised as a kid, I can't put her through that again.'

'Right, then you still need to tell her about Justin and Thomas. Just leave out the other bit. Tell her he's someone you knew from your days on the beat and that he's a bad 'un. Jesus, girl, you can't let her marry this fuckin' boy!'

Once they had finished speaking, Laura thanked Trina for hearing her out. If anything, she felt worse after the call, not better. But she had needed some clarity to be sure she was doing the right thing.

The day dragged. Candice's last lecture usually finished at four on a Monday and as the hands on the clock crawled around to four-thirty, Laura's heart was pounding. She knew that unless Candice had stopped off at the library, she would be home any second. Laura had resigned herself to the fact that she needed to speak to her daughter, but she'd start off by taking a soft approach and see how it went.

Then she heard Candice's car pulling up and braced herself for a difficult conversation.

55

When Candice walked in from university, she could tell her mother had something on her mind. She had that worried look about her. 'What is it?' she asked.

'Sit down, Candice. I need to talk to you about something.'

Candice did as Laura instructed then waited for her to begin.

'It's about Thomas. I think you might be rushing into things a bit too soon with him. Maybe it would be better to call off the engagement until you know a bit more about his family.'

Candice was shocked. Where the hell had this come from? Then she realised what had prompted it. 'Aah, right. Is this about his dad having a criminal record?' she asked.

'Kind of, yeah. But it's more than that. I think he's behind the vendetta against the shops and Thomas may have been involved too.'

'Thomas? Why the hell would you think that?'

'Well, I think he's working with his dad.'

'Hang on a minute. So, let me get this straight. Just because Thomas's dad has a criminal record you've jumped to the conclusion that him and Thomas are behind the attacks on your shops. What the hell?'

'No, Candice. Like I said, it's more than that. Think about when we went to see the CCTV footage, when you mentioned Thomas being five eleven and the police started asking questions about him. It could easily have been him on camera.'

'Are you crazy? I only said that to show them that Ethan was quite a bit taller than five ten. I never thought for a minute that the image was Thomas. That's why I put the police straight there and then. What the hell has got into you? Are you back on the drugs?'

'No, I'm not back on the bloody drugs. I haven't touched anything for years.'

Candice could tell that the reference to drugs had angered her mother, but she didn't care. She was furious herself to think that her mother could possibly suspect Thomas! 'Then why the hell are you accusing Thomas of attacking your shops?' she asked. 'He'd never do anything like that!'

'I'll tell you why if you give me a minute…'

'No!' Candice cut in, her temper now boiling over. 'I don't want to hear it. You're nothing but a hypocrite. It's alright for you to have a dodgy past but when it comes to Thomas's father having one it's another matter.'

'It's nothing to do with that!' Laura yelled. 'I can explain if you'll give me a bloody chance.'

'No way. I don't want to listen to any more of this bullshit! How dare you accuse Thomas of something like that? He'd never do anything to hurt me or you.'

Candice picked up her college bag and fled from the house and then into her car. Despite her rage she drove until she had reached the centre of Altrincham. Then, realising she needed to calm down, she parked up while she mulled everything over.

It was hard to believe her mother would make such an accusation. She knew that the stress of the past few months had got to her, but this was something else! Candice realised now why her mother had got herself into such a state at the dinner party and then demanded that she left with her. She must have had this sick idea in her head then. And if she had been taking drugs then that would also explain why she was having difficulty eating and didn't feel well.

Her mother had had her share of problems in the past, and she'd forgiven her for all her transgressions during her childhood. The fact that Laura had worked so hard to make it up to her ever since had helped. Once her mother had got off the drugs and stopped working the beat, they had enjoyed a good life together. Until now.

She dreaded to think that her mother's recent difficulties might have driven her back to drugs. It was the only reason she could think of for her flawed reasoning, and Candice dreaded the thought of Laura dragging them back into that life. But, whatever happened, she vowed to herself that there was no way she would let her mother's failings come between her and Thomas.

Laura could have kicked herself. She'd handled it all wrong. Candice was bound to go off the deep end as soon as she said anything negative about Thomas. She should have known; not only was Candice crazy about him but she had also inherited her mother's temper. It would have been better to focus on Justin instead, especially as she was certain of his involvement whereas with Thomas it was just a suspicion.

She went to the kitchen and poured herself a glass of wine. She knew she shouldn't, *but extreme situations called for extreme measures*, she thought. As she replayed the conversation in her head, she hammered her fist on one of the work surfaces in frustration.

Laura went back to the lounge. She decided to give both herself and Candice time to calm down. Then she would try again and see if she got through to her this time. For the next hour she planned in her head what she would say. Then, with shaking hands she rang Candice's mobile number. But there was no reply.

For the rest of the evening, she sat worrying. She thought about ringing Trina again but knew there was nothing she could say that would make her feel better. She needed to sort this out herself.

Laura hoped Candice hadn't gone to Thomas's. She couldn't settle as she thought about the danger her daughter might be in right now. Should she ring the police? But, if she did, Candice might take against her even more. And she needed to get things back on track with her.

After ringing her daughter a further two times, Laura gave up and went to bed. But she couldn't sleep until at ten past twelve she heard Candice's key in the lock. She had obviously decided not to come home until she thought her mother was in bed. Respecting her wishes, Laura stayed where she was. It was enough just to know that she was back home safe. She'd tackle her in the morning.

But when Laura got up the next day there was no sign of Candice in the house. She must have left early for university, and it was apparent to Laura now that her daughter was avoiding her.

56

Laura was relieved when Candice came home the following evening. 'Hi, love, are you OK?' she shouted as she heard her daughter in the hall.

But she ignored her and went straight upstairs. *Never mind*, thought Laura. *She's bound to come back down again for her dinner. I'll talk to her then.*

It was a while later and Laura was in the kitchen preparing their evening meal when she heard footsteps on the stairs. She walked through to the hall, eager to see Candice and make up with her. But she was astonished to find her carrying a suitcase.

'What's going on?' she asked.

'I've decided to stay at Thomas's for a while. I'll come back home when you've sorted yourself out and got back off the drugs. They're making you paranoid.' Then she tutted. 'I suppose it'll be a while yet.'

'For God's sake! Don't be ridiculous. You can't stay there. You're putting yourself in danger.'

'Mother, will you stop it! Are you really that jealous of me being with Thomas that you're willing to make up some pathetic story about him attacking your shops? Listen to yourself!'

'No! You listen to me, Candice. Justin's a bad person. He's done really bad things, not only to the shops but in the past too.'

'Stop it, Mother! I don't want to hear any more. You're so bloody possessive that you can't cope with the thought that I'll be getting married and leaving home. But you're driving me away. You need to let go.' Then she turned away from Laura and as she opened the front door, she added, 'Contact me when you're clean.'

Laura watched in despair as her daughter headed down the drive and popped open the boot on her car, roughly throwing the case inside. For a few moments she stood rigid with shock. It felt like a bad dream; surely this couldn't really be happening to her. Then she snapped to. She had to stop Candice. She couldn't lose her! And she dreaded to think what might happen while she was under Justin Foster's roof.

Laura ran down the drive. By this time Candice was behind the wheel and had started the engine. Heedless of the danger, Laura rapped on the side window. 'Candice! Candice! Come back. I need to talk to you. Just hear me out, please!'

'Let go of the car, Mum. I'm setting off. Stand back, will you?'

Then the car moved slowly away from the kerb and Laura jumped back so the motion wouldn't knock her to the ground.

'Candice, come back!' she shouted down the road. 'You need to know about Justin!'

But Candice kept driving and Laura's eyes filled with tears as she watched the car disappear into the distance.

*

When Laura got back into the house she was trembling and for several minutes she sobbed bitterly. How could her Candice treat her like this? Her wonderful, precious only daughter. She had thought that she'd repaired all the damage of the past and that they now had a solid stable relationship. But how wrong she had been.

Once the tears had abated, Laura began to think about her next move. Surprising herself, she didn't reach for the bottle. It was as though she wanted to prove Candice wrong about her. Turning to drink would have been predictable. But she was determined not to be that person who her daughter seemed to think she was. Instead, she needed to do something positive to put things right.

Knowing there was no point in ringing Candice while she was driving, Laura sent her a text, pleading with her to let her explain everything. She hoped that when her daughter arrived at Thomas's she would look at the text and give her a call. But when Candice hadn't responded after half an hour, Laura texted again and later in the evening too. Then she tried ringing, but all her calls and texts went unanswered.

After checking her phone for the umpteenth time, Laura dialled the number DS Worrall had given her. Unfortunately, he and DI Carson were unavailable, but Laura wasn't going to let that deter her, so she asked to speak to someone else on the team and was transferred to a female officer called DC Reid.

Laura began to relate to her all that had happened while DC Reid listened sympathetically. Unfortunately, as soon as

Laura mentioned the fact that her daughter had gone to live with the man who had attacked her so savagely, she became upset again. She tried to tell DC Reid the rest of what had happened in between sobs. But her tale was disjointed as she rushed to fit in all the details including the vendetta and all that had happened years previously leading to Justin Foster's arrest.

'Right, let me just slow you down for a minute. I am familiar with the case so let's start with the attacks on your shops, shall we?'

Laura realised that she must sound hysterical, but she was desperate to get the police to take action. 'No, I need to tell you about my daughter first.'

'Alright, you said she had gone to live with your attacker. Is that right?' She spoke slowly and deliberately as though addressing a child.

'Yeah, Justin Foster. She's engaged to his son, Thomas,' said Laura trying to make herself better understood.

'And your daughter is how old?'

'Twenty-one.'

'So, did Justin Foster force her into his home?'

'No!' Laura found herself shouting. 'But the point I'm making is that this man is dangerous.'

'So, did your daughter go to live at his home of her own accord?'

'Yes, I suppose she did.'

'Well, in that case, I'm afraid there's nothing we can do. She's past the age of consent.'

'But you don't understand,' Laura cried. 'I'm frightened of what he's gonna do to her to get back at me. I had him arrested, you see.'

'Yes, and you said he's already served his time?'

'Yeah, but he's still dangerous. He's been attacking my staff... and... and vandalising my shops. Well, he was behind the attacks. He got a man called Milo Swain to do it for him, and I think Thomas might be involved too.'

'Milo Swain. Ah yes, I know the name. We've looked at the case extensively and there was no evidence of anybody else's involvement. Milo Swain fits the profile. We believe he was the man spotted on CCTV and he was also picked out by the witness Caitlin Percival. Added to that is the fact that since his death the attacks have stopped.'

'But that's because Justin Foster is crafty. He wants you to believe that Milo Swain did it all, but it was him who put him up to it.' She paused, knowing that she was coming over as a bit unstable, but she had to somehow convince the police of Justin's involvement. 'And now he's getting at me through my daughter. Please, you need to do something. I think she's in a lot of danger.'

'I'm sorry but we can't spare police resources to go out on a limb. Like I say, we've already found Milo Swain responsible for the attacks on your shops and staff and, other than that, there is no crime.'

'But there might be. Justin Foster could be doing anything to my daughter right at this minute for all I know. Look at what he did to me...'

'Yes, I understand your concerns, but he's served his time for what he did in the past.' Give me a moment...' Laura could hear the officer tapping away at her keyboard then she said, 'Yes, I've just had a quick look at his record. Since his release he has kept his nose clean and we've no reason to suspect him of any other crimes.'

'For fuck's sake!' yelled Laura, her frustration taking over. 'You're not listening to me.'

'Let me stop you there,' said the officer firmly. 'I've already explained to you that we have no reason to suspect Justin Foster of anything so there's nothing more I can do. If the situation changes, let us know.'

Then she cut the call and Laura screamed into her mobile. 'You stupid bitch! Why won't you listen?' But there was nobody on the other end of the line. Laura cried tears of frustration and thought again of all the terrible things Justin could be doing to her daughter right at this moment.

Then her mind flew back to the attack. Her flashback was so real that she could almost feel the pain as he pummelled her with his fists again and again, and his teeth sank into her tender flesh.

She had a sensation of choking just like she had back then when she had cried so desperately that mucus clogged her nose and throat. Subconsciously she clawed at her face as if trying to remove the gag that was making it difficult to breathe. But when she realised that it was her imagination playing tricks on her, she tried to take deep calming breaths.

She needed to hold it together. There must be something she could do. Then she had an idea. She'd find details of Justin's trial and text the link to Candice. Maybe then her daughter would believe her.

It took her an age to find the press report on the Internet. She had to wade through pages of recent headlines before she reached the historical news items. But finally, there it was. She copied the link on the top of the screen and sent it in a message to Candice.

Please read the attached news report. It will explain a lot.

But again, there was no response. Laura couldn't understand it. Surely, by reading the news report she would know what Justin had done, unless she hadn't bothered reading it. She couldn't see that being the case though. Natural curiosity would have prompted her to follow the link and, once she did that, Justin's crimes would quickly become evident.

Then she realised that it wasn't just a case of her daughter not reading her texts. She hadn't even seen them. Because, in all likelihood, she'd blocked her.

57

'Here you go,' said Justin, putting the coffees down for Candice and Thomas then returning to the kitchen to get the drinks for himself and his other half. He sat down next to Pam then turned to Candice and asked. 'Did you give any more thought to my offer of a permanent job?

'Yes, it sounds good,' said Candice, 'but I want to finish my course first. I'd like to see what results I get.'

'Oh, don't worry about that. You'll pass with flying colours. I'm already aware how smart you are. I could give you a start now if you want. One of my showroom managers is a bit useless. Maybe we could put you with him. You'll soon excel and probably take over from him eventually.'

'Thank you,' said Candice, 'but I still want to finish my degree.' When Thomas's dad looked at her pointedly, she added, 'I mean, there seems no point in having come this far if I'm just going to waste it, does there?'

'Fair enough – it's up to you. Anyway, while I've got you both together, there's something else I'd like to run by you. There's a new development just up the road. The houses are smashing. From what I've seen, I think they would suit you two just fine. Why don't we arrange to view them this weekend?'

'We're not ready yet,' said Thomas.

'Well, no time like the present is what I always say. I mean, you are planning on living together before you tie the knot, aren't you, so why wait?'

Thomas laughed. 'Are you trying to get rid of us?'

'No, not at all. You can stay here forever for all I care. I'm just thinking of you two. Prices are going up, so it's best to get on the property ladder as soon as you can.'

'We haven't managed to save a deposit yet, and there'll only be one of us working for a while.'

'That's not a problem – I can lend you the money for a deposit. Just pay me back when you can. And if Candice was to take up my offer of a job, then you'd have two incomes coming in, wouldn't you?'

Justin watched while Thomas and Candice shared a glance. From studying their body language, he could tell that his son was thinking about it, but Candice was perhaps not so keen.

'Erm, we'll have to have a chat about it,' said Thomas.

'OK, but don't take too long. Houses are selling like hot cakes now and the prices are only headed in one direction.'

He smiled to himself. It was only a matter of time until they gave in to him. After all, what he was offering was too good to refuse. While Candice was living with him there was a good chance she'd eventually go back to her mum. And he didn't want that. He wanted to create as big a wedge as possible between Laura Sharples and her daughter.

Candice was a good kid, and he had no objections to his

son marrying her. In fact, he welcomed it because it gave him a lot of control over all their lives. But Laura Sharples was another matter, and he wouldn't be happy until he'd made that bitch suffer as much as possible.

'How is she?' asked Tiffany when Trina walked back into the lounge of their Altrincham home after checking on Laura in one of the spare rooms.

'She's asleep, thank God. I'm glad I insisted on her going to bed before she hit the bottle again. The booze isn't doing her any good at all, especially now she's on anti-depressants.'

'At least the tablets are helping her sleep,' said Tiffany.

'Yeah, which is better than what was happening before.'

'I know – she looked shocking.'

Laura had now been staying with Trina and Tiffany for three days. It had been a week since Candice had left home and Laura still hadn't had any contact from her.

'I really feel for her,' said Trina.

'I know. I just wish there was something we could do.'

'Well, I don't think there is now. We've already tried everything. Candice won't answer my calls either, probably because she knows I'd be ringing on behalf of her mum. And when I tried to see her at Thomas's house, his dad wouldn't let me near her. He knew who I was straightaway because I went to watch the court case with Laura when he was sent down years ago.'

'Perhaps I could go round there,' said Tiffany.

'No. I don't want you anywhere near him. He's a right nasty bastard. We just have to hope that Candice will ring her mum. And the sooner the better before Laura has a full-blown breakdown.'

Tiffany grimaced. 'I can't believe she hasn't contacted her yet to be honest. I didn't think Candice could be cruel like that.'

'Well, it's not all the kid's fault. She genuinely thinks her mum is back on the drugs and...' She lowered her voice so that Laura wouldn't hear her from the bedroom. 'She has been through a lot in the past when her mother was high on drugs and pissed half the time. And there's no way she wants to go back down that route, which is probably why she finds it easier to blank Laura.

'Don't get me wrong, Laura's a good person. She just trod the wrong path for a while like a lot of us did. But she regrets it now and she's spent years trying to make it up to her.

'Candice is head over heels with this lad and she can't cope with any criticisms about him. The trouble is she doesn't realise that by doing what she's doing she's playing right into Justin Foster's hands. He's a nasty, manipulative bastard who will be revelling in Laura's pain.'

'I just hope Laura will come out of it all right.'

'So do I,' said Trina. 'Because the last thing any of us wants is her going back to her previous life.'

58

Candice was confused. Ever since she'd gone to live with Thomas, his dad was putting her under increasing pressure. She was pleased that he was so good to her, and she loved her fiancé to bits, but things were moving a bit too fast. She was only twenty-one and had planned to wait a couple of years before she got married.

Candice had always thought that Thomas was of a like mind. But since his dad had been putting all these ideas into his head, he was changing. They were now in his room, and she knew he would want to discuss what his dad had proposed.

'So, what do you think?' he asked. 'Would you like to go and view those houses? I've seen them from the outside and, to be honest, they look really nice.'

'I'd rather wait, Thomas. It's too early yet. I want to finish my degree before we buy a house.'

'Well, there's no harm looking.'

'No. I don't want to be tempted, not when we can't even afford the deposit yet.'

'It's not a problem, Candice. My dad has already said he'd lend us the deposit.'

'Yeah, but we'd still have to pay it back.'

'There's no rush; Dad would let us take our time, honest. He wouldn't see us without. In fact, he's said before that he'd help us with the mortgage too until you're working.'

'I don't want to start off in debt, and I don't want to feel like a burden while I'm still at university.'

'OK,' said Thomas. 'Don't worry. I get where you're coming from. If you want to take a bit longer, that's fine.' Then he smiled at her. 'You're well worth waiting for.'

Candice was relieved. At least he could appreciate her concerns. She'd been feeling pressurised during the past couple of days, and it was unsettling her. But there was another reason she was feeling unsettled: she was missing her mum and was beginning to regret her hasty decision to ostracise her.

She loved her mum to bits, but she loved her fiancé to bits too. When her mother had tried to implicate him in the attacks on the shops it had felt as though she was trying to come between them. Candice couldn't entertain that thought, which was why she had reacted rashly.

When she and Thomas had finished chatting, she nipped to the bathroom. On her way back she came across Pam on the upstairs landing.

Pam smiled. 'I'm glad I've bumped into you,' she said. Then she lowered her voice, 'I wanted to have a word. I noticed you've not been looking so happy for the last day or two. Are you missing your mum by any chance?'

Candice nodded, surprising herself when she felt a surge of emotion and had to fight back tears.

'Erm, I thought you might regret your decision to block her calls. Why don't you just send her a text and let her know you're alright? I know how close you and your mum were and it would be a shame if you were to lose contact. I'm sure she's missing you as much as you're missing her, and it might make her feel better knowing that you've not fallen out with her altogether but that you just need a bit of time.'

'Erm thanks. I might do,' said Candice, rushing back to Thomas's room so she didn't have to continue the conversation.

She was finding it difficult but, nevertheless, what Pam said had hit home. Perhaps she had been a bit hasty and maybe she should send her mum a text. She'd sleep on it and see how she felt, realising that despite her mother's faults, she didn't want to cut ties with her altogether.

The following morning, Laura was in Trina and Tiffany's lounge watching breakfast TV with them when her phone pinged. She rushed to see who the text was from and grew excited when she saw Candice's name on the screen.

'It's from Candice,' she announced. Then she opened the text and quickly scanned through it.

'Go on, what does it say?' Trina urged.

Laura relayed the message on the screen.

Hi Mum, just thought I'd let you know I'm OK but I'm not ready to talk yet. I hope you're looking after yourself.

Her face dropped with disappointment.

'Eh, that's good,' said Tiffany. 'At least she's been in touch.'

'Yeah, but she still doesn't want to see me.' After a

moment's thought, she added, 'I'll give her a ring now she's unblocked me, see whether she's come round yet.'

'No, don't,' said Trina. 'You need to give it time. It's a start but if you overdo it, you'll risk pushing her further away. And anyway, I'm not having you sitting here brooding now that she's got in touch. Come on, me and Tiff are taking you out shopping. It'll take your mind off things.'

Laura wasn't really in the mood to hit the shops. But Trina was right: it would take her mind off things and stop her from flinching every time her phone made a sound.

An hour or so later they were in the centre of Altrincham. She was glad they'd gone shopping locally when she spotted somebody she knew in one of the fashion shops. Laura had only met the woman once, but she recognised her straightaway. Without thinking she left the company of Trina and Tiffany and walked over.

'Hi, Pam, how are you?'

Pam looked surprised to see Laura but her expression of astonishment was soon replaced by a smile. 'Hi, Laura. I'm good thanks. How are you?' She seemed to realise it was a silly question and quickly added, 'Sorry, I know it must be difficult for you with Candice staying at Justin's.' Then she patted Laura on the arm. 'Don't worry – she's fine. I know she's missing you and I'm sure she'll soon come round.'

'Thanks,' said Laura before asking, 'Did she tell you why she'd left?'

'Not exactly, no. Justin mentioned something about you disapproving of Thomas and said Candice wasn't happy about it. But she's at that age, isn't she? Head over heels and won't hear a thing said against her boyfriend.'

Laura forced a smile. 'Do you mind if we have a chat? I can grab us a drink at the coffee shop if you like.'

Pam looked at her watch. 'Ooh, I'm not sure. I need to be on my way soon.'

'It won't take long, honest, but there's something I need you to know.'

'Alright then. I can spare half an hour.'

'Good, thank you. Let me just tell my friends where I'll be,' said Laura, spotting Trina and Tiffany heading towards her.

'Hi, this is Pam,' she announced. 'We're just going for a coffee while we have a chat. Can I call you when we're finished?'

'Well, we're just about ready for a coffee ourselves,' said Trina. 'Mind if we join you?'

'Not at all,' said Laura, and Pam nodded meekly.

They all trundled out of the shop and found the nearest coffee bar. Trina and Tiffany offered to buy coffee and cakes while Laura found some seats, and once she and Pam were settled, she wasted no time in coming straight to the point.

She began by telling her why Candice had left home and told her about Justin, and possibly Thomas, being behind the attacks on her businesses. When Pam shook her head in disbelief, Laura detailed the conversation she'd had with Justin at the top of the stairs when she had come to his house for dinner. Then she explained why he was out to get her and didn't miss anything out.

'No, I don't believe it,' said Pam. 'Justin would never do anything like that.'

By this time Trina and Tiffany had joined them at the

table and Pam was reaching nervously for her handbag under the table.

'No, don't go yet,' said Laura. 'I can prove it to you.'

'Pam's eyes flitted nervously around the group, and she fiddled with the handles on her bag. 'I think I've heard more than enough, and I'd rather not hear any more.'

'At least let me prove it,' said Laura, scanning through her phone in search of the news article relating to Justin's trial. 'You see, you're the only chance I've got of getting through to Candice. She just thinks I'm on drugs and talking nonsense, and I need somebody to put her straight.'

'Yeah, hear her out,' Trina growled. 'Then, if you still don't believe her, you're free to do as you please.'

Pam looked startled by Trina's gruff manner, and she placed her bag neatly on her knee. 'Alright, let's see the proof,' she said.

Laura was relieved when she managed to call the link to the trial up on the screen. 'There you go,' she said, handing Pam her phone.

She watched as Pam read through the article and her face blanched. 'Oh my God! Oh my God!' she kept repeating.

Then she looked up at Laura with a horror-filled expression. Laura, despite being relieved that the truth was out in the open, couldn't help but feel some pity for the woman sitting facing her who seemed so nice. But she deserved to know the truth.

'Sorry but I just want to add that I'm not taking any drugs,' said Laura. 'Candice was wrong. I expect that like you she found it hard to believe.'

'No, she isn't on anything. I can vouch for that,' said

Trina. 'She's been staying with me and Tiff because she's been so upset, and if she was on drugs, we'd know about it.'

Laura waited a moment, allowing Pam a few seconds to take in the devastating news before she asked, 'I wonder if you wouldn't mind explaining to Candice that he was behind the attacks? But please don't mention the trial. I'd prefer to tell her about that myself.'

Pam carried on staring in shock at Laura. Then, suddenly, she stood up and slung her bag over her shoulder, saying. 'I'm sorry but I can't deal with this now.'

As she spoke her voice was trembling, and Laura felt bad for putting so much on her all at once. She was just about to apologise when Pam fled from the coffee shop without looking back.

Laura turned to Trina. 'Shit! What the fuck do I do now?'

59

Candice had noticed a change in Thomas's dad. Suddenly, he seemed moody, and he wasn't as friendly as normal. It felt as though he was struggling to hold something in and had to make a big effort to be pleasant. Instead of his politeness flowing naturally, it now felt forced, and the sullen expression on his face didn't always match his words.

Something else she noticed was that Pam hadn't been around the house for the past three days and, as far as she and Thomas knew, Justin hadn't been to see Pam either, which was unusual. In the time that she had known Thomas, she had noticed how close his dad and Pam had become, and it was rare for them not to see each other on most days.

She had asked Thomas about it, and he had noticed too. Thomas had deduced that they must have had a row and that it must have been a bad one for them not to see each other for three days. But he didn't know what the row was about and nor did he want to invade his father's privacy by asking.

Candice just hoped that whatever it was, they would sort it out soon because the atmosphere in the house was awkward. In fact, it made her think that she might have been better off staying at home. But then she thought about the accusations her mother had made against Thomas and decided that she wasn't going to forgive her altogether yet.

It was Saturday and Laura was now back at home. Trina had tried to insist that she stayed a bit longer but, despite being grateful to Trina and Tiffany for offering to put her up when she had been at her worst, she missed having her own space. Trina had relented when Laura told her she was feeling much better since Candice had been in touch.

But now, as she looked at the latest text from her daughter, Laura felt downhearted. Ever since Candice had got in touch a few days previously, her texts had been short and to the point. It had upset Laura because it felt as though there was now an impenetrable barrier between her and Candice. Instead of sharing their familiar closeness, Candice had been treating her almost like a stranger. And it hurt.

Laura had been so tempted to ring her, but she was afraid of pushing her too soon. She knew how hot-headed Candice could be and the last thing she wanted was another row that they might not recover from.

Today, Candice's texts had been a bit more friendly as she told her how she and Thomas were going out to Manchester tomorrow and meeting her friends Emma and Alicia for afternoon tea. Laura had dared to hope that they were finally getting back on track but in her latest text Candice had told her about Justin offering her a permanent job at one of his car showrooms, which she had turned down.

Before their fallout Laura would have spoken to Candice and advised her about the future. And Candice would have taken her advice on board. But she felt that she could no longer do that without fear of upsetting Candice even more.

Laura's fear was that Justin Foster would put pressure on her daughter till he got his own way. She didn't want her working for a crook. He was probably involved in all sorts of dodgy deals. Not only could his businesses fold at any time if the police caught up with him, but she didn't want her daughter implicated if they did.

For years she had worked hard to provide for Candice, and she wanted the best for her. But now she felt as though she was slipping further and further away, and it was killing her.

She thought about her encounter with Pam three days ago and couldn't understand why she hadn't heard anything further. Surely there would have been a backlash from what she had told Pam.

But what if Pam had told Candice about everything including the trial and the events leading up to it? That would mean Candice now knew about Laura's involvement. Since Laura had tried to send Candice the link to the trial herself, she had thought better of it because she was worried about how her daughter would react. Did she know everything now? Was she keeping Laura at a distance because of it?

Deciding she needed to know, Laura sent a text to Candice:

I bumped into Pam last Wednesday. I was just wondering whether she has said anything to you.

Candice was quick to reply:

She hasn't been here for days. Said anything about what?

Shit! thought Laura, knowing her daughter wouldn't thank her for spelling it out. After a moment's thought, she texted back:

Nothing in particular, just that she'd seen me.

She didn't hear anything further from Candice after that and she was becoming increasingly worried. If Pam hadn't been round to Justin's house, then it must be because of what she had told her. But it was also apparent that she hadn't said anything to Candice, which left Laura with a dilemma.

As far as she was concerned, for as long as her daughter was staying under Justin's roof she was in peril. She couldn't get through to her about the danger she was in and now it seemed that Pam wasn't prepared to tell her either. That only left one course of action. She would challenge Justin herself. Sod the risk! It was worth taking if it meant she would protect her daughter.

Tempted as she was to confide in Trina, she decided against it. She knew her friend would try to talk her out of it. But Laura's mind was made up; tomorrow while Candice and Thomas were out, she would go round to the house in the hope of catching Justin alone.

60

On Sunday morning, Pam heard the chime of the doorbell and a tremor of fear pulsed through her. She peeped from behind the curtain, a habit she'd got into ever since she'd found out the devastating truth about the man she had been in a relationship with. To her dismay, there on the road in front of her house was Justin's car. Pam quickly ducked out of the way, desperately hoping he hadn't spotted her.

She was terrified of a confrontation and had been avoiding him for the past four days. The things Laura told her had shaken her to the core. There was no room in her life for someone like him. The mere thought that they had been together, and slept together, made her feel physically sick. And she was having difficulty coming to terms with what she had learnt.

Now she couldn't stand to see him. She had broken the news to him over the phone, merely saying the relationship wasn't working for her. Then she terminated the call. But Justin wasn't taking no for an answer. He wanted an explanation and he had plagued her with unwanted calls and texts.

All his messages had gone unanswered, and Pam had

naively hoped that he would eventually get bored and leave her alone. But the fact that he had turned up at her house told her he wasn't going to give up so easily.

She plonked herself down in the space behind the exterior wall of the living room, knowing he wouldn't be able to see her from there. A shadow passed over the window and she could sense his closeness. She visualised him cupping his hands above his eyes while he stared through the living room window trying to spot any trace of her.

When he shouted her name, she jumped in shock. 'Pam! I know you're in there. I want to talk to you. Can you open the door please and let me in?'

Pam felt a sense of panic, wondering if there was any sign of her presence. Her car was in the garage so that wouldn't give her away. With pounding heart, her eyes flitted across to the coffee table. Thank God she had cleared her mug away!

Pam knew now that he was calling her bluff. He didn't really know whether she was in or not. If she could just ignore him for long enough, he would hopefully go away. Then she heard the booming sound of his voice again.

'Come on, Pam. The least you can do is talk to me.' She could hear his tone of exasperation when he asked, 'What's this about?'

Then his voice changed again. He was now becoming annoyed. 'For God's sake, Pam! What *is* your problem?'

She heard him muttering angrily but couldn't pick out the words. Her heart was pounding now, and her gut was churning. *'Please go away!'* she kept muttering to herself. Then she heard the angry stomp of footsteps. They were becoming fainter, which told her he was moving away from the house.

Pam heaved a sigh of relief but stayed where she was. It was several seconds later when she heard the slamming of a car door then the thrumming of an engine. Still, she stayed there, not wanting to risk him catching a glimpse of her through his rear-view mirror.

She gave it a few minutes longer before she crawled out of her hiding place. Pam was shaking with fear, even though he had done nothing more than demand an explanation for their failed relationship. But it wasn't what he had done to her that had terrified her, it was the knowledge of what he could do.

Once Pam had found out about him, everything seemed to fit into place. She remembered the first time she had slept with him when, in the throes of passion, he had slapped her hard on the backside and tugged at her hair. Pam had been so horrified that she had pulled away from him and refused to stay the rest of the night.

But Justin had been so apologetic and had inundated her the following day with calls and texts. The day after, an expensive bunch of flowers had been delivered to her house. When she finally agreed to speak to him, he had explained that a lot of women enjoyed it and he hadn't wished to offend her.

The way he explained it made her feel like a prude and, in the end, she agreed to carry on seeing him provided he kept to her boundaries. There was no way she wanted a repeat of that performance which, deep down, she saw as unnatural.

He had kept to his word, but now she realised that he wouldn't have felt fulfilled in their relationship. A man who had the propensity to hurt a woman would be driven to do it again and again. And because she wasn't satisfying his perverse needs, he was probably going elsewhere to carry out his weird fantasies. From what Laura had told her, it didn't matter to him whether the woman was a willing party or not.

But what about Candice? Didn't she deserve to know the type of man whose roof she was living under? Her mother had obviously thought so when she had begged Pam to tell Candice about Justin because Candice wouldn't listen to her. What if Laura had still not been able to get through to Candice?

Pam had been wrestling with her conscience for days, telling herself that it was best not to get involved. Maybe it was the terror of hearing him at her door that made her realise how selfish she had been. And now she realised that she had to do something.

Candice was a lovely young woman, and she would never forgive herself if any harm came to her. She had to warn her. So, she fumbled inside her handbag until her shaking hands felt the cold hard glass of her mobile phone. Then she pulled it out and called Candice's number.

61

Laura waited until three o'clock on Sunday afternoon, confident that by then Candice and Thomas would have left for Manchester and, hopefully, Justin Foster would be home alone. She was terrified at the prospect of facing him. But she was also angry. And it was her anger that was pushing her to behave so recklessly.

This man had tried to destroy her, with his ruthless campaign to terrorise her staff and vandalise her businesses. And now he was stealing her daughter and doing his best to turn Candice against her. But he wouldn't get away with it. Because today she was going to give him an ultimatum. Either he got Thomas to break up with Candice and sent her home, or the world would find out just what sort of a man he was.

When Laura pulled up outside his house she was tempted to turn around and go back home. She was so nervous that her hands were clammy on the steering wheel and her mouth was dry. She'd been nervous the last time she'd come here too, desperate to make a good impression in front of Thomas's father. But the nerves she felt now far outweighed anything she had felt before. Because now she knew who he was.

After he had been safely locked up behind bars years previously, Laura had been relieved, thinking that she would never again set eyes on him. The attack had haunted her for years even after she'd turned her back on her life of prostitution. And yet here she was, visiting him in his own home for the second time.

She crept tentatively up the garden path, her heart thundering inside her ribcage. All the while she was willing herself to go through with it. She had to. It was her duty to protect her daughter as well as her businesses.

Laura rang the bell and waited for him to answer. When she heard his footsteps coming down the hall, she thought her heart would burst out of her chest, it was beating so frantically. But then she took a deep breath, squared her shoulders, and prepared herself to face her nemesis.

When he answered the door and saw Laura standing there, he laughed raucously. 'Well, well, to what do I owe the pleasure?'

Laura tried not to let him wind her up as she came straight to the point. 'Can I have a word please? It's about Candice.'

He stood back and waved his hand with a flourish, being overly dramatic as though taunting her. 'Come through.'

Laura went straight to the lounge and waited for him to follow her. She listened for signs of other people inside the house but heard nothing. 'We're alone,' he said, reading her mind, and even though Laura had planned to tackle him alone, hearing him say the word sent a fresh shiver of fear down her spine.

She took a deep breath. 'Good. That means I'll be able to say what I need to say.'

'Go ahead.' He held his hand out towards the sofa, indicating that she should take a seat.

'No thanks, I'd prefer to stand.' Then she moved nearer the window so she was in full view of anyone who might happen to pass by.

'Tell me…' she said, 'was Thomas involved in the vendetta against me?'

'That would be telling, wouldn't it?' he said, tormenting her.

'I think you should encourage Candice to return home,' she said.

He laughed again. 'Do you now?'

'Yes, I do.' Laura could feel her stomach muscles tense as she tackled him. 'It's obvious you're trying to turn her against me. I have a good relationship with my daughter, and I don't want you ruining it.'

'It's a bit late for that,' he said. 'From what she's been saying about you lately, she doesn't think very much of you at all. And she did leave your home of her own accord, didn't she?'

Laura was surprised that Candice had confided in him to that extent, but she tried not to show it. He smiled slyly and she fought to hold it together. 'That's because you're poisoning her against me. She'd think very differently if she knew you were the one behind the attacks on the shops and my staff, wouldn't she?'

'It's a pity for you that she doesn't believe you then, isn't it?'

'She doesn't believe that Thomas is involved but I haven't told her about you yet.'

'Why not, if you're so convinced that she'll accept it?'

Laura thought about how unapproachable her daughter had been since she'd tried to suggest that Thomas might have been involved in the attacks. She knew she'd been tiptoeing around Candice, afraid of upsetting her more and afraid that if she told her about Justin the whole truth would spill out.

Laura didn't want Candice to know the part she had played in past events. If she should ever find out, she might turn against her altogether. And Laura couldn't bear the thought of never seeing her daughter again.

He continued to goad her. 'Because, deep down, you know that your own daughter wouldn't believe you. And why should she? After all, I'm a respectable businessman who has always treated her fairly. My son is educated and has had a good upbringing. And then there's you: a reformed drug addict and prostitute.

'No wonder she didn't believe what you told her about Thomas. And that's before you begin to look at the facts as she sees them. As far as your daughter is concerned, Milo Swain was at the root of the vendetta. And since his death there have been no further attacks, which makes it more convincing, doesn't it?'

He smiled arrogantly and Laura's nerves became buried in a mass of seething anger. 'Oh, you think you're so bloody clever, don't you? Well, you won't be feeling so smug when everyone finds out who you really are. I bet your employees and customers don't know about your prison record, do they?'

'Don't bother threatening me. I mean, who's going to believe the word of a cheap tart? Your daughter didn't, so why would anybody else?'

Laura was so angry by now that she knew she'd have to play her trump card heedless of the consequences. 'Because there are news articles relating to your trial. I could easily send a news clip to Candice. She might be so blinded by your son's charms that she can't see what a conniving pair of bastards you really are! But she will do, in time. And if you're not willing to tell me whether Thomas is involved, then I can only assume he is. And, in that case, I want her as far away from the pair of you as possible.'

To Laura's consternation, it was as though he had read her thoughts when he said, 'But you won't send the news clip, will you? Because you're frightened of her finding out the part you played. And, believe me, I'd make sure she knew,' he threatened, taking a menacing step towards her.

'I don't care anymore. I just want her safely away from you.'

She realised she had slipped up in mentioning the news item. He had guessed at her reluctance to share it with her daughter up to now, and he knew why.

Laura was about to leave his home. She had wasted her time coming here and knew she would have to do things the hard way now. It would break Candice's heart to find out everything and she probably wouldn't thank her for it. But she had no choice.

'Hang on a minute,' he said before she had chance to get away. 'You met Pam at the engagement dinner, didn't you? That means you would recognise her if you were to bump into her. Or maybe your daughter told you a little more, and it gave you enough information to track her down.'

Laura knew what was coming. She could see the look of recognition on his face before he added, 'It was you, wasn't it? You dirty fuckin' whore! You told Pam about me, didn't you? That's why she won't see me.'

Laura felt a surge of intense fear. She could tell how angry he was as he stepped towards her. She stiffened, expecting him to attack but, to her surprise, he walked round her. She realised what he was doing when she heard the loud swish of the curtains being shut. It was so nobody could see what he was about to do.

Then she ran.

62

Thomas cursed the traffic as he made his way back from the city centre. He could have done without this on a Sunday afternoon. But he had promised to drop Candice off, and he didn't like to break his promise.

He had been due to meet Candice's friends with her for afternoon tea. But, because of the rift within the group, Emma and Alicia were the only two going. Thomas didn't really want to be the only guy in a group with three girls. After giving it some thought, he had suggested to Candice that she go without him but had agreed to drop her off. And now, as he neared home, he was looking forward to watching some sport on TV, maybe with his dad if he was in.

Laura made it to the hallway. She could sense him gaining on her and then she felt his hot breath on the back of her neck before he grabbed the collar of her coat. It was unbuttoned, so she quickly wriggled out of it and raced to the door.

She scrabbled at the bunch of keys hanging out of the keyhole, desperate to escape. But as soon as she clasped them and tried to open the lock, he caught up with her. One hand was clamped around her mouth, the other clawing at her hand as he fought her for the keys.

He managed to pull the keys out and they crashed to the ground. Laura bent to retrieve them. But he pounced on her, dragging her along the floor and away from the door. Then he pinned her down, punching at her face and body till blood spurted from her nose.

Laura squealed with pain but tried to fight back as he lowered his hand and tried to unfasten the belt on her trousers. 'No!' she yelled, anticipating another savage rape, and pushing his hands away.

'Oh yeah. If you thought last time was bad, then you've seen nothing yet. And I'm gonna enjoy every fuckin' minute of it!'

Those same feelings came rushing back to Laura. Dread. Fear. Repulsion. And she knew she couldn't go through that again. Using all her force, she raised her knee and managed to connect.

'Aw, you fuckin' bitch!' he yelled, clutching his testicles.

She tried to throw him off her but, despite his pain, he remained there. Laura knew that as soon as he recovered, he would resume his attempts. Giving him a mighty shove, she tried to escape. She was halfway there, with only her legs stuck underneath his bulk when she felt the weight of his fist in her face again.

Laura screamed and scratched and kicked. But she couldn't break free. Amidst the cacophony of her screeching and his shouting, she didn't hear the front door opening. And the first she knew of Thomas's presence was when he shouted above the din.

'For God's sake, Father! What the hell is going on?'

Appearing shocked, Justin quickly got up and turned to face his son. At last Laura was free. She prised herself off the hallway floor and stood unsteadily then wiped her hand under her nose to stem the blood spillage. Thomas stared, astonished, at the crimson mess that sullied her face.

'Don't pretend you don't know what he's like!' she yelled. 'You knew he'd served time. Candice told me.'

The ordeal had angered Laura and, regardless of the ongoing danger, she demanded answers. 'Why did you fuckin' lie to her and tell her it was because he dealt in cannabis? You knew what he'd really done…'

'Hang on,' Thomas cut in. 'What on earth are you talking about? I don't know anything more than that.'

'Stop lying, Thomas. I know you're in on it with him. You've been helping him by wrecking my shops. Then you both set this whole thing up to reel Candice in. Do you realise how much she fuckin' loves you? It'll break her heart when she finds out you were just using her.'

'I'm not using her!'

Laura was so angry and distressed that she didn't pick up on his body language. 'Stop it! Stop it!' she yelled. 'Just tell the fuckin' truth for God's sake. You're as despicable as him.'

She looked at Justin who was staring wildly back at her. 'Take no notice of her, Thomas. She's a cracked-up junkie. She's off her head, doesn't know what she's doing. I let her in the house thinking it was a social visit then she goes and bloody attacks me. I had to defend myself.'

'You believe what you want,' she screamed at Thomas, rushing past him till she had almost reached the door. 'But don't go spinning your lies to Candice about cannabis dealing and your mother dying of a fuckin' heart attack. We all know she topped herself because of the shame.'

Still desperate to break free, she dashed through the door, leaving Thomas with his mouth agape and Justin with a lot of explaining to do. It wasn't until she was on her way home and was beginning to calm down that she realised something: Thomas had genuinely been shocked when she had mentioned his mother's suicide.

All the time she had assumed that Thomas had been lying to Candice. But what if it had been Justin who had fed him the lie and Thomas had only been repeating what he had been told? If that was the case, then it was a dreadful way to find out and she felt terrible for breaking the news to him like that.

But it also meant that Thomas might have been unaware of his father's vendetta. In fact, Thomas might have had no involvement whatsoever in any of his father's dirty dealings.

63

When Laura reached home, she did her best to clean up her face. She wiped the blood away with a damp cloth but there was still a bruise under her eye and signs of swelling. She hadn't been home long when she heard somebody at the front door. Still reeling from her experience at Justin's house, her adrenalin began pumping fiercely around her body and her ears pricked up.

The next thing she heard was the sound of footsteps in the hallway. Her heart was pounding, and her first impulse was to escape. Maybe Justin had come to finish the job off. But before she could figure out how to get away, the footsteps became louder. They were outside the living room door now. Her heart seemed to stop beating as she waited for the inevitable.

And then Candice walked in.

'Jesus Christ!' said Laura with her hand over her heart. 'You scared the bloody life out of me.'

'Sorry,' said Candice, sitting down on the sofa. Then, looking more intently at her mother, she said, 'Oh my God! What's happened to your face?'

'Never mind that,' said Laura, 'what's happened to you? Why are you home?'

'Thanks, that's a lovely greeting.'

'You know what I mean, Candice.'

Her daughter looked shamefaced. 'You were right... about Thomas and his dad. Pam rang me while I was in Manchester. That's why I've come straight home. I can't face seeing Thomas right now.'

As she spoke her voice trembled and Laura went straight over and put her arm around her, stroking her back. 'Aw, love. I'm so sorry you had to hear that.'

'It's not your fault,' said Candice, calmer now. 'Pam said you showed her something that proves what sort of a man Justin is, but she wouldn't tell me what it was. She said you needed to tell me yourself. What is it, Mum?'

Laura knew it was time to tell her everything. Candice deserved to know the truth even if it meant Laura would have to deal with the consequences.

'Well, for a start,' she said. 'There's a chance Thomas might not be involved with any of it.'

Candice's face brightened a little. 'Why?'

'It was his lies that made me suspect him, but it wasn't his fault the story he told you was wrong. His mother didn't die of a heart attack.' She paused a moment then took a breath before adding, 'She committed suicide because of what Justin had done.'

When Candice's jaw fell open, Laura said, 'I saw Thomas at the house earlier when I had a confrontation with his father. I thought Thomas had lied to you about his mother, and about the reason his father was banged up, but when I had a go at him about it, he looked just as shocked as you are now. That was when I realised that he might not have been lying. Perhaps he'd just been telling the lies Justin fed him.'

'Is that how you got the marks on your face?'

Laura lowered her voice. 'Yes, Justin did it. I went to see him, hoping I could persuade him to send you home. I was desperate and I couldn't stand the thought of you living in a house with such a dangerous man.'

'Aw, Mum,' said Candice. 'I'm so sorry. I didn't realise how bad Justin was, honestly. And I'm sorry for not believing you.'

Laura shrugged. 'That's understandable. After all you'd been through in the past, I suppose it would be only natural for you to assume I was on the drugs again, but I'm not. And you were right for not wanting to hear bad of Thomas. I think he's probably another innocent victim in this whole bloody mess.'

Candice didn't seem to want to discuss Thomas, and Laura understood that it would be difficult for her to get her head around it all. Instead, she asked, 'What did Justin do that was so bad that Thomas's mum committed suicide?'

Laura took another deep breath. Then, slowly, trying to remain detached, she detailed the attack that had taken place in that hotel room all those years ago.

Then she added, 'The other lie Justin had fed to Thomas was about why he was put in prison.'

Candice was staring at her, inquisitively, digesting her every word in her eagerness to get to the truth.

'He told you his father was imprisoned for dealing in cannabis. But he wasn't.'

'Was it because of the attack?'

Laura shook her head. 'No. Unfortunately I couldn't prove it. But Justin did something else after that. And what I showed Pam was a news clip about the trial. I just hope that you'll be able to forgive me when I tell you what it was.'

64

Laura tried to steady herself as she prepared to continue with her story.

'After the attack from Justin Foster, I'd had enough. I was sick of the abusive treatment by clients. That's why I took his credit cards and cash. I went on a bit of a spree, and it felt good knowing I was getting one up on the bastard who had attacked me so viciously. What I didn't realise when I took his things was that there was also a list of names. I kept it with me 'cos I thought it might come in useful.

'I was high on drugs and booze most of the time in those days, and I was still grieving the loss of your father. I wasn't in my right mind for a while. Then I had to appear in court for soliciting. I couldn't believe it when I recognised the judge. He was only one of my bloody clients, wasn't he?

'I was even more surprised when he gave me a backhander so that I wouldn't tell anyone about his secret life. I took it as well. That's what I was like back then. I'd have done anything to get my next fix.'

She stopped and looked nervously at her daughter, fearing her judgement, but Candice's expression was giving nothing away. Taking a deep breath, Laura continued, avoiding eye contact while she spoke.

'Anyway, that set me thinking that maybe other clients would pay me for my silence. So, I set out on a mission to rob and blackmail them. I was trying to get my revenge for what they'd put me through. I carried on working the beat for a while, but I had a plan. I hated that life, so I started putting the money away until I had enough to go into rehab. Once I was clean, Trina lent me the money to set myself up in business.

'I regret what I did in a way, but those men deserved it. They were the very worst clients: the nasty ones, the perverts, and the weirdos. I suppose I was doing it for all those girls who had suffered at their hands. But I was also doing it so that we could have a better future. I wanted to come off the beat and for you to be proud of me.'

She made eye contact with Candice again, relieved when she gave her a nod of encouragement.

'Unfortunately, I didn't realise just how vindictive Justin Foster was or how badly he wanted that list of names. It was a list of all the lowlifes he dealt with: drug dealers, addicts, bully boys and even a bent copper. He and his bunch of criminals were involved in bringing drugs into the country and then distributing them. And we're not just talking cannabis either.

'But that wasn't what he was sent down for. Unfortunately, the courts couldn't prove all the counts against him. There was one crime they could prove though because he was caught in the act, thanks to me. And I'd do it again because what he did was horrendous.'

Laura's voice was shaking now and her heart was beating rapidly. She knew that she was about to uncover the most traumatic part of the story, and she hoped to God that Candice wouldn't hold it against her.

'When you didn't return from school that afternoon, I just knew there was something badly wrong. It didn't take me long to find out that Justin Foster was behind it. He'd been trying to track me down ever since he'd found out I'd stolen his money and the list of names.

'It took me a whole two days and nights before I found you in a mangy old barn full of bloody rats and insects.

'I hardly recognised you when I found you. All your clothes were filthy, and you looked manky. You looked really skinny and frail too, maybe because they'd let you go hungry or maybe you looked drawn because of the stress of it all. You were in a right state, and it took months of counselling to get you right. You probably remember going to see Mrs Thompson every week.'

Candice nodded again, but now Laura could see tears in her eyes.

'Justin had got his bully boys to grab you off the street then keep you in that bloody dirty barn with just a bit of food and water. The only time you came into contact with him was when I tried to escape with you. You might remember three men turning up in a four-by-four. But you were either hidden behind me or inside my car, so it doesn't surprise me that you didn't recognise him. We tried to escape while they were shooting at us, and I think that with everything that was going on the last thing on your mind would have been to look at the three men inside that car.'

By the time she had finished her tale, Laura was trembling. 'I'm so sorry, love. If I hadn't taken his things to get back at him then he wouldn't have retaliated by kidnapping you.'

She looked at Candice, willing her to speak, but she was in a state of stunned silence and the tears were streaming down her face. While she waited, Laura took a sip of the glass of water standing on the coffee table and tried to compose herself.

It was a while before Candice spoke. Then she asked, 'Are you going to report him for what he did today?'

'There's no point. I've got no proof. He told Thomas he did it in self-defence because I came to the house and attacked him. He would only tell the police the same thing and they'd probably believe him because they knew how desperate I was to get you away from him. You see, I'd already rung them, but they wouldn't take me seriously.'

Candice nodded. Then she said solemnly, 'I can't believe Thomas's dad was my kidnapper. You should have told me!'

'I know, but it's not an easy thing to tell.'

Candice shook her head but didn't say anything more. Instead, she stood up and walked straight out of the room and up the stairs where Laura assumed she had gone into her own bedroom. She had expected her to be upset. After all, it was an awful lot to take in.

Candice must be feeling a whole range of emotions. Shock. Bitterness. Anger. And Laura realised that the best thing to do now was to give her some space so that she could come to terms with it all.

65

'What the hell has been going on, Dad?' Thomas demanded as soon as Laura was out of the house.

'Well, I opened the door, and the woman was like a screaming banshee, demanding that I get you to finish with Candice. Bloody hell, I can see why Candice left home now. The woman is deranged. I'm sorry I had to hit her, son, but it was the only way I could control her. She had her hands round my throat.' He ran his fingers along his neck to emphasise his words.

'And what about what she said? Did Mum really commit suicide?'

Justin had to think fast. If he lied to him, he knew his son could easily check the Internet. Thomas had never previously had cause to check the facts, but that was before that bloody whore had started spilling her vitriol.

'I'm really sorry, son.' As he spoke, he forced himself to look contrite, hanging his head low and adopting a pained expression. 'Me and your grandparents we… we… we were trying to protect you. We decided that we didn't want you and your sister thinking of your mother as a woman who was weak enough to commit such a selfish act, so we came up with the story about the heart attack.'

'Who did? Whose fuckin' idea was it?'

'Well, all of us really. I – I think it was your grandfather who suggested it. But we all agreed. We thought it was for the best. Much better for you to think of her death as natural causes than…'

Thomas cut in, angrily, before he could finish. 'And what did you do that made her so ashamed?'

Justin knew he couldn't afford to tell him the truth this time. Thomas would never forgive him if he knew about the kidnap of his fiancée. He'd have to take the chance of sticking to the same story. 'Oh, she lied about that. It *was* cannabis. The woman isn't right in the head.'

Thomas stared at him. He could tell his son's face was full of doubt, so he quickly said, 'Look, I know this has all been a shock. I'm really sorry for what I did in the past. And the fact that it was only a mild drug doesn't make it any better. I still broke the law and I hold my hands up to that. Your mother obviously couldn't take the shame of me being locked up. I've regretted it every day since. I'm so sorry, son, and if there was anything I could do to make it up to you, I would.'

Thomas still didn't say anything, but his expression remained stern.

'Why don't you sit down?' asked Justin. 'I'll grab us both a beer from the fridge and we can watch a bit of sport, take our minds off things.'

'Do you really think I'm in the mood to sit watching TV after all that?' asked Thomas.

The conversation was interrupted by the bleeping of Thomas's phone. He pulled it from his pocket and looked at the screen. His facial expression changed again, his eyebrows furrowing as he read the message.

'What is it, son? What's happened?'

Thomas spoke slowly and Justin sensed from his tone that he was trying to hold himself together. 'It's Candice. Apparently, she doesn't want to see me anymore. It's because of the vendetta against her mum's shops. What the hell is she talking about?'

'You're joking!' said Justin. 'It'll be her bitch of a mother trying to poison her against you. Why on earth would you be involved with the vendetta? That's ridiculous!'

'But why? She was fine with Candice seeing me before.'

'Because she was losing control over her daughter and couldn't handle it.'

Thomas nodded. 'I'm ringing her,' he said, and he made the call so quickly that Justin didn't have chance to talk him out of it. But it rang out unanswered. 'I'm going round there.'

'No, don't do that!' said Justin, worried that if he saw Laura, she would tell him everything.

'Why not?'

'Well, look what happened just now. I think her mother's a very dangerous woman, son. You could be walking into anything. Perhaps it's better to leave it a bit, let Candice calm down and then tackle her. It's obvious that whatever lies her mother has been telling have left Candice terribly upset. She'll come round; you'll see. I know how much she thinks of you.'

Thomas frowned but Justin could tell he was mulling over his words. Then he sighed and announced. 'I'm going out.' When Justin looked at him, alarmed, he added, 'Don't worry. I'm not going round there. I'm just pissed off. I'll probably call for Jamie and go for a pint.'

Once he had gone, Justin poured a drink for himself. He needed one after all that. It had been a close shave, and in a way, it was good that Candice wasn't speaking to Thomas. Her mother had obviously said something to her, and his worry was that Candice might convince Thomas that her mother had been telling the truth.

As he sat there knocking back beer, his thoughts eventually turned to Pam. He was missing her and wanted things to be right between them again. He knew that the only way that would happen was if he could convince her that Laura had been lying. That damn woman wouldn't be happy until she had turned everyone against him, and he knew he had to somehow turn things around. He had to convince them that she was the one lying, not him.

Knowing Pam would ignore his calls, he was tempted to go round there now. But he'd already had a drink, so he'd have to leave it till after work tomorrow. But he was determined that when he did call round, he'd make sure he brought Pam round to his way of thinking.

It was Monday and Thomas had had a rough day at work. He'd stayed out far too late on Sunday evening trying to drown his sorrows after everything that had taken place that day. Then he'd stayed at his friend Jamie's house and gone straight to work from there. After filling Jamie in on some of what had happened, his friend had invited Thomas to stay with him for as long as necessary.

He'd hardly been able to concentrate at work that day. Not only did he have the hangover from hell, but he also couldn't stop everything from whirling around inside his thumping head. First there had been the shock of seeing his dad grappling with Candice's mum on the hallway floor, then the revelation that his dad had lied about his mother committing suicide and then the callous way Candice had finished with him by text message and refused to speak to him.

Something was going on, but he wasn't sure exactly what. He felt at odds with his father now. Things didn't add up somehow. If he had lied about something as big as his mother's death, then maybe he had lied about the reason he had served time too. And maybe Laura was right. He knew that the only way he could get to the bottom of everything would be to visit Candice, so he went straight to her home after work.

'I hope you don't mind me calling round,' he said tentatively when Laura answered the front door. 'I wondered if I could have a word with Candice, please.'

'You'd better come in,' said Laura, leading him into the living room. 'Before you speak to Candice, I just wanted to say that I'm sorry for breaking the news about your mother's suicide to you like that. I honestly thought you knew.'

Thomas nodded but didn't say anything. He could hardly respond that it was alright, could he?

'I need to let you know that Candice hasn't been herself since yesterday,' Laura continued. 'You see, I told her a lot of things, and she's finding it hard to deal with.'

'What things? I don't understand. Why would you

suddenly come to see my dad? He says you attacked him, and then there was all that stuff about me wrecking your shops. I'd never do anything like that. You didn't really think that, did you?'

Laura smiled wryly. 'I did, but I don't anymore.'

Thomas was still confused. 'Is that why Candice doesn't want to see me? Does she think I wrecked the shops too? Why? I don't understand why you would both think that.'

'I think she's just confused after everything I told her. There's a lot you don't know, Thomas. But I think it's about time you knew the truth. I must warn you though, you're going to be just as shocked as Candice was. She's still coming to terms with everything I told her. But if you'd like to sit down, I'll make us a drink then I'll go and get Candice and we can talk.'

66

Although Pam knew Justin was keen to get back with her, she wasn't expecting two visits in as many days. She was therefore a little more relaxed than she should have been, and despite it being early evening, she still hadn't drawn the curtains. Neither did she hear the sound of a car pulling up outside her house as she sat watching TV.

The first Pam knew of Justin's arrival was when he appeared outside her living room window. She jumped at the sight of him, making her spill a little of her coffee over herself. For a moment she deliberated over what to do. But then she realised that now he knew she was at home, he wasn't going to go away without speaking to her.

The familiar sight of him made her more complacent. This was the man she had been so close to in every respect. And in all the time she had been seeing him, he had never physically hurt her apart from that one occasion at the beginning of the relationship when she had put him straight about her boundaries. Maybe it was best to speak to him. Then perhaps he would get the message and leave her alone.

She went to the front door and let him inside. There was no way she was going to discuss private business on the doorstep. Once they were in the living room, she offered him a drink and invited him to take a seat.

Pam went through to the kitchen to make him a coffee and was surprised when she turned round to see him standing next to her. 'Why, Pam? Why did you end it?'

'I was going to tell you once I'd made you a drink.'

'Sod the drink! Tell me now. I want to know.'

She noticed a glint of menace in his eye that she'd never seen before, and fear clutched at her insides. She had to tell him. There was no way out of this now. She just hoped he'd accept it.

'I... I bumped into Laura in Altrincham,' she began nervously. Justin raised his eyebrows, and she continued, cautiously. 'She wanted to talk. I thought it was about Candice because she seemed upset about her leaving. So... so we went for a coffee.'

'I might have known she was involved. The woman's deranged!'

'I was shocked by what she told me, Justin.'

'What? What did she tell you?' he demanded.

'About you being behind the vendetta against her because of what happened in the past.'

'Oh, for God's sake! Not that again. Y'know, she's even got into Candice's head. The girl rang Thomas today to say she doesn't want to see him anymore. The poor lad's done nothing wrong. He thought the world of that girl, despite her upbringing.'

Pam knew she had to deflect him from his rant, so she spoke up. 'That's not all she told me, Justin. She said you attacked her years ago.'

'Me? Attacked her? Why on earth would I want to do that? I didn't even know her before the engagement dinner! The woman's a fantasist.'

'Oh, I think you did, Justin. You visited her when she was a prostitute and that's when the attack took place.'

'Are you serious? Would you honestly believe the word of someone like that over me?'

Pam could tell he was becoming increasingly irate. But she had to see this through, get everything out in the open. She knew he wouldn't take no for an answer until he knew why she had ended the relationship. In a way she was sorry she had let him inside the house, but once she had said what she needed to say she would ask him to leave. And that would be the end of that.

'I didn't believe her until she showed me the link to a news article from years ago.'

Pam saw his face pale. She already knew Laura had been right although she had still been struggling to accept it. But his expression confirmed her worst fears.

'You kidnapped Candice, didn't you?'

'Rubbish! Why would you believe that?'

'It was your name in the article: Justin Foster.'

'She's obviously found somebody with the same name and decided to use it to her advantage. It wouldn't surprise me if she's told her daughter the same tale.'

'No, I don't think she's told Candice yet, Justin. But I told her that you were behind the vendetta against her mother.'

'You what?' he yelled. 'So, you believe the word of a fuckin' whore over mine? I'm the man who loves you. I spoilt you rotten, even wanted to marry you. And this is how you repay me? By conspiring with a fuckin' lowlife drugged-up prostitute!'

Pam could see the mounting rage in him now and decided not to say anything more. His eyes were bulging, the tendons in his neck were protruding, and his complexion was ruddy. She noticed the sheen of perspiration that covered his face, and the way spittle flew from his mouth as he yelled at her.

'You fuckin' traitorous bitch! After all I've done for you.'

Pam tried to cower away, but she was trapped between him and the granite work surface behind her. She thought of slipping to the side and freeing herself from him. Then she could make her way to the front door and hold it wide open while she asked him to leave.

But before she had the chance, she felt the weight of his hand as it grasped the left side of her face.

'Please Justin, no,' she begged.

But he carried on relentlessly, smashing her head against the worktop. Her back arched uncomfortably and her arms flailed around, trying to steady herself as her feet slid beneath her.

His hand remained fast as he smashed her head again. And again. Her legs buckled with the force of it. There was an intense pain in the back of her head. It felt like it was going to explode. She slipped towards the ground. Then she hit the floor with a thud.

Laura was dreading telling Thomas everything. It had been bad enough telling her daughter. Since then, Candice had stayed up in her room for most of the time and hardly spoken to anybody, including her and Thomas. And Laura realised that she must be feeling betrayed by those closest to her.

She went through to the kitchen and flipped on the kettle with shaking hands. Then she made a drink for each of them, including Candice. She set the drinks down on the coffee table in the lounge and said to Thomas, 'I'll just go up and get her.'

She found Candice lying on her bed, and she could tell she'd been crying. 'Candice,' she whispered softly. 'Thomas is here. He's very confused. I think we both need to speak to him. Will you come down?'

Candice agreed more readily than she thought she would. Her daughter followed her down the stairs and when Laura took a seat in the lounge opposite Thomas, Candice took the other armchair. Laura tried to ignore the way Candice eyed Thomas warily as she said, 'I think Thomas is as much in the dark as you were, love. So, first of all, I want to tell him everything that's happened. He deserves to know.'

Candice nodded but remained silent. Then Laura cleared her throat and began speaking. She told Thomas everything she had told Candice the day before, from the attack at the hands of his father several years prior, to her subsequent revenge mission, and then on to his father's kidnap of Candice and the fact that he was behind the recent vendetta against her.

Thomas looked shocked when she mentioned the kidnap, so she showed him the news article as she had done with Pam and Candice. 'I know it's a lot to take in,' said Laura as she looked at the tears in his eyes.'

'I can't believe it,' he said. 'I knew Dad had done some bad stuff, but I never thought he'd do anything like this!

And I can't believe how he and my grandparents lied to me and my sister about my mum's death.'

'To be fair to them, I think they were trying to protect you,' said Laura. 'It was probably easier for you to accept that she had died of a heart attack than the real reason would have been.'

He sat in stunned silence for a while, and it was Candice who spoke next. 'I'm sorry, Thomas. When Pam told me about everything, I thought you were involved too.'

'Is that why you didn't want to see me?' he asked, with tears running down his face.

'At first, yes. But then when Mum said you might be innocent, well, I just needed some space. I needed to process it all. It was such a shock.'

'You should know me by now, Candice. Although, to be fair, who could blame you for thinking badly of me with a dad like mine? I still can't get my head around what he's done.' He turned and looked at Laura. 'Do you really think he was behind the attacks on your shops?'

'Yes,' said Laura. 'He told me he'd employed Milo Swain to carry out the attacks.'

'Shit!' muttered Thomas, burying his head in his hands.

Candice raced over to the sofa, plonked herself next to him and then wrapped her arms around him. 'I'm so sorry,' she repeated and for a few moments they both cried in each other's arms.

Laura had a lump in her throat. She really felt for them. It was awful for such a lovely young couple to have gone through so much. She decided to leave the room to give them a bit of time but as she stood up to go, Candice raised her head and addressed her.

'Mum, I just want to say that I'm sorry for how I've been with you since yesterday too.'

'That's understandable, love. You were bound to be upset about things.'

'I know, but I don't really blame you for Justin kidnapping me.' As she spoke the words, Laura noticed Thomas flinch and her heart went out to him. Candice carried on speaking, 'You told me why Justin had kidnapped me for my sake. Because you wanted to be honest about everything so that I'd understand why Justin was behind the vendetta. And you did that for me even though you risked me going against you.'

Laura smiled wryly and Candice said, 'When you took revenge on Justin, you weren't to know that he would do something like that, were you?'

'No, of course not.'

Then Thomas looked up at Candice. 'But I can't understand it, Candice. Why would you stop seeing me when your mum had explained that I couldn't have been involved?'

'I was just in shock, and I hadn't heard the full story at first, not when Pam told me.'

'Hang on. Pam told you?'

'Yes, I told Pam,' said Laura. 'Although, she didn't tell Candice about Justin being responsible for the kidnap, just about all the other stuff.'

'Does my dad know Pam told you?' Thomas asked Candice.

As soon as he spoke, Laura knew what was on his mind, and she could have kicked herself for not thinking of it sooner. Now that Justin knew she had told Pam all about his past, would she be safe?

Thomas mirrored her thoughts when he said, 'I think we should call the police and tell them everything that's happened. I know he's my dad, but the police need to know.'

67

DI Carson and DS Worrall were on their way to the home of Justin Foster. They had sat in astonishment in Laura Sharples' lounge while she brought them up to date with everything. Her daughter and her daughter's boyfriend had occasionally chipped in to give more detail. Now the DI just wanted to get round to Foster's house as soon as possible.

'Quick as you can,' he said to his sergeant as he slid into the passenger seat next to him. 'We need to get hold of this man before he does anything else. If what they say is true, then the girlfriend could be in grave danger.'

They made it to Justin Foster's house in record time but, to DI Carson's dismay, there was no sign of anyone inside the house when they arrived.

'What now?' asked the detective sergeant. 'The girlfriend?'

'Yes, quickly.'

Thomas Foster had already given them the address, so it didn't take long before they were on their way. DI Carson had a bad feeling about this. He wasn't familiar with the case from nine years ago but judging by what the witnesses had said the man sounded like a nasty piece of stuff with a penchant for attacking women.

Ten minutes later they arrived at the home of Pam Springer in Sale, a suburb of Manchester not far from Altrincham. There was a car on the drive and as DI Carson hammered on the front door his sergeant rushed to the window.

'There's no sign of anyone in there, sir, but the TV is on and there's a half-empty mug on the table.'

'OK, give it a couple of minutes. She might be in the bathroom,' DI Carson said, pressing the doorbell then hammering on the door again.

But it soon became evident that they weren't going to get a reply and the inspector's feeling of disquiet intensified.

'Should I try round the back, sir?' asked DS Worrall.

'Yes, come on.'

The DI led the way. There was a path down the side of the house. He followed it round to the back door and tried the handle. But it was locked. Before DS Worrall had chance to quiz him on their next move, he walked to the window, and the sergeant followed.

'Jesus!' he said on seeing the body of a woman on the floor. Then he shouted to his sergeant. 'Get the door open!'

DS Worrall ran to the back door and rammed it with his shoulder. It took a few attempts before the wood finally started to give. Carson helped him give it one last shove and, after pulling away the shards of wood that criss-crossed from one side of the lock mechanism to the other, they pushed their way in and dashed through to the kitchen.

The body was sprawled on the floor at a strange angle with its legs bent underneath the torso and the battered head cocked to one side. Judging by the angle DI Carson guessed that she must have gone down like a sack of spuds.

And he also surmised that her fall must have followed a bash on the head.

He stepped closer to examine the body. Her head had one side caved in and was covered in blood, which had also flowed onto the kitchen floor. But strangely, it was the underside of her head that was battered. The scarlet pool was beginning to set, telling him she had been there for some time. It was also punctuated by skid marks where her feet must have slipped as she went down. That meant the floor must have already been soaked with it.

DI Carson bent over to get a better look at that side of her head. It hovered several inches from the floor, propped up by her shoulders with her torso and arms folded underneath. Even with his experience the sight made him flinch. He deduced that it must have been a savage blow or number of blows that had felled her, as he could see splinters of bone poking out through the gaping wound.

He straightened up and noticed the state of the worktop. It was caked in blood. A closer examination told him that there were also tiny fragments of bone embedded in the viscous matter. That was when he realised that she hadn't been bashed on her head. No. Whoever had done this had used her head like a battering ram against the granite surface.

'Bastard!' he cursed.

Carson had no doubt that she was dead, and he signalled to the DS to stand back. He needed to preserve the crime scene, so he took a few paces away from the body where he carried on surveying the scene for any other clues. Taking his phone out, he began tapping buttons while he said to DS Worrall, 'I want you round at Justin Foster's home to see if he's back yet. Call for backup and don't go in till they arrive. He's obviously a dangerous man.'

He could hear a voice on the other end of the phone, but he finished instructing the DS before he switched his attention to the caller. 'I'll wait here for the pathologist to arrive.'

'OK, sir. I presume you want him brought in for questioning.'

'No, I don't. I want the bastard arrested! And I'll organise a search of his home and business premises while I'm waiting for the pathologist. I have a feeling this isn't the only murder he's committed. So, let's be clear on this, we're looking for something that connects him to the murders of Pam Springer and Milo Swain. I'll catch up with you once I've finished here.'

Over an hour later, DS Worrall looked across at the man seated in front of him in the interrogation room: Justin Foster. The man was broken. Devastated! Because he'd brutally killed the woman he loved in a fit of temper.

When he and a team of officers had raced round to the home of Justin Foster, DS Worrall had been prepared. He'd expected the culprit to put up a fight or at least protest his innocence. Instead, he'd sat there sobbing into his hands as they'd read him his rights and then led him away.

But the DS didn't have any sympathy for Justin Foster. So many people had suffered because of this vicious man. He'd also broken the law on several counts, and DS Worrall was determined to nail him.

He regretted what had happened to Ethan and his suicide

had caused the DS many sleepless nights. It was a mistake to have suspected the lad, let alone to have pursued him so doggedly. DS Worrall had been desperate for a result but now it seemed that Ethan had been completely innocent.

Despite his regrets, all the extra hours he had worked on this case now seemed worthwhile. He felt sure that he was going to get his longed-for promotion now that he had made the arrest. But his glow of satisfaction wasn't just about that. It was about making sure that scum like Justin Foster was taken off the streets. And that was worth more than any promotion.

Today DS Worrall had come to realise why officers like the DI stayed in the job for so long. Because capturing the Justin Fosters of this world gave him a buzz like no other.

68

February 2022

Laura smiled as she smelt the aroma of garlic coming from the kitchen. She had pulled out all the stops tonight and was proud of what she had achieved. A choice of starters to suit everyone, a sumptuous main course, which Candice had approved of, and a choice of three different gateaux for dessert. And, of course, the wine and champagne would be flowing.

It had been three months since Justin's arrest. Following evidence obtained from each of the witnesses, the police had searched all his premises and carried out a thorough examination of Pam's home. It seemed that he must have fled Pam's house in a panic as he had left fingerprints on the worktop. The police had also found a phone he had hidden in his loft and, although he had deleted any text messages between him and Milo Swain, technical police specialists had uncovered the incriminating data.

Once they had gathered enough evidence, the police had

charged him with both murders, and investigations were ongoing into his corrupt business practices. In the meantime, he had been remanded in custody. Laura was relieved to think that they were safely out of his clutches for now.

Candice and Thomas had both been through a traumatic time, and the murder of Pam at the hands of Justin had taken its toll. At first there was little trace of the carefree couple they had been, but as time went on things were improving. Candice was busy focusing on her studies although she was still managing to fit in time to see Thomas.

It had been difficult for Thomas to accept what kind of a monster his father was, but he had finally washed his hands of him. He had told both Candice and Laura that he would never be able to forgive him for driving his mother to suicide, and he didn't want any connection with the kind of man who could viciously rape, attack and kill women as well as kidnap a young and frightened child. The fact that the child was now his fiancée made him even more resolute in his decision.

For Laura things were also improving. She was gradually rebuilding her businesses and preparing her Wilmslow shop for a future reopening. Aside from that, she was feeling more relaxed in herself now that she wasn't constantly in fear of an unknown attacker.

As she was examining the food, she heard the doorbell. 'I'll go,' shouted Candice, and she could hear her trundling down the stairs and then chatting excitedly after she had opened the door.

Once she had put the finishing touches to the starters, Laura walked through to the dining room to find her guests already seated around the table. She was pleased to see Candice pouring a drink for them and making them feel at home. Candice turned to her then made the introductions.

'This is my mum, Laura. And this is Marion and Dennis.'

Laura smiled and said hello to the elderly, smartly dressed couple who greeted her in return. 'Thank you for inviting us,' said Marion. 'You've got a lovely home. I must make sure Dennis is on his best behaviour.'

'Hehe, she's the one you need to keep your eye on,' said Dennis, and Marion dug him playfully in the ribs.

'What would you like for starters?' asked Laura, reeling off the list of dishes she had prepared.

'Ooh, you're spoiling us,' said Dennis. 'You shouldn't have gone to so much trouble.'

Marion laughed. 'Not on our account anyway. Dennis'll eat almost anything.' She patted his rotund stomach.

'Eh, I've been nurturing this for years,' Dennis responded, rubbing his hands around his midriff. 'And I always think it's best to carry a bit of spare.'

Laura took a list of what everyone wanted and smiled to herself as she went through to the kitchen to fetch the food, aided by Candice.

'What do you think?' Candice asked.

'Oh, they seem lovely. Very down to earth, aren't they?'

'Yeah, I told you they were.'

Laura had taken to them straightaway. They did seem a lovely couple who both had a friendly manner. The banter between them carried on throughout the meal, making everyone laugh as they batted witty comments to and fro. Laura could tell there was no animosity between them, and she immediately felt relaxed as they all tucked into the food and drink.

It was the first time she had met Thomas's maternal grandparents, and she had felt on edge prior to the meal. It was important to her that they all got along well, especially after her disastrous experience of Thomas's father. Thankfully, they couldn't have been more different from him.

As the evening progressed, conversation turned to Justin and his crimes. It was obvious from what Marion said that neither she nor her husband had a lot of time for Justin, and never had done. They were very forthcoming in their criticisms and had never forgiven him for the death of their daughter. To Laura it felt like she had found two new allies.

Once the analysis of Justin was out of the way, the atmosphere became more relaxed as they all chatted amicably. Dennis was an interesting character who had led a full life, and both he and Marion were very witty.

Thomas waited until they had all finished eating before he took an unused fork and tapped it against his glass several times to get everybody's attention. 'Me and Candice have got an announcement to make,' he said.

The room went quiet as they all focused on Thomas and waited to hear what he had to say. Laura noticed that he had a look of immense pride.

'We've fixed the date for the wedding,' he said. 'We're going to tie the knot on the 15th of July next year. That will give us a year after Candice finishes uni so we can get some more savings behind us.'

'Hurrah!' shouted Dennis, and they all raised a glass to congratulate them.

As Laura looked around the table, she felt content. Thomas was a lovely lad with none of his father's flaws, thankfully. It was obvious to Laura that his mother and grandparents had been responsible for his upbringing and had shaped him into the fine young man that he was today. She couldn't have been happier to welcome Thomas into her family and was confident that her daughter would have a wonderful future with him.

69

Laura was sitting in the public gallery at Manchester Crown Court with Candice by her side as well as her friends Trina and Tiffany. To the other side of Candice sat Thomas. Justin was being tried for various crimes including the murders of Milo Swain and Pam Springer, organising the attacks on Laura's shops and staff, the attack on Laura inside his home and his corrupt business practices.

It had been a week-long trial, which had been stressful for all of them. They had all given their evidence against Justin Foster. Laura had personally found it very nerve-racking, but she knew it had been worse for Thomas in view of his emotional attachment to his father.

The evidence against Justin was overwhelming, and as the week progressed it had seemed that he wasn't going to get off lightly. But it had still been galling to see his defence lawyer try to twist all the evidence against him and portray him as a good character.

The trial was coming to a close, and they had been called in to the courtroom to hear the verdict. Laura was trembling as she sat and waited, and her hands were clammy. If Justin got off lightly, she didn't know how she would cope. And, although she knew there wasn't much chance of him getting away with his crimes, doubt still clouded her mind.

As the judge began to speak, she inhaled sharply, and Trina squeezed her hand. 'Relax,' she whispered. 'He hasn't got a fuckin' prayer.'

'Could the foreman of the jury please stand?' said the judge.

A small man wearing spectacles got to his feet and gazed around the court with a smile on his face and an air of importance.

The judge read out the first count. 'For the murder of Pam Springer, what is your verdict?'

'Guilty,' announced the foreman, staring directly at Justin. He spoke loudly as though he wanted to make sure there was no doubt about the pronounced verdict.

A murmur of voices went round the court and the judge called for order then went on to read the next count. Laura could feel her heart racing, her head was fuzzy and there was a pounding inside her ears. She was in such a state that she didn't take in all the judge's words, but the verdicts came in loud and clear. 'Guilty. Guilty. Guilty.'

'Yes!' said Trina, giving Laura's hand another squeeze then raising it high. 'They've got him. They've fuckin' got him!'

Laura gazed around the courtroom. There was a general air of excitement with people fist-pumping and yelping with delight. Across from her she noticed Justin scowling then he muttered angrily as he was led away. Thomas and Candice sat quietly.

'Are you OK?' Laura asked Candice.

Candice nodded solemnly then whispered, 'I'm just thinking of Thomas.'

'I know,' said Laura.

Her heart went out to the lad. It must be heart-breaking seeing people so overjoyed at the prospect of his father being put behind bars for a second time. But for her it was a different story. For the past few years, it had been difficult to accept that Justin had got away with the vicious rape and attack he had previously carried out on her, even though he had been imprisoned for the kidnap of Candice.

But this time he had been found guilty of every single count against him including the attack on her at his home. And once sentencing was pronounced, he would be facing a very long time behind bars. By the time he was released he would be an old man – that's if he survived his sentence.

This man had caused so much pain and anguish in the lives of Laura and those around her. But now, relief flooded her body. She knew that she was unlikely to ever have to deal with him again. Justice had finally been served.

Acknowledgements

I would like to begin by thanking my publishers, Head of Zeus, who have supported me in many ways. It has now been five years since I published my first book with Head of Zeus in July 2017, and it has been a pleasure working with them. They are a fantastic bunch of people, and I am flattered and extremely grateful for their continuing belief in me as an author.

Particular thanks go to Laura Palmer who has backed me from the start, my structural editor Martina Arzu for helping to shape the novel, Peyton Stableford for all your help and advice, Helena Newton for a great job on the copy edits and all the rest of the team who work hard on book design, PR, promotion, marketing, and a host of other tasks.

Thanks to my agent, Jo Bell, for all your support. I would also like to thank all the staff at Bell Lomax Moreton for your ongoing help including John Baker, Sarah McDonnell, and Lorna Hemingway.

Although my research for this novel has been secondary, everything I learnt during my primary research for The Working Girls series has been of value and I am sure I carried that knowledge through with me when writing

Guilt. I would therefore again like to thank all the people who were so willing to chat with me and answer my queries during the writing of The Working Girls series.

Shortly after finishing the first draft of this novel, I attended my first literature festival as a panellist where I connected with other crime authors and crime fiction aficionados. The crime writing community is so welcoming, and it was a joy to meet other writers and chat with some of my readers. I look forward to meeting more of you in the future.

Thank you to the wider crime reading community including book bloggers, reviewers and all the people who give up their free time to run social media groups where crime readers and authors can connect and share their enthusiasm and recommendations for crime novels.

Lastly, as always, I would like to thank my family and friends for your continuing support and for always being there for me.

About the Author

HEATHER BURNSIDE started her writing career more than twenty years ago when she worked as a freelance writer while studying for a writing diploma. As part of her studies Heather wrote the first chapters of her debut novel, *Slur*, but she didn't complete the novel till many years later. *Slur* became the first book in The Riverhill Trilogy, which was followed by The Manchester Trilogy then her current series, The Working Girls.

You can find out more about the author by signing up to the Heather Burnside mailing list (eepurl.com/CP6YP) for the latest updates including details of new releases and book bargains, or by following her on any of the links below.

Facebook: www.facebook.com/HeatherBurnsideAuthor/
Twitter: www.twitter.com/heatherbwriter
Website: www.heatherburnside.com